THE AGREEMENT

BETHANY-KRIS

Published by Bethany-Kris

www.bethanykris.com

ISBN 13: 978-1-989658-45-1

Editor: Elizabeth Peters

Cover Design © Mignon Mykel

For all those Russian Guns fans … you've waited long enough. XO.

CONTENTS

PROLOGUE

"It started with a bit of cocaine."

A dark chuckle sounded from Demyan Avdonin's left before his friend—one of his oldest—replied only, "Don't all the best stories?"

Side by side in matching leather bucket chairs that faced a familiar landscape, in one of the best parts of New York City, the two men shared a laugh that Demyan hadn't realized he needed. He wasn't the type to spill his family's secrets—or their problems.

His adult son was certainly one of those.

"If only it stayed that way, though," Demyan added after a second.

Maxim hummed under his breath. "This is a life of temptation, and we're men made for it, Demyan."

Maybe so.

Sighing, he told Maxim, "I don't think I ever taught him how to tell himself no."

He didn't need his friend to say what he already knew—
that was a lesson no man in their life could afford to miss.
Except, apparently, if it was Demyan's son.

Roman Avdonin had a knack for pushing every limit—
testing each line drawn for him. It didn't matter the man or
the establishment making the rule, he swore his son was
born to break them.

Men, that was.

Better men than him, anyway.

And rules.

Couldn't forget those.

Demyan didn't have a proper excuse as to why he felt the
need to discuss his personal issues with Maxim during the
man's very short visit to the city, but here he was—*who the
fuck else is listening?*

At his left, Maxim jerked a hand his way, the cigar between
the man's fingertips losing an ash on the way. It fell to the
shiny floor of a townhouse Demyan used for occasions just
like this. A last-minute meet up with an old friend in the
business—the mafia. It wasn't often that the bosses of rival
bratvas became friends, even if their business rarely
overlapped.

The two were an exception to the rule—mutual respect, a
bit of distance between their territories, and easy
conversation helped the friendship along. He didn't
particularly like all the man's business, but he'd also never
dropped it on Demyan's doorstep, either. Maxim never
asked questions that probed too deep unless Demyan
offered—especially about his family—and he handed back
the same courtesy.

Claire, his wife, liked to say Demyan didn't have *enough*
friends, and he should make the effort to keep the ones he
did.

Or at least the ones he liked.

Maxim was that friend—so, yes. He dropped everything
for a fifteen-minute conversation in a mostly empty
townhouse in a room full of cigar smoke because his
counterpart never went anywhere without one at his lips.

Demyan didn't really mind.

THE AGREEMENT

"He's found himself some trouble, then, no?" Maxim asked.

Demyan kept his gaze on the bay windows overlooking the Hudson, and the view across the river. Boats skipped fast and slow over the water, and for a moment, he said nothing as he watched them go.

What was there to say?

He's a grown man.

Roman can make his choices.

My son might get himself killed.

All of those were true, and more. They were also very telling about how Demyan felt, and he wasn't keen on going *there*. No man in his position did, considering the risk.

"Nothing that he hasn't managed to find his way out of," Demyan eventually muttered. "So far."

"I could help with that."

The offer made Demyan still in his chair. He didn't glance his friend's way, but as his mind mulled over the offer—and implications—he already knew his answer. He didn't really need to think about it.

His love was loyalty.

It would always be his weakness.

"I'm not interested in setting up my son to get him under control, old friend," Demyan murmured, reaching for the glass of vodka on the table between them."

"Well, that's the best part," Maxim replied, striking a bemused grin. "Nobody said you had to do a fucking thing."

Demyan sipped his drink, and said nothing—he didn't agree, or otherwise.

Well, he thought, *so be it*

3

ONE

Roman Avdonin had never learned when enough was enough, and he blamed it on the fact that no one thought to step in and teach him. That was undoubtedly why his father's men didn't bat an eye at the Bratva Prince of Brighton Beach stepping outside the Pakhan's three-story colonial estate to nab a baggie of ivory powder from his best friend.

Marky Thompson—the right-hand man to Roman's car theft and chop shop scheme—held his drug of choice out the driver's window of his pearl black Ferrari without concern for who watched. All it took was one look at Marky's shifting gaze for him to know the man's true feelings on being called in to deliver Roman's drugs on a day like today.

"I know how you don't like being told what to do…" Marky started, tilting his head out of the window a little more.

"Then don't."

ᵀᴴᴱAGREEMENT

Roman snatched the baggie, encompassing it in his palm and slipping it into the pocket of his grey jeans. He didn't look over his shoulder or at the bulls walking around the estate. The bratva enforcers had their eye on everything. They saw *everything*. It wasn't like he was trying to hide it. They knew who he was. Everyone knew who the fuck he was. Maybe a man different from Roman, would have felt a sense of responsibility given the circumstances of the day. Maybe even some shame.

Not Roman.

He didn't give a single flying fuck, and he was pretty sure his family didn't, either.

"Well, I'm just trying to make a suggestion, man," Marky continued.

Roman grinned—it took the edge of the irritation already starting to simmer below the surface of his constantly short fuse—but only because he knew what was coming. This was one of the things he hated most about this place. About his world—*this life*. Everyone was so damn predictable. He waited a few beats, knowing Marky would continue speaking, but he wasn't about to jump in and encourage his friend to go ahead and get told to fuck off faster than the guy wanted to.

His prerogative, and all.

"Maybe today is not the day to piss off your papa."

Right.

Was there ever a day for that?

Shit, Roman had been making that a daily occurrence since his ass hit puberty. Here he was, a grown ass man, and not much changed. He'd stopped worrying how Demyan Avdonin would feel when it became apparent that the disappointment of others didn't do very much to or for him except cause him unneeded shame.

Giving Marky a shrug, Roman said, "Listen, everyone around here is acting like the world is going to crash down on us just because some middle-aged men from Chicago are showing up in town."

Marky drummed his fingers on the steering wheel. He looked past Roman's shoulder to the bulls leaning against the estate's gates. "They are more than just some middle-aged men. Even you know better than that, *Prince*."

Nice, Roman thought. The emphasis on the *prince*—as if he needed a reminder about the men he came from when he stood where he did—felt like a joke that didn't quite land.

"Roll your eyes and you might just start sounding like a fifteen-year-old girl."

Marky snickered at that, and Roman finally looked back over his shoulder at the men still lingering too near for his tastes. Two of them, the ones standing closest to the gate, looked quickly away when his stare met theirs, and Roman got the feeling that they were talking about him.

Why wouldn't they?

He had a pretty good idea of what they thought of him. The only son of a formidable, long-standing Bratva Pakhan. A brat from the moment he was born. Destined to have more control and power in their chosen life than them from the second he was *conceived*. The Prince of Brighton Beach. Little Odessa's Devil.

He didn't have to work half as hard as them to get where he was, but that didn't mean he hadn't put in the blood, sweat, and tears to still do it. They knew it, too, and he was sure that his privilege alongside the reputation he'd earned— his violence was swift and severe when barely provoked— aided in the silent understanding he had with these men.

They shouldn't be saying shit about him, not unless they wanted to die for it, too.

"Where is he?" Marky's question snapped him out of his thoughts, and brought him back to the conversation.

"Who?"

"Who else?"

"Probably still in bed with my mother," Roman muttered, adding lower, "Whispering sweet nothings, or whatever the fuck they do."

By all appearances, though, his mother enjoyed that from her husband. Loyal to a fault and content in her place as the boss's wife, why would she complain that she had him eating out of the palm of her hand?

{}^{\text{THE}}AGREEMENT

"Why do you shit on your father for being in love with his woman?" Marky asked.

"*Being in love*—do you even fucking hear yourself?"

Roman laughed. It rose up his throat like a snarl. Sometimes, he didn't even remember why he was still best friends with Marky—the guy could be dense as fuck when he didn't feel like putting his brain to good use.

"He's the only bratva man we know who has one woman. No girls in the city when he wants. Not even a woman on the side. What else would you call that?"

"You're forgetting about my grandfather," Roman said dryly.

There were a million other things he would rather do instead of having this conversation, but Marky was determined to see it through. The fucking *idiot*.

"So it clearly runs in the family."

Marky got that ridiculous twinkle in his eye, one that made Roman want to punch his friend in the throat. They both knew the entire conversation was a joke. Roman with one woman—tied to her for life? Answering her every beck and call like his father did with his mother, his grandfather with his grandmother? Waking up to see the same face over and over again? It made him laugh. He couldn't remember the last time he wanted *one thing* of anything.

Everything tasted better in large quantities.

Most of all: *pussy*.

"And just like everything else, I'm going to disappoint my father in that regard, too," Roman replied with a chuckle while Marky shook his head. "Another family tradition gone straight to hell."

"One of these days you're going to wish you listened to me."

He doubted that.

Highly.

"And one of these days you're going to wish you didn't waste my time."

Marky sighed like he had something more to say, but Roman didn't want to stand around to listen. It was only because he counted Marky as a friend that he gave the man a pass more often than anyone else—today was one of those days.

"Just get the fuck outta here," he commanded light-heartedly.

After all, friends did not mean equal. Marky knew it just as well as he did, and while they did well to sometimes pretend like the two of them were squared up in the life they lived, that just wasn't the case.

Behind him, he heard Marky's Ferrari roar to life. He wasn't the type to wave, so he didn't. He just kept walking. When he passed by one of the bulls, he reached over and drummed his fingers on the man's shiny bald spot. The man instinctually ducked away but then caught himself and stood still.

Who did he think he was?

Flinching at the Prince.

It was *comical.*

Roman had grown up around these men. All his life, he treated them exactly the way he wanted to, nobody told him he couldn't, and he wasn't about to change that now.

Inside the house, the soles of his shoes squeaked on the polished marble floors. His mother was particular about a lot of things. Whose shoes went where, who could be in the kitchen when she cooked ... *cleaning.*

She liked the house maintained just-so—no fingerprints on any glass, no dust dancing in streams of sunlight, and certainly no dirty shoes on her floor. She dared to tell him that would change *only* when she was given grandchildren to spoil.

Another thing he doubted.

She just wanted grandbabies.

He glanced at the clock on the wall in the grand foyer, taking note of the time. Hanging down along the massive, winding staircase, the crystal chandelier swung gently like someone had just been dusting it. One of the maids probably did while he was outside, but the staff in the mansion were as smart as the men who watched it outside. They stayed out of the Avdonin family's way.

Especially his.

ᴛʜᴇAGREEMENT

Demyan was late to start his day. Still in bed, no doubt. Roman took the spiral stairs up to the second floor with silent steps, two a stride. His father was free to take as much time as he wanted. It allowed him a chance to put the baggie to good use without yet another lecture about his private activities.

In his childhood bedroom, he shut and locked the door. Not that anyone would enter without knocking or asking his permission. Not much had changed about the space that he had officially moved out of ten years ago, shortly after he turned seventeen.

There was a glass-topped night table on the left side of the four-poster, king-size bed, and he was going to put that to good use, too. Sitting on the edge of his bed, he emptied the baggie on the table, and then spent a few seconds looking for the credit card he wanted from his wallet.

What would this day look like if he didn't do what he was about to?

He really didn't care to find out.

• • •

Everyone looked twitchy, Roman thought, with their eyes darting everywhere.

On high alert.

Two bulls in the front, while his father sat in the row behind him. He watched familiar streets pass by the dark-tinted windows of their Mercedes SUV. The muscle behind the wheel, and the one in the front passenger seat kept their eyes focused outside to monitor every car and passerby to find the danger they were sure was there.

Total bullshit.

Roman could have laughed at their paranoia, but *someone* wouldn't appreciate that. Except his lack of concern as they drove through the city wasn't escaping Demyan's notice while the man chatted on the phone with his own father.

Why the fucking eggshells?

Cocaine certainly had a way of making Roman think he was bulletproof, but he still figured they were making a bigger thing out of this whole day than it needed to be. Had his father ever been chill in his life? Demyan's voice droned on in the background of Roman's thoughts, the mention of his grandfather's name, Anton, almost making him tune into the private conversation.

If there was anyone in the world Roman couldn't say no to—one person whose word might count when spoken—it was his grandfather. But even the prospect of joining the conversation wasn't enough to drag him from his annoyance at the day.

What was the big deal?

Well, he knew.

Three bratvas—New York, Jersey, and Chicago—coming together to discuss business was enough to put an entire city on edge given the right circumstances. Usually bloody ones. This wasn't supposed to be like that, though. Their business had managed to exist independent of each other for decades other than the mutual work between the Avdonin Bratva in New York, and the Vasin organization in Jersey—proximity sometimes worked to their benefit. A marriage between the two families helped that shit out, as well.

Chicago wasn't quite the same. They minded their own business, and rarely ever stepped on the toes of anyone outside of Illinois. However, for the first time in more years than he could remember, the Yazovs wanted to meet with them.

New York, specifically. Then they had to go and ask for the Vasin Bratva to get in on the chat, too. That was when Roman's father started to get serious about how he wanted to ensure safety while their visitors were in town—especially since the Yazov organization made it clear they weren't discussing anything unless it was face to face.

Nothing good came from demands.

Men like them were also careful by nature.

So to speak.

The sound of his father calling his name—short and low—snapped Roman out of his thoughts. The phone call with his grandfather had come to an end it seemed.

ᴛʜᴇAGREEMENT

"You could stop ..." Demyan trailed off, glancing him over before adding, "Well, the twitchiness. Add that to the way your pupils look, and it's a dead giveaway."

Roman dragged the back of his hand over his upper lip. How did his father figure it out? He suddenly noticed the way he was furiously tapping the floor with his feet; his fingers had been drumming a constant beat to the leather-wrapped armrest. Cocaine tingled with an electric pulse through his veins. He could feel it at the back of his head—a throbbing burst of heat. That, and an inexplicable urge to grab someone and thrash them against the floor of the vehicle until they couldn't breathe, and he finally *could*.

He didn't reply to his father, but apparently, he didn't have to.

"Don't look so surprised, son, you left the baggie sitting on top of the damn trash can. *In the kitchen.*"

Right.

Fuck.

Sometimes, he didn't think shit through. At the same time, he couldn't find it in himself to care.

Demyan continued despite Roman's silence in the row behind him, saying, "Your mother would have seen it if I didn't find it first."

Shame.

"She would have survived the horror."

His twisted smirk only earned a shake of Demyan's head, and nothing more. Cellophane. That's what he was to his papa. Transparent to a fault.

Roman often wondered how Demyan did it—how he unravelled his son with barely any effort at all no matter how tightly he wore this suit of chaos.

Even as a child, Roman was aware of the significance of his position; the unique relationship he shared with his father that few could understand. They couldn't be only father and son when they were also a pakhan and a vor. He didn't know if it was equally strange for Demyan to not only train and punish his son, but to also have to love him because he was his own blood.

But it had certainly shaped the way Roman perceived the world around him, and the relationships he chose to have inside of it.

Demyan clicked his tongue, his gaze darting back to the windows like he was over the moment of unsurprising disappointment, and already moving on. "You're losing your touch, Roman. The least you can do for your mother's sake is clean up the evidence."

"Maybe you don't know her as well as you think you do. She sees everything, she knows everything," Roman replied.

His father breathed in deeply and nodded. "Trust me, son, I know that very well." Then, Demyan grinned indulgently— like a vision of his wife had filled his brain, and he was blown away somewhere else. It didn't last long before the sharp, unapproving stare flicked back his way. "Back to *you*, though."

Roman's jaw clenched. His father tended to stay out of his habits, so why was he mentioning it now? Besides, it wasn't like the drug-use was an actual problem for him. Certainly not something he couldn't keep under control. Sometimes, he would end up going weeks without touching it. Then, something would pull him in again—usually boredom.

Shocker.

The Prince of Brighton Beach had very little else to do when he wasn't boosting cars. How many secret raves could he go to? He started when he was barely sixteen. It had been over eleven years by now that he was living this life he made, stacking his own money. His nickname—dubbed by the reporters who had the balls to put his name to paper—of Little Odessa's Devil hadn't come out of nowhere.

He had never needed his father or the bratva to pay for his indulgences, he made his name in the streets before they could do it for him, so what gave Demyan the authority to call him out on anything?

Most importantly, and the one fact his father should have cared most about—Roman never got in the kind of shit he couldn't get out of. It was the only rule he made an attempt to follow. He had all the cops he needed under his belt.

ᴛʜᴇAGREEMENT

Nobody was going to point a finger at his dad; their corrupt control of New York had spanned decades.

The Avdonins hadn't been built overnight.

So, what was the fucking problem?

"You're stewing in your own rage, Roman," Demyan murmured, his tone softening just enough to remind him that more often than not, this man was his father before anything else. "There has to be a reason *why*. Is there something you want to tell me?"

There he went.

Again.

Reading his mind like an open book.

"We usually keep out of each other's shit, don't we?" Roman asked, determined to keep his tone calm even though the cocaine made that really hard.

"I need you fully present today, son."

"What do you think I'm doing here, then?"

Demyan shook his head again, and nothing else. Christ, that aggravated Roman even more, and he wasn't entirely sure why. Not that it mattered. The conversation was over because they were already pulling up to the side of the road.

The Avdonins had selected the meeting spot. An eatery run by them, so it would be an environment they could control. As Roman shifted in his seat to ready for when his father chose to exit, more cars pulled up around them. A half a dozen, and then more soon after, with the same opaque windows as theirs.

Everyone had arrived, it seemed.

Right on time.

Roman wanted to say more to his father, but the boss was already stepping out of the car. Cool, calm, collected, and ready to handle his business. He wished he could say the same.

It had never served him well to leave anything unfinished—especially not with Demyan—and the conversation had left him with a bitter taste in the mouth.

Or *shit* …

Maybe that was still the cocaine.

TWO

Roman's eyes fixed on Anastasia's long legs as she sat beside him, her perfectly slender thighs crossed over each other. The smoke from his cigarette curled and swirled around his fingers when he gestured her way, and she passed him a smile. A smile that told him many things—one, that she was bored of this scene, and two, that she enjoyed the way he looked at her.

She was a paid whore.

Added to the scenery.

Just like the other women who dotted the restaurant's floor. Women the other men of the bratva had brought along with them to either show off, or entice someone for one reason or another. Games were constantly in play, and Roman didn't pretend like he cared to understand or indulge in any of them.

Dressed to the nines; their faces caked with makeup and in clothes that cost just a little less than their boob jobs—the women added to the entertainment while the men discussed important business. And every single one of them knew they were here because they weren't good enough to actually be wives. There wouldn't be sparkling rings on their fingers. No mansions behind gates and little babies to soak their affection and attention on while their husbands did … whatever they wanted to do.

None, that was, except his mother, Claire.

His father had arranged for a separate car to transport Claire to the venue, some time after everyone else had settled down. Some might consider it a huge disrespect to Claire that she was invited where no other wife of important men in the criminal underworld would go. Like it meant *she* wasn't good enough, either. His mother once told him she didn't care what people thought about where or with whom she spent her time. He believed her.

Roman gazed at his mother across the floor. Claire Avdonin, Irish enough to color her up, defined herself in ways others didn't. He figured, some of his personality had definitely been formed by that, even if he took it to an extreme. Her class, style, and natural warmth was unparalleled by everyone she met—no one compared. Not another man's wife, not passers on the street, and certainly not any of the other women here. She was the kind of woman who was born to stand beside the man she did. Except when asked, she liked to say it had been learned. Nonetheless, her very nature made her a perfect hostess for the dinner that had been able to immediately make everyone feel comfortable in their surroundings.

These were rival, *criminal* bosses … and their men. Important men from all sides, really. Loud as a habit. Difficult by nature. Dominant in their power.

Yet, their chauvinistic, tattooed, crass selves melted into smiling, softer spoken gentlemen when Claire came around with her high-voltage smile, and her melodic, kind voice. She didn't intrude, was a sight to see, she never asked questions, and people trusted her.

She set them off guard.

Every single time.

If nothing else, Roman had to hand it to his father for selecting the right woman to have by his side.

His mother looked at him across the room like she sensed he was watching her. She smiled at him, quick and fleeting, and he gave her a nod in response. Then, Anastasia's hand on Roman's knee brought him quickly back to the table he was sitting at.

This shit was purposeful.

It had to be.

His father arranged to have him stuck at his current table with these two—maybe to punish him for their earlier conversation, or just because he thought Roman could use a lesson in self-control.

Whatever the reason, he wasn't thrilled. He didn't like the idea that his father had arranged for him to be at this table, with a paid whore and Dima Kuznetsov, son of Leonid Kusnetsov. A Vor from the Chicago Bratva, there was something about Dima that rubbed Roman wrong. He didn't have to know what it was for it to be there—it being there was enough.

Anastasia moved her hand away from Roman's knee before Dima noticed it there. After all, he was probably the one who paid for her—maybe she was one of his women that he trusted enough to travel, who fucking knew—and it was obvious to Roman that he was trying to establish himself as the bigger man at the table.

Yeah.

It was going to take more than comparing cocks in whatever way Dima felt like it to make Roman even *consider* weighing whether or not the man was worth the effort. He already knew the answer anyway.

Dima wasn't.

Insignificant, Dima's voice was a nuisance at the table. Dragging at the back of his mind, fraying his already taut nerves. The topic at hand would have interested Roman, maybe, if he was just trying to inform him about the business, but he wasn't.

Anastasia was good at pretending to hang off his every word. Her bright red hair matched the color of her plump lips. The blindingly shiny silver dress also matched her stilettos. She glanced at him from time to time, every chance she got to look away from the man who had an arm around her delicate shoulders.

"But you see, sweetheart, I know where to put my money so I can make more, yes? You get it?" Dima asked, speaking only to Anastasia but loud enough that his other companion at the table was forced to grit his teeth through it.

Roman's molars were going to crack.

Surely.

He did his best to keep the cocaine buzz going, but that shit was slowly starting to fade. If he didn't slip away somewhere to get back into the right headspace, nothing good would happen. Except people would notice. More specifically, his father. It almost made him want to do it more, just for the reaction. Maybe that would trigger Demyan in to finishing the conversation he instigated in the car.

He still wasn't over that.

"You are *so* smart," Anastasia said.

A smile curled the corners of her lips as she threw Roman a knowing glance. She was making it too obvious, and yet, it flew under Dima's radar. He chuckled—the pride thick and clear—while he nodded to her compliment.

Dima winked, saying, "I was born into this business. Multiplying my capital is in my blood, hmm?"

And so is the flesh trade; Roman wanted to add but he chewed on his words—mainly because he didn't want to direct Dima's attention to himself. He refused to engage unless required …

Or provoked.

Anastasia drawled on, her voice sultry in Dima's ear with praises and compliments that stroked the man's ego but with just enough suggestive sarcasm to keep Roman mildly amused. Then, he had to go and notice the way she flicked her tongue over her lips.

Yeah, sure, he wouldn't have minded bending her over a table and having his fill. Sex was sex—he enjoyed feeding the urge—and he didn't feel very much shame about it.

Never had.

Consenting adults could do whatever the fuck they wanted, as long as it felt *good*. And hell, even if it didn't.

He just had to like it.

In fact, he imagined getting his fill from Anastasia within yelling distance of Dima—there was no better way to ruin a man's reputation than fucking his woman—and it seemed like a good idea. Rubbing his hand over his upper lip again, he sniffed.

Across the room, he briefly listened to the conversations passing between his father, and the other bosses at the table. The meeting was turning out to be a success. Demyan was being offered trafficking connections to help grow the network for the Avdonins beyond their current reach. It looked like he would even accept the offer. He would have to be a fool to turn that down.

Roman wondered what Maxim Yazov from Chicago wanted in return, though.

Three bratvas working together in harmony was unheard of, but if they could make it happen, it was better than one working alone. Even Roman knew that.

"I mean they're all a ripe, young age to listen, you know?" Dima continued.

Jesus Christ.

How was he still talking?

Roman's irritation bubbled as he was forced to pay attention to what the idiot playing pretend said. Anastasia shifted in her seat, and this was the first time she displayed a reaction to the content of this conversation.

"So, it's not like they can exactly put up a fight, yeah? We move them quickly between cities. Within a few weeks there's no trace of them."

Dima didn't even try to hide his pleasure at stating that fact. A creep move to Roman. Anastasia threw him another look of discomfort, but he didn't know what she wanted him to say. Sure, she had to pretend to drool over every word that left Dima's mouth, but trafficking teenage girls for the sex trade and then bragging about it—was not exactly an easy pill to swallow.

ᴛʜᴇAGREEMENT

Dima was searching Anastasia's face to make sure he had made an adequate impression on her, and then he turned to Roman.

"Eight. States, no? Six months and a hundred million dollars," Dima bragged.

Roman grinned right back. "That all?"

Those were the first words he had spoken in a while. It startled both his companions at the table.

"Did you say something to me?" Dima hissed.

Ah.

Hit a nerve?

It made Roman's grin grow wider.

"That's how much I made from three chop shops in New York alone," he told Dima.

A vein had popped up in the middle of the other man's forehead, his eyes turning bloodshot-red. Dima wasn't pleased with that statement.

So?

"Anyone can steal cars and make a few bucks," Dima shot back.

A little too late for the impact to hurt, though.

"Then, why haven't you done it yet?"

Anastasia's stare whipped Roman's way, her painted-red lips widening like her eyes, but he didn't care about her.

Roman's easy counter matched the unwavering stare he leveled on the man. He silently dared Dima to have enough balls to admit he couldn't make the kind of money Roman did in front of the woman he had paid to stroke his ego and cock. Even in his shame, Roman would have the decency then to offer the man an ounce of respect.

Surprise.

Dima doubled down.

"Because the thrill doesn't last long enough, yes?" Dima added a short, dark laugh, and turned to Anastasia again when he said, "You steal a car and that's done. It's a single payment, one transaction. A girl, well, she can be used again and again. You break a girl, and she's broken forever. So, what does it matter?"

19

Anastasia had to force herself to smile with Dima's gaze still firmly locked on her, but only weakly. It was only her discomfort with the conversation that urged him to stop provoking Dima in to giving even more information about his business that would *really* unsettle the female at the table.

This shit didn't get better.

Just bad.

The meeting was still going well. Roman tried to pay attention to what was being said, but he could barely hear them anymore. It sounded like the formalities were over at least. Things had gone smoothly, which meant that nobody would be looking for him anytime soon. He could make a smooth exit … if he wanted.

He returned Anastasia's smile when she glanced at him again. Boredom stared back at him. She wished she was somewhere else—anywhere other than within Dima's breathing distance. Roman wished the same.

Being the Chicago Pakhan's right-hand man, alongside his own father, Dima was called away for a private conversation with his boss.

Perfect timing.

Dima reluctantly headed away from the table, momentarily glancing back with a narrowed, icy stare loaded for Roman. He stared right back, unchallenged. Anastasia took the opportunity to immediately lean toward him once her companion had been distracted with more important men.

"I heard a rumor about your nickname," she began.

Oh?

"What did you hear?"

"You're called Little Odessa's Devil."

Roman stubbed the cigarette into a smoky ashtray between them, and met Anastasia's eyes, smirking all the while. "Do you want to find out why?"

• • •

Marky, despite his earlier warnings, didn't even bother to hide his incredulous grin when Roman slipped out the back door of the restaurant, with the redhead on his arm. "You're fucking nuts," he remarked with a slap to Roman's back.

"That is exactly what I want you to take care of," he told Anastasia with a wink.

She threw her head back and laughed. Out of Dima's view, the woman wasn't as flighty and ... *fake*. Although, he was sure those tits of hers were bought and paid for.

The deserted alley at the back of the restaurant worked fine for him and what he planned to do. Roman had made sure he wasn't going to be noticed by anyone who really mattered when he walked out. The meeting was still in progress, but things had turned more casual amongst the bratva men.

Marky knew exactly what to do without being told. He stood to the side with his back to the wall, keeping watch while Roman busted a nut down Anastasia's throat.

Anastasia's tongue danced along the seam of her top lip when Roman grabbed her by the back of her neck, pulling her down to her knees in front of him. A wicked smile spread on her face while she clung to his muscular arm. She liked his rough handling.

He had to do nothing after that, which was fine with him. She was the one who undid his belt and pulled down his pants. His cock throbbed and grew hard at the sight of her red mouth coming dangerously close to the head of his cock with white teeth baring slightly. She opened wide and licked her bottom lip while she stroked him in preparation.

Fuck that.

He didn't need foreplay.

He twisted one thick bunch of her red hair around his hand so he could hold her in place, murmuring to her, "Just fucking suck me—*don't play.*"

Her hands found his thighs for support, and that painted-red mouth of hers took him in. He plowed his cock deep down her throat and began thrusting. Slurpy sounds followed her moans of delight with every push.

He should have just closed his fucking eyes and got his rocks off, but getting head in a dirty alley was the least exciting thing he'd done that week. The distraction of busting a nut wasn't enough to keep Roman from noticing the marks on her wrists where her bangles had slipped down her arms.

Bruises.

Blue and fresh.

He had a good idea who put them there, too. Dima had her eating out of the palm of his hand. He hurt her; maybe it was some shit he got off on, or maybe it was just because he could. Either way, she had to sit there and listen to him boast about all the other women he was using—or trafficking.

Fun times.

And he needed to get his head out of that headspace. Fast.

Roman tried to focus on the way her tongue moved over his cock instead of the imprints of bruises he could still see even after he closed his eyes. After a while, it started to work. She sucked him hard. He controlled her hair like reins around his hand. Yanking and tugging her while he fucked her mouth exactly the way he wanted.

When he came, he filled her mouth with his sticky cum until it dribbled down the side of her mouth while her tongue was still flat to the base of his cock, and she stared up at him. Only then did he pull away. Anastasia wiped her lips with the back of her hand. Her perfect red lipstick was smudged now.

She eyed him with her big green eyes while he pulled up his pants, waiting for something, maybe. What, he didn't know.

Did she expect something?

He wasn't Dima—wouldn't hurt her. Roman also wasn't a saint; the furthest thing from it really, and he got what he wanted here. Everything else was over.

Staring back at her, it was the first time he noticed the smattering of freckles across her cheeks and nose. He allowed himself that one moment to feel sorry for her—whatever her circumstance—before he reached down and fished the key out of the front of her dress. She had wedged it deep down her cleavage, but he had a pretty good view of it the entire time.

^{\text{\tiny THE}}AGREEMENT

He'd noted the Bugatti emblem on the keychain at first glance. It wasn't the kind of car he could forget, and while he might have had other things on his mind earlier when they first arrived, he didn't miss the vehicle when Dima pulled up, either.

He had to hand it to Anastasia. She at least tried to make a grab for the key. Roman held it out of her reach with a dry chuckle, and a little shake of his head.

"I would apologize, but I don't think you really care," he said.

"Of course, I care … he's going to kill me!"

Anastasia scrambled up from the ground, following him on shaky legs as he walked past her without a glance backward. Marky turned when Roman approached, and he tossed the key his friend's way with a laugh.

There was no way that Dima drove all the way from Chicago in a Bugatti. It was pretty obvious that it was a rental. He was already delighting at the thought of chopping the car down and shipping it overseas to one of the clients on his list. Roman had spent the past decade adding up a trusted roll-call of clients who would drool at the vehicle he was about to have in his possession.

"What are you going to do with it?" she called behind him.

"What do you think I'm going to do?"

"Steal it for your chop shop?"

He gave Marky a look from the side, his tone mocking when he said, "She's got *brains*, man. Imagine."

Marky barked a laugh. "Shut up, asshole."

Roman only shrugged, but even that wasn't enough for Anastasia. She followed him down the alley while Marky went ahead of him with the key swinging from his index finger. It would have been easier if the chick disappeared by now. He half-expected her to go running to Dima or the others from his bratva to warn them of Roman's plan.

Instead, her heels clicked on the cobbled alley while she tried to keep up with them.

"Please, I'm serious. *God*. Christ, listen to me! He *will* kill me, this will be all my fault," she cried out again, a tremble in her voice making Roman hesitate.

When he turned to her this time, she was holding her arms out for him to see where she had shoved up the sleeves of her dress. There were more than just the bruises he had initially noticed. Cuts and deeper looking wounds, some fresh and others starting to heal, marked the insides of her arms.

Roman swallowed hard. "You're not any better than any of the other girls he ships from state to state—you're just paid."

She didn't reply, but the stuttering breath of air she released told him more than she could, anyway. He wasn't up for playing hero with a woman—*any* woman, really. No one had time for that shit, but …

Roman mulled over what to do. When he threw a look at Marky over his shoulder, his best friend gave him a raised brow and a tilt of his head in Anastasia's direction like he was silently saying, *Come on, Roman.*

Jesus.

"Fine," Roman told her, "you can come with us, but see yourself gone before morning."

Relief swept over her face when she nodded wildly. "Yes, thank you, that's all I need. Just a head start tonight."

"Then, hurry the fuck up," he growled.

Because he didn't have time to keep being *nice.*

Marky had already made his way to the Bugatti parked at the side of the restaurant, opened the driver's door and got the vehicle running. Ready for Roman to jump inside, and get gone as fast as he could. While there were bulls everywhere, keeping a watch on the premises, nobody even glanced his way when the Avdonin Prince slipped into a parked car. The key of which he already possessed.

Nothing looked out of the ordinary.

Anastasia climbed into the passenger seat, exhaling deeply as she tried to catch her breath. Roman caught her eye as he pressed down on the accelerator. She smiled back.

He didn't.

She would give him anything he wanted.

That much was clear.

The problem?

He was already bored.

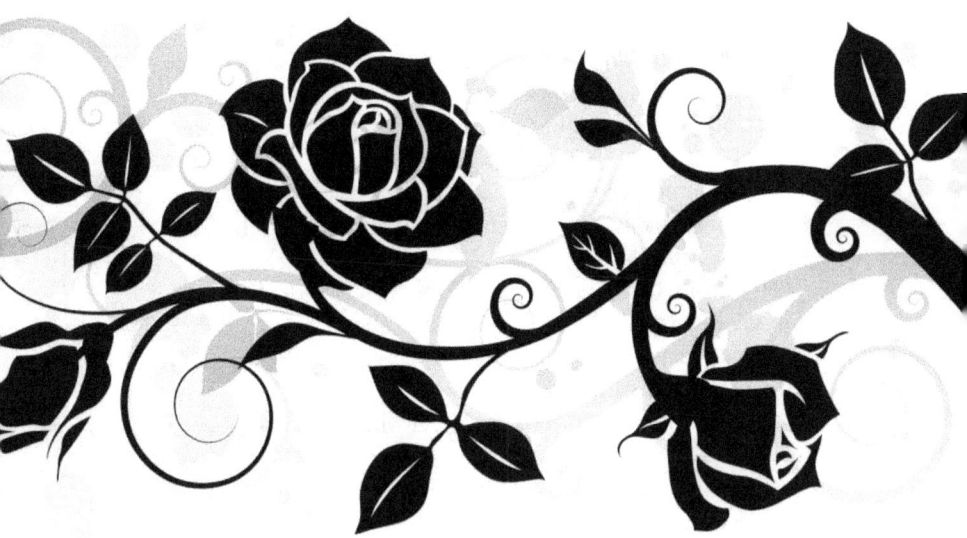

THREE

"So, you haven't picked a woman yet? Or one hasn't been picked for you?"

Anastasia's soft question had Roman's hand clenching tighter around the steering wheel. He hadn't expected that from her. The word choice suggested that maybe her involvement with Dima allowed her insight on bratva men and their way of life. He didn't dare to indulge her curiosity, if that's why she brought it up.

With an arm dangling out of the rolled-down window, and a lit joint between his lips, he reveled in the smell of the heavy smoke filling the interior of the car. It clung to the air between them, every breath dragging into his lungs tasted like weed and expensive leather.

He might have offered her a hit, but he wasn't in the mood to share. And shit, hadn't his good deed for the day been enough?

She was *there*.

"No," he eventually said, offering nothing more.

The way her mouth opened to say something else had Roman rolling his gaze toward the window at his left. She kept trying to get him to talk—he didn't have shit to say.

"You're just … doing whatever with whoever, *whenever*, then?"

"Something like that."

"You're lucky. You do what you want and go wherever you like. *Free.*"

Her tone had dipped from sadness to almost *dreamy*. It made Roman's throat tight—people always assumed that his life was easy. He walked on water while they drowned. He imagined what a life like that would look like.

"What makes you think I'm free?" he mumbled under his breath.

She still heard him loud and clear.

"You *are* Demyan Avdonin's son."

"*And?*"

"Come on, don't play stupid. Dima wouldn't shut up about you—*the Prince of New York*, he said. He tried to laugh it off, said you were just a spoiled brat with too much control who hasn't grown up yet, but—"

Roman's gaze cut to her, the fire burning bright enough to stop her words instantly. "What else?"

Her throat bobbed. "I—"

"*What else?* He must have said something else—you said it, not me. So, what else?"

"Nothing."

Roman didn't believe that for a second. He was, however, fine with letting her drop the conversation if she was finally going to shut up. *Fuck* Dima. That piece of shit wouldn't last a month in New York with Roman to contend with on the streets. Better men than him had already tried.

And failed.

Anastasia fiddled with the sleeves of her dress, silent in her thoughts and unaware that Roman had turned his gaze back on her. He could have said a lot about her assumptions regarding his life—it was just easier for someone to see him from an outside perspective and judge or believe what they wanted.

THE AGREEMENT

But …

Fuck.

His shoulders ached sometimes. From the expectations he knew his people kept hanging around his neck like a noose, and the responsibility of his position. He worried more often than not that he was an embarrassment for the men who shared his last name, and he wondered if his mother wished she had raised him differently.

God knew …

Claire tried.

With him, she tried *really* hard.

His half-sister, Vera, was perfect in every way, and he was at the other end of that rainbow. She certainly hadn't put their parents through the kind of shit he had over the years.

Still was, honestly.

The burden of not having turned out quite the way his parents pictured his life—or so he believed—kept Roman in a state of constant limbo. Numb because he was who he was, and he liked that person, but also just distant enough from the people who loved him that he hoped it hurt them less to see him this way. He never swung too much one way or the other; he stayed right in the middle, unwilling to figure out how to fix it.

Or if he wanted to.

When his family looked at him, did they see their legacy in ruin—was that all they saw?

"What's on your mind?"

Anastasia's voice broke through his thoughts. A throb at the back of his head reminded him why he didn't like females for more than a quick fuck—they never stopped talking.

Roman's stare cut her way. "Let's get something clear, otherwise, at the next stoplight, I'm kicking your ass out of this car."

She sucked in a fast breath.

He didn't wait for her to respond before adding, "We're not here to talk. I'm taking you to my shop, and then you go on your way. *Disappear.* I don't need to see you again. I don't want to."

Cold, yes.

But it was the truth.

At least, he was a decent enough man to offer her that. He couldn't say much else for the rest, though.

She sat with her long legs crossed, and her fingers tangling and untangling in her lap, the nervous actions making him more and more unsettled as the quiet seconds ticked on. He didn't care where she went or what she would have to do to get back home after this. Wherever her home was. He just wanted to wash his hands of her.

"I really *am* grateful to you," Anastasia whispered. "If I didn't leave with you ... he would never have let me go."

Roman groaned in response. He didn't need her gratitude. He just wanted to be left alone.

"And you didn't have to do this for me, except you still did. I know the asshole act is just to make it clear where we stand—and I do. You know, but maybe you're not the man you keep telling yourself you are, Roman Avdonin."

Or maybe he was exactly that man.

She didn't have the first clue.

Roman whipped his face around to look at her. "You don't fucking *know* me."

His voice and expression should have been cold enough for her to get the hint and shut the fuck up. His respect for her dared to notch up when Anastasia tipped her chin upward slightly, and stared him down, unafraid.

"No, I don't—someday, someone will, though. And when that happens, what will you do then?"

The words hit him right in the chest.

She didn't know ...

Couldn't.

But that terrified him.

The only thing that did.

• • •

Roman hadn't noticed the phone that sat between them in the console until the damn thing started to ring. *Through the Bluetooth speakers.* He hadn't put the radio on, but apparently, the speakers were turned up loud enough to make the ringing pierce through his eardrums.

"Is he as deaf as he is stupid?"

"It's his phone," Anastasia informed, glancing toward the phone.

Clearly.

Roman growled under his breath as he turned the volume down to a bearable level. Not that it did anything for the ache in his ears. "Why the *fuck* did he leave it in the car?"

"Paranoid. He thinks they're bugged, and someone might be listening. He doesn't like carrying them around everywhere."

"Them? He has more than one?"

Anastasia shrugged. "He only ever gets burner phones and switches them out every week."

Jesus.

He understood the need—many guys in his line of work replaced their phones often—still, not to that extent. Dima sounded more and more like someone who was constantly looking over his shoulder. Always afraid of getting caught with his pants down.

Why?

The obvious reason was rarely the right one.

The ringing finally ended, and then a few moments later, the screen on the dash blinked with a voice message. He didn't know why, but the message started auto-playing through Bluetooth.

Shit.

Maybe the car wasn't a rental.

Roman startled when he heard a soft, but annoyed, voice echo over the microphone.

"It's me. Katee. There. I called you back. Are you happy now?"

She sounded like ... a *girl.*

Young.

Maybe ten.

Silence spread through the Bugatti when the message ended abruptly.

He really shouldn't ask.

Roman's mouth worked before he could stop it. "Who the fuck was that?"

"I don't know. She calls him a lot, though," Anastasia replied. "Maybe his sister?"

Maybe.

Either way, Roman didn't give a shit. And because he couldn't afford another distraction like the phone call, he didn't waste time rolling down the window and tossing the device to the racing pavement below.

All he cared about now was getting the car to the shop where he would hide it until it could be cut down.

• • •

Despite owning three different chop shops across New York, the one in Brighton Beach was the one he preferred working at because it was also technically his home. One of two. He kept an apartment in the city—just because.

His loft was situated right above the chop shop. When someone from the bratva needed to find him, this was the first place they came to do so. And now it looked like *the cops* knew it, too.

Later, when he had time to think the situation over because he had nothing else to do except stare at the cement walls of a jail cell, Roman would blame the comfort he felt in the safety of his home for his distraction. He used the clicker to open the warehouse's shutters before driving straight into a goddamn mess.

At first, when Roman saw the three armed cops standing there—weapons already drawn and pointed at him through the windshield—he thought it was a joke. Not once had his shops been raided in the past year. And even before that, the amount of police he had on his payroll ensured he could do business without worry they were going to constantly come up on him without enough warning from his sources to keep his side of things covered.

Except it wasn't a joke.

And he was *fucked.*

"Oh, my God," Anastasia whispered, horrified.

ᴛʜᴇAGREEMENT

Roman's foot had hit the brakes on the car to stop it all of three feet away from the legs of the officers. His other foot twitched with the urge to jam down on the gas, but a rational part of his brain kept him from making an even worse mistake than he already had tonight.

"Hands up—*step out of the car with your hands up!*"

"Now!"

Shit, he hadn't even put the car in park. Roman's heart raced like thundering hooves in his chest as his gaze darted from the cops in front of him, and the rapidly closing garage door behind him in the rearview mirror.

He could have made it—*would have*—if not for Anastasia reaching over and digging her red stiletto nails into his arm with enough force to drag Roman's attention away from the danger he still faced.

"What the fuck are you—"

She didn't even finish her sentence before the windshield was shot out of the Bugatti. Roman had enough sense to turn his face away from the exploding glass, but he couldn't say if Anastasia had been smart enough—or quick, for that matter—to do the same. His low *fuck* hissed through the car when he turned his head just in time to see brass knuckles coming for the driver's side window.

It was over, then.

Roman knew it.

His hands went up, and all he said, hoping Anastasia would hear, was, "Be *easy*, shit."

Two cops went for him immediately—one must have got the car in park because the damn thing didn't roll away when he found himself some distance away from the car, face down to cement with hands on his back and shoulders.

A knee found the middle of his shoulders, too.

"Nice place, Roman," he heard one of the cops say above him. "Always wondered what it looked like inside."

Christ. "This was a setup," Roman hissed as he watched the scene unfold.

Anastasia was pulled from the car, too, but it only took one pig to do the job on that side of things. The horror filling her face as tears streamed down her cheeks did nothing to ease the rough handling of the officer that dragged her to Roman's side on the cement floor. It also didn't stop her from fighting the man every step of the way.

He had to give her that.

Somehow, Roman got the feeling that she didn't know what role she had played in this scheme—if that's what this had been—but if she did … he would make her wish she hadn't.

Roman tensed when the weight of the officer's knee came firmer into his back, the pain spearing through his spine instantly. "I said fucking *easy*, asshole."

The cop only laughed. "It's going to be a long night for you, buddy."

Stale breath wafted over his shoulder. He'd have given anything to be able to drive his fist through the man's rib cage in that second.

Life didn't work that way.

And this wasn't his first rodeo.

Roman was well aware what a stunt like that could potentially cost him, and already, he could count the charges he was going to have piling up.

Anastasia was the one who still hadn't got the memo to stay still, say nothing, and let the ball roll. Her unholy fit continued with the same cop who did his best to keep her contained on the floor.

"Let me go. You have to let me go! They will kill me."

Her screams flew over the cops.

Unheard.

Not for him, though.

She'd mentioned her idea of freedom earlier, and the word was still lingering in the back of his mind. As the cops barked back and forth—waiting for their back-up down the block, apparently, yet another sign this had been a planned event—he turned to the screeching redhead at his right.

"You wanna be free?"

Anastasia sucked in a shuddering, sobbed, "*W-what?*"

He wasn't going to be a parrot—didn't have time for it, considering their circumstances. Under his breath, Roman told the chick, "Keep your mouth shut—say you were my

32

whore. Picked you up in Odessa. You'll get twelve months, max. Chicago ... Dima, none of them will touch you when it's that long. Twelve months, and you can start over."

Her wet, green eyes searched his, but there wasn't anything left for her to find. Her red lips trembled like she was going to say something, and he was sure he saw her mouth *thank you* when the two cops gripping Roman yanked him up from the floor without warning. He didn't fight being led out of the warehouse. He figured there was a cop car parked outside. Somewhere discreet on the side where he didn't notice it when he zoomed past.

Like a fucking idiot.

The whole thing was a setup. He knew that now. Right from the Bugatti key, and Anastasia with the big tits and long legs to catch his self-indulgent eye. This was the reason why Dima was trying to dominate the conversation, determined to divert attention to the female on his arm and how desirable she was. He hoped to get on Roman's nerves, to inadvertently challenge him in to falling for the redheaded bait.

The motherfucker had figured him out—and knew Roman would not be able to resist the car or the woman when he had something to prove.

Pride was a bitch.

Especially his.

The better question was *why*.

Roman wouldn't waste time on being hit where he was weak—he only cared about the reason it happened in the first goddamn place. Those answers were going to have to wait. Unfortunately.

The grip of the police tightened on his shoulders as Roman whistled a happy tune, the cop car finally coming into sight. He knew that would infuriate them.

What did they expect?

"Knock it off," the cop at his left muttered.

Roman continued instead, and celebrated a silent mini-victory.

Whatever they did next, well ...

He'd probably suffered worse.

FOUR

As another round of chills started to creep through Roman's aching frame on the hard metal slab that was now his bed in the jail cell, he reminded himself that this was nothing he hadn't done before. He had been in jail for minor shit over the years. Months at a time, even. Protection wasn't something he concerned himself with, either. His last name guaranteed nobody with half a brain cell would or could touch him.

Not without dying for it.

He just wanted to be left alone.

It had been four days since his arrest, and he spent most of that time in his cell, staring up at the ceiling from his bed, blankly. At least, he was alone in the cell, but that was the only comfort he was allowed.

The effects of withdrawal had started rearing their ugly heads forty-eight hours into his incarceration. By three days, he was sure his neighbor in the cell next door to his was tired of hearing him pace as the headaches and shivers started. He could sense what was going to come. The puking. Fevers and chills for days. His heart already raced, but that would get far worse, too, until he was sure the organ might explode from the stress on it.

This was only the beginning.

Four days without the little baggies Marky supplied, and Roman was reminded all over again why he kept telling himself it was the last time *every time* he put the coke back down. Then, a fucking voice in his head that sounded a lot like himself would say he could handle it when he knew that white powder would make shit a whole lot better, and he'd be right back at it again. Still, he wasn't new to withdrawal. He just needed to wait it out. Wait for his body to flush it, and then he would be fresh again.

He'd been here, done this.

Just not in jail at the same time.

The best thing he could do for himself was to stay out of trouble. At least for a few days until the storm had passed. It wasn't like the officers in the jail would or could do anything to help with the symptoms—shit, they had active users in the jail cells who had drugs brought in for them to contend with. Somebody sweating out their withdrawal in a cell was a common sight.

He didn't have to worry about confronting his family—his parents would never visit him in jail. His family weren't traditionalist in following the bratva rules, but when police got involved, the rules and expectations were the same all across the board. *Everyone* stayed out of sight until shit was handled.

Demyan Avdonin and his wife would not be seen in a place like this, getting their photo taken and plastered across every rag in the city. It was attention the Avdonins didn't need, and his father's bratva couldn't afford. He had just handed his parents one more reason to add to the growing pile of concerns.

He gripped the edges of the metal bed while waves of nausea rippled through his body with the next round of shivers. His jaw clenched, feeling the rise and fall of his insides, in an effort to hold back the vomit promising to spill his stomach contents.

Deep breaths.

One more.

He might be able to breathe through it. A few more minutes, and the shaking would hopefully stop. His skin was glazed, damp with sweat. The sweat seeped through the faded buzz of his black hair—greasy to the touch. That was the least of Roman's problems.

He wasn't sure if his last name afforded him a bit of dignity and respect from the officers in the jail, but the guards hadn't forced him to leave for a shower. Or shit, maybe it was the opposite, and somebody was teaching him a lesson.

Fine.

It was well-learned.

The turning of a key in his cell door had Roman jumping up to sit on the edge of the bed. *Bad move.* He rocked himself back and forth, uncaring and not knowing who watched him from the door because that was the only way to keep himself from hurling his stomach contents on the floor.

Then, he looked up.

Fuck.

Through swimming vision, his grandfather, Anton, watched him from where he stood in the open passageway, slapping one of the guards on his shoulder. He even had a fucking smile on his face as he stepped into his grandson's cell.

Roman should have known.

Visitation rules didn't apply to the Avdonins.

Money talked.

Bullshit walked.

Anton was brought directly here. Despite the shaking and convulsing, it was instinctual for Roman to stand up. The respect of the matter, because his grandfather was in the room, and nothing more. Something he had done from the time he was a boy, and despite being a twenty-seven-year-old man in a bit of a messy situation, it bore no effect on the respect he offered to Anton.

ᴛʜᴇAGREEMENT

That, and a little bit of love.

Love made him stand, too.

In his seventies, one wouldn't think that looking at his grandfather, Anton wore the age badly. In fact, he carried it quite well. Deep lines in his face and the gray that colored his jet-black hair gave his severe nature a bit more wisdom and color. He was feared by many, but growing up under his grandfather's feet taught Roman one important thing about the man.

He was still just *that*.

A man.

"Roman, you look like shit, yeah," Anton said when the guard stepped away from the cell, and out of his sight entirely. "Sit down, my boy."

At least, he didn't look worried.

That was a win.

Roman would take what he could get.

And then his grandfather had to go and say, "Well done—you've thoroughly terrified your mother."

"Kick me when I'm down, Grandpapa."

That's how it was done.

Anton only shrugged.

Roman couldn't stand the silence. "What are you doing here?"

He sat back down, but not because his grandfather suggested it or because he really wanted to. His knees were already giving up on him, and the floor had started to spin.

Goddammit.

"I'm admiring the scenery," Anton said, a dark chuckle echoing with his words. "What the fuck do you think I'm doing here?"

Roman let out a grunt that tasted like bile. "Okay, *why* are you here?"

"Can't a grandfather visit his grandson in jail?"

"Not if he's Anton Avdonin." Roman tipped his head to the side, meeting his grandfather's gaze as he uttered through chattering teeth, "*We stay the fuck away from cops, always. A guy goes in, we work to get him out, but we don't fucking touch him until he is.* That's what you always told me."

37

And his father. Any bratva man that cared enough to teach Roman about their life. All of them. He knew how this worked. He expected nothing different for him *because* he was who he was.

So ...

"Why are you here?" he asked again.

His grandfather moved to stand against the wall, arms crossed over his wide chest. Like Demyan, Anton had that ability to scrutinize him and read him easily. *Old souls*, they had muttered between each other from the time Roman could remember. His father said they were all the same, just a little different. Anton never denied it.

Roman wondered *how*.

He had yet to figure it out.

"Are you going to ask me how they are?" Anton murmured instead of answering his grandson's question.

Stay out of my fucking head, he thought.

Still holding onto that stupid pride, Roman replied, "I'm going to ask you what they're saying about me, yeah."

Anton sighed deeply, shaking his head. It should have bothered Roman more that he was becoming accustomed to the look of disappointment on his family's faces. They thought he was out of control.

Hell.

They weren't wrong.

"Your mother worries, anyway, but this—"

"She has nothing to worry about," Roman snapped, refusing to let his grandfather even go there.

He wasn't doing this. And certainly not *here*—in a jail cell with a guard that was probably still close enough to overhear their private conversation. He stood up too quickly, making his legs turn to jelly. For a few minutes, he'd almost managed to forget that his body was revolting against his mind.

A war raged inside him.

Could his grandfather see it?

"No, you're right, Roman. Why would your mother worry—you're perfectly *fine*."

THE AGREEMENT

The sharp edge to Anton's voice was the only thing that kept his grandson from thinking he was speaking to himself. "You're in withdrawal."

A laugh escaped Roman's lips, and he rubbed his hand over his nose—a habit he hated. "I'm in prison. I'm bored. I was so close—that car would have pulled in three mil, *easy*."

The harder Roman tried to brush his current condition off, the darker Anton's face got.

"Listen to yourself."

"Grandpapa, just—"

"You're in *denial*."

Anton rarely yelled, and he certainly wasn't in the habit of raising his voice in public. But for a brief moment, he dropped the facade when his words snapped louder and felt like whips cracking down on a stoic Roman.

Never lose control, Roman.

Don't let people find the parts of you that react—or the things you'll react for. They'll always hit you where you're weak.

Those were Anton's words, so for his grandfather to make time to visit him here, alongside his outburst, it didn't mean anything good. Self-control was sometimes a very fickle thing for Avdonin men.

Roman was not the exception.

"I am fine," Roman assured, his throat dry. "I just need a few days."

"Your eyes look like they're bleeding."

"Do you want to sleep in this fucking joint, or …?"

"You're shaking. Has the puking started yet—the shits, maybe? God knows that steel toilet is going to be a lot harsher to sweat this round through than the cushioned seat in your bathroom at the loft, hmm?"

Right for the gut.

Like only his grandpapa could do.

Roman breathed through the pounding in his skull and vomit bubbling in his stomach, choosing his words carefully and letting them out slower than he cared to admit. "I'll survive it. This is nothing. I've been through worse."

"And yet, you keep insisting you don't have a problem. *Look* at you."

"My problem is that all of you expect me to be like—" Roman jammed his teeth together, forcing the words back down so he could mutter, "I know it's bad."

Anton raked a hand through his hair, staring at Roman with a blue gaze that matched his own. He hated the pity he found there when his grandfather looked him up and down once more. "Your hubris, my boy. How does it feel to arrive?"

"I—"

"You'll have a reckoning for this. You'll answer for it; you'll sacrifice more than you want."

Death, maybe?

If so …

"I'll welcome it with open fucking arms."

At this point, what else did he have to lose? Their very conversation and the way it unfolded told Roman everything he needed to know. Anton's chiding click spoke of his disapproval without him needing to voice it in another way, yet again.

Roman didn't expect anything different.

What had he ever done to make him proud? He wasn't Demyan. The perfect son. The perfect husband. He wasn't *always* in control; constantly the unwavering pillar in the storm that was their life. He enjoyed the chaos more than he should, and he didn't know how to stop doing that.

Anton had every reason to be proud of the man *he* had raised, while Roman was a whole other story.

"I don't think you understand," Anton warned, stepping closer to Roman once more.

"I think I understand you perfectly well, actually."

Roman swallowed the lump forming in his throat, refusing to dig deeper into the emotions slicing at his surface. Instead, he stared into the eyes of a man he had grown up admiring. One he knew he would never be able to become—so he hadn't even ever bothered to *try*. Not a single man who knew Anton could disrespect him, not if they truly sat down and allowed him five minutes to speak. He was *that* kind of man.

That was his legacy, and here was his grandson.

A car thief.

THE AGREEMENT

… with a drug problem.

What else was there to say?

"I'm sure you have some idea what this has done to your father," Anton said after a moment.

"I can't exactly picture him crying for me, let's be real."

Anton's eyes flickered with fleeting amusement, and the edges of his lips twitched like they might break into a grin. "I *meant*, the position you've put him in here. The Yazovs consider this as a mark of disrespect, and I don't blame them. Had this been done to me when I was a boss, I would have strung you from the telephone wires by your intestines. You tried to steal from them. The son of the Avdonin Pakhan—you *blatantly* stole from them. The balls on you, Roman. Jesus Christ."

"An opportunity presented itself to me. Tell me, in my position, you wouldn't have at least *considered* doing the same."

"But it's not me sweating out my coke habit in this cell, is it?" his grandfather returned just as swiftly. "*And* you fucked one of their whores. One of Dima's whores, no less. The good news for her is that information came from your friend—Marky—and it doesn't appear as though they're interested in chasing her through the system."

Roman wished he cared.

Irritation flickered in Anton's eyes at his grandson's obvious disregard for the mistakes he had made. "But who the fuck cares, Roman, right? Are you even listening to what I'm saying to you? That position you put your father in—the Yazovs suddenly have demands."

Wouldn't it be just his shit luck in that moment for another wild wave of shaking and chills to overtake Roman. It was intense enough to knock him back, and he had to turn away from his grandfather. Just so he wouldn't see the way his face twisted from the intensity.

"You think you're going to be able to hide this from me? What this is doing to you?" Anton asked.

"I have nothing to hide."

"No. No, you don't." When Roman faced his grandfather again, the man was clenching and unclenching his fists. "We let you go on for too long like you did. We're just as much to blame."

"You know they set me up, right? The whole thing was a setup."

"Which you fell for," Anton deadpanned.

"What do they want from us now?"

"You'll see when you get out. I only came here to offer your mother some sort of comfort because your father absolutely refused."

Right.

Demyan and his lines.

Roman didn't want to give his grandfather the impression that he was desperate to get out, but he stifled the urge to ask when he would be released, or even ... when a lawyer would show up on his behalf. He opted to keep his damn mouth shut. This was turning out to be the perfect place for him to ride out the storm of withdrawal.

Considering everything.

Anton was already moving to the cell door, tapping on it lightly with his wedding ring before he looked over his shoulder at his grandson again.

"Good talk, Grandpapa." Roman managed a sardonic smile through the sweat dripping down the sides of his face, and the muscles screaming in pain. "Tell my ma I'm fine. Nothing else."

Anton nodded once, and he knew his grandfather would keep his word on the news he delivered to Claire. As he strolled out of the cell, he called over his shoulder, "But someone should have told you to get your shit together a long time ago, Roman."

The cell door closed behind him, and he was alone.

Again.

Yeah.

"Yeah, someone should have given a shit," he murmured to himself.

• • •

⅋AGREEMENT

His stay didn't even last a week. Two days after his grandfather's visit, and Roman was led out of his cell, and freed to the streets. No explanation, and he knew better than to ask questions. The forces of the Avdonin Bratva, connections constantly working behind the scenes, had undoubtedly made it happen. There were a few perks to being who he was.

Even if he sacrificed for it.

A black car with the dark tinted windows, and a bull with a door already held open for him to slip into the backseat waited outside the jail for him. Roman squinted up at the sun, letting the warmth spread over on his face. At least, the shaking was gone. He still felt a gut-deep shudder from time to time, a clawing, irresistible urge to make a run for it.

To go find Marky.

A few more days of resistance and that whispering voice of cocaine still slipping through his veins would hopefully be gone, too.

Roman followed the man who was there to lead him to the car, saying nothing. Not that the bull minded—he didn't speak, either. He didn't know who he was but figured he was sent by Demyan to collect him. At one point, he'd stopped paying attention to all the men who surrounded his father. It was all a sea of fucking same-faced soldiers, anyway. Guys who weren't going anywhere but right where they already were at the end of the day. It was easier if he didn't make friends with people who eventually came to realize it was the men like him who kept them neck-down on the ground.

Under their boots.

In the car, he sank down in the seat. A few years ago, when conversation still flowed easily between his mother and him, she would have admonished him for sitting like that. *Like a cranky teenager.*

The scenes of the city passed him by—familiar streets he'd called home forever—and he couldn't help but wonder if he would miss this place if he ever had to leave. As much as he loved New York, and his family, he hated it all, too.

Too much.

Roman was surprised to find his mother waiting at the door as he took the steps up to the house two at a time. The bulls who guarded the estate had their attention turned to him. The Prince was back, and he'd brought trouble with him.

Everywhere he went.

Claire stood in front of him—mixed emotions marred her face. The flickering anger dancing over her trembling lips was fleeting, though, because the sadness was just as quick to come in its place. His mother had never raised a hand to him—*wouldn't*. She didn't hit her children, but he wondered if she wanted to right then. He would have deserved it.

Then, she smiled.

Soft, and sweet.

The relief taunted him. He would never have admitted that he was happy to see her, too. As a kid he remembered being affectionate, clinging to his mother's legs and gazing up at his father with pride. He laughed freely, and didn't worry about what people wanted from him. Life's experiences had knocked that bullshit out of him eventually.

"*Roman.*"

She spoke in her trademark quiet voice, leaning forward to put her arms around him. He let her hug him—that was as far he was going to allow it to go because anything more felt like a betrayal to her when he was still the cause of her pain. He breathed in his mother's familiar scent, allowing himself a sense of comfort. When she pulled away, her gaze searched his six-foot-five-inch frame.

Looking for marks?

Bruises, maybe.

Some sign of *jail*.

Who knew?

He was glad she didn't have to see him in the state that his grandfather found him a few days ago. There were conversations he never wanted to have with his mother, and the state of his addiction was *high* on that list.

"Your sister was about to fly down all the way from Russia," she said, still holding him by his shoulders at arm's length.

"Why would she do something as stupid as that?"

"Because she cares about you and loves you. She thought she would have been able to help. Or ... *do* something—you know how she is."

Yeah, he knew exactly how his sister was. Vera would get there, end up making a huge fuss, and meddle in every aspect of his life where she wasn't supposed to interfere. He loved Vera, probably much more than she knew, but she was who she was. She took her big sister role too seriously considering their ages. He was glad she didn't turn up at the jail for his little stint. A flight from Russia wasn't worth that.

Roman pulled away from his mother, and headed into the house. The last thing he needed was her sympathy or probing when it wouldn't do anything for his situation, and any answers she managed to pull from him would only leave her feeling far worse.

Silence worked better.

Even if it hurt.

In the foyer, the booming voice of the Yazov Pakhan, Maxim, carried down the winding staircase. He recognized the voice, not only from the restaurant meeting, but because he had heard it a handful of times in the past. The man's distant, but known and very *real*, friendship with Demyan afforded Roman the unfortunate luxury of knowing the man's tone on the spot.

It instantly irritated him. He may not have reacted that way under any other circumstance, but he couldn't quite say that considering his recent stint in jail because of one of Maxim's fucking men.

Well.

Roman had a big hand in that, too.

Not that it mattered.

"What the fuck is he doing here?" Roman asked his mother, his sharp tone making her wince. He really didn't expect an answer, and instead of waiting for one, followed the source of the voice. It led him to his father's office upstairs.

Claire stayed right on his heels. "Roman ... leave them be. Calm down a bit before—"

He ignored his mother, hot anger spiraling into his gut as he charged through the doors of the office to find his father in friendly conversation with the boss of the Chicago Bratva. Both men sat with swirling bourbons in their crystal glasses in each of his father's favorite leather bucket chairs. The ones Demyan liked placed directly in front of the bay windows so that he had a view of the birds in the spring and summer months. Both men turned his way at the abrupt— and rude, although he didn't give a damn—entrance.

"Son," was all Demyan remarked.

His expression remained undecipherable.

Blank like paper.

Roman couldn't tell if his father was happy to see him or not as he stepped further into the room. He didn't turn to make sure his mother was gone. She knew to disappear and not interfere when *vory* were in the house, but especially when they were in his father's office. Claire had been playing this game for far longer than even Roman. Her voice was loud in private, but she knew when that time was, too.

Maxim Yazov sat staring at him, resignation pulling his face in a more somber expression—the kind of look an uncle might give their favorite nephew for breaking a vase. Roman knew the man from his childhood, but he wouldn't go as far to say he held *real* affection for the man in the same way he might for his uncle, Koldan, the boss of the Jersey Bratva. As far as he remembered—Demyan and Maxim kept a friendship, but not a particularly close one. They had a decent working relationship, and Roman was brought up to respect Maxim because of it, but also as a man who had earned his rank in the bratva. A *boss*.

But he wasn't Roman's boss.

That's what counted today. One of his men had set him up, and sent him to jail over a *car*. Petty bullshit, really. None of his business with the car boost would really affect business between the organizations. Brigadiers fought amongst themselves all the time, *especially* between bratvas, and as long as it didn't hurt any withstanding deals or cross some obvious line, then nobody gave a shit.

What made him different?

ᴛʜᴇAGREEMENT

Roman couldn't be sure if Maxim had a role to play in his arrest, too. He intended on finding out, though.

"Do you want to explain to me—"

Demyan arched a brow, and the second his mouth opened, Roman's words came to a halt when his father said, "The first words out of your mouth should be *thank you* and nothing else, Roman."

"Excuse me?"

"Maxim here," Demyan explained, a hand waving in the direction of the quiet man, "pulled some strings, and got you out of the doghouse way sooner than we would have managed."

Roman didn't even blink. "I could have waited it out—let's not pretend like they were going to press charges that actually fucking stuck. Name a brigadier you know that wants his name on a police record as the *victim*. I was fine."

His father gave him that look—one that spoke volumes. A frequent, silent order that had accompanied him since childhood, and it pissed him off even more because of it. *Be grateful, Roman*, it said.

For what?

Getting clean on a jailhouse floor?

Unneeded police attention on his work?

Right.

Grateful.

Roman knew what was expected of him, and only because he didn't care to make the situation more difficult for himself than it needed to be, he turned to Maxim and gave him a nod. That was as far as he was going to go. The words *thank you* would not be pried from his living, breathing mouth.

"You *wouldn't* have been fine," Demyan noted, then, turning to Maxim with a nod of his own. "As I've said already, your help *is* appreciated, of course."

Roman *almost* flinched at that statement.

Anton would *never*.

Demyan was stooping—bending to another man in a position of power, even if it was in private. That went against everything he had ever known about his father, and what the man taught him. Roman seriously doubted the Yazovs had

47

anything that interested his father enough to essentially put him on his knees—even hypothetically.

So, why?

What was he trying to prove?

Apparently, Demyan wanted to prove something to Roman if his next words were any indication. "Maybe there is some way that my son can explain his actions. For once, I would enjoy hearing *that*."

His gaze turned on Roman, cold but patient.

Waiting.

So did Maxim's.

He had fucking news for them—not that they would *like* it. The two were going to keep waiting for something Roman didn't have. Or rather, something he didn't plan to give at all. Everyone in the room knew exactly what—and why—it had happened.

This was all a charade.

He refused to play into it.

"I'm not going to make excuses for myself," Roman said simply.

Maxim sat forward on the edge of his seat, almost as if he couldn't stop himself from watching the train wreck happen right in front of his face. Demyan drummed his fingers on the armchair, the line of his jaw tensing in a way that meant he was losing his calm demeanor, and *fast*.

The only noise?

Ice cubes swirling in his father's glass.

What else did he expect from Roman? Groveling? Going down on his knees and fucking apologizing to this man like he was the *lesser* between them?

Absolutely not.

When Demyan glanced at Maxim once more, a look was exchanged between the two that said there was something else at play. Something he wasn't privy to, and he didn't like that. It immediately put him on edge sharper than he could handle. He should have known his father wasn't going to just let his actions go with a half-assed non-apology.

This wasn't *new* for Roman.

It was just getting old.

⁊ᴇAGREEMENT

"Fine, then if my son doesn't feel like humbling himself, it only seems fair to allow you to do so, old friend," Demyan said, keeping his head tilted toward Maxim though his gaze rammed hard into Roman. "How can we repay you for this unfortunate incident?"

At that question, he faced Maxim directly and ignored Roman like he wasn't even in the room.

"Damages to the car, yes?"

"Of course."

"What fucking damages?" Roman snarled.

His father and Maxim continued as if he wasn't in the room.

Still.

"And Dima wants—"

Roman interrupted that bullshit from Maxim before it went any further. "I am *not* apologizing to him. You'll rip every bone from my body before I'll say fuck all to that piece of shit."

"That can be arranged," Maxim murmured.

He stared back at the man, unaffected.

So be it.

The thing people didn't realize about Roman?

He'd die on his hills.

Every fucking one of them.

His father tossed a warning look his way—what was that supposed to do?

Roman clenched his fists at his sides, noticing the throb behind his eyes where it was beginning to feel like his brain was contracting. Rage was a real problem he had never quite learned how to handle—why would he when letting it free felt so much better? He'd always been big on shit that felt good.

Right then, there were so many things in the room he would have loved to pick up and break. *Hurricane Roman,* his grandmama used to call him when he was younger and threw an unholy fit. If he ever had a chance to trash this room …

This was where his father exercised all his power—that authority Roman had grown to despise. Where he was constantly reminded of the fact that he was not like Demyan.

Not like Anton.

"He doesn't have to apologize to Dima, no, I have a better idea, anyway." Maxim spoke in a cool voice, like he knew where this conversation was headed from the moment he began. Unsurprisingly, Roman bet he did, too. "From what I hear, your chop shops are ... quite lucrative, yes?"

What does that fucking have anything to do with you?

His shops, the car theft ring ... that business he had built from the ground up, starting when he was still practically a fucking kid, was sacred to him in ways he couldn't explain. *He'd* done that.

It was his.

Fuck anyone who assumed differently, or thought they could take it from him.

He dared them to try.

If only Roman felt like letting his thoughts slip out of his mouth would do him good then he might consider it, but he was well aware that wasn't the case. Maybe it was the absence of the coke in his veins that made him feel less invincible, or even his recent stint in jail. One way or another, he knew his better option at the moment was to shut the fuck up until he understood what was really going on.

Maxim continued speaking to the room, unconcerned about Roman's silence. "I want the car theft scheme moved to Chicago. We can hire a new crew—or you can bring your own from here, no?—and we'll do whatever it takes to make it as successful as it has been here. *Eventually*—perhaps—I'll consider allowing *you* to return to your business here if things are beneficial on my side of things there."

Demyan glanced at his son, his silent anger vibrating through the room; the unspoken words he wouldn't say out loud were still clear to his son. *Do you see what you have done? You did this to yourself.*

Was he hearing this correctly?

Maxim Yazov wanted his own chop shop ring in Illinois, run exactly the way Roman had been running it here?

Why—he kept coming back to that goddamn question. He bet there were a handful of guys in Maxim's Bratva that were perfectly capable of running a boosting scheme. Maybe they wouldn't make as much money as Roman could—at least, not right away—but that was only because he had a ready set of connections to get shit off the ground. And he worked *years* for that.

The very fact he'd built his business the way he had allowed him a sort of freedom within the Avdonin Bratva that many other brigadiers didn't have. Roman did it all himself.

For what, now?

Chicago's benefit?

It certainly wouldn't be like New York, he bet.

"But you know, Maxim, I've had no role in Roman's work," Demyan murmured around the rim of his glass before taking a large gulp. Setting the glass back down to the table between the two men, he added, "Technically, he's not had to answer to or for anyone—he makes his money, pays his dues, and doesn't rely heavily on the direction—or *correction*—of his boss. It's ... worked better that way, you know?"

The rage coursing through Roman rendered him stone-still. He didn't expect Maxim to have the balls to suggest something like this to his father—or for his father to react in this way. Another bratva was suggesting stealing his son's business from right under his feet. So what, when Maxim was happy his scheme was up and running, making good money, then he'd boot Roman back to New York with a *lesson well-learned?*

Sounded like bullshit.

"That's what I was told, yes," Maxim said, nodding in agreement. "Which means it will have to be Roman running the show, but I don't mind. As long as the money is worth it, and he doesn't make me regret it."

"You're fucking kidding me."

Demyan shrugged, unfazed by his son's outburst. "Move to Chicago—get acquainted with a new scene? Sounds like it might be exactly what you need to ... start out clean. If you hear what I'm saying, I mean."

He heard him perfectly well, actually.

His father was trying to sell him this plan, having worked it out in advance with Maxim before Roman's arrival. *No doubt.* Another fucking setup. So this was how his father was spending his time while he was left to tough-it-out in jail.

Another teachable moment.

As if it had ever worked before.

"And in return you'll gain access to some of our trafficking routes, Demyan. I'll make sure it is worth your while. We can have our spies work that out between themselves, no?"

Demyan tipped his head once, saying only, "Works for me."

Wait …

"You can't just demand I—"

"And how long do you think this will last?" Demyan asked, interjecting before his son could get a decent word in edgewise. "Roman in Chicago, I mean. For his mother's peace of mind, give me an estimate."

Demyan was asking all the questions for him, as if this was a regular job interview or some shit. Except there was nothing regular about this, and it wasn't just *any* job. It was repayment. A lesson being taught to a truant son.

Roman saw through all of it. All the terms and conditions had been discussed before he had even stepped out of the jailhouse, he was sure. He wasn't going to get a say here—that much was clear.

"For as long as it takes," Maxim replied, offering a wave of two fingers in Roman's direction. "And so, I suppose it really comes down to him, no? And how dedicated he is to making it *work.*"

Roman said nothing.

What was the point?

That didn't seem to bother his father.

"This will be good for us all," Demyan added.

"For *whom?*"

Roman's sharp words—the only ones he could manage without saying something he might seriously regret—went unheard by the men.

"New things are on the horizon, Roman. *Good* things, maybe. A challenge, a new environment … friends to make, even?" Maxim offered him that as if it was something he might enjoy. "It's not a bad way to spend a year or two."

"Or longer." Demyan steepled his fingers under his chin, saying more, "This is the only way we can make the legal issues go away currently—the Yazovs will handle that as long as you do what you need to for them. Quite a *big* pile of legal shit that you have got yourself into, considering."

"I didn't *ask* for help to get out of it. I have managed to single-handedly get out of every other pile of shit just fine," Roman snapped back.

"Have you ever faced something like this before? You're looking at eight or more years in prison," Maxim interjected. It took every ounce of control he possessed to keep himself from pouncing at the man. "And that's if I tell my legal side of things to back off on applying pressure to the police I have in my pocket. If they keep digging beyond the hole you've already dug for yourself … Roman, it only gets worse from here, I assure you."

Then, Maxim smirked wickedly. "But move to Chicago for a few years and all this goes away, yes? *See*, simple. And I can make it happen."

Now it was a *few* years?

Right.

He knew better than to ask for options.

There weren't any.

His feet moved in the direction of the door before he truly comprehended what he was even doing, the heaviness of disbelief still thick enough to keep him quiet for the moment. One didn't just walk out of a room where two pakhans were in conversation. He should have waited to be dismissed, but what were they going to do—shoot him? By the sounds of it, Maxim needed him.

Demyan had long ago given up trying to educate his son in the proper displays of respect when it came to better men. And still, his father's angry, dark shout hit his back as he retreated from the room. "*Roman!*"

He let the door bang hard enough to echo on his way out. It was only the sight of his mother, standing at the end of the corridor, that made him pause long enough to subdue the sudden urge to trash the entire hallway.

"Can we talk?" she asked, the high pitch of her tone making him wince.

Claire was the kind of woman who put decorum and order above everything else. For her to drop that act, considering who was in the house, well it didn't spell out anything good. He assumed her anger was with him, but Roman stilled in place when she rushed toward him, clutching at the long string of pearls around her neck.

He was tempted to simply walk past her, and ignore the pleading in her eyes. But then she reached for him when she was closer, curling her fingers around his left bicep and gazing up at him with *love*—pure love from a mother. Emotion so raw, it always made him want to look away when she leveled it on him. Roman had always known his mother loved him. It was inexplicable—something he just *knew* when she was around him. A tangible feeling beyond the understanding. There was a part of him that thought it weakened him because he loved her, too. But he had never been able to say that love was enough to keep him from causing her pain.

Demyan was the king of New York, wielding unimaginable power over an entire state in the country. From the time he could walk, Roman found himself under his father's feet constantly, and yet as a child, it was with his mother where he felt safest.

Somehow, that hadn't changed.

"What do you want to talk about, Ma? Please, don't act like you didn't know. He wouldn't keep something like this from you."

Claire's grip on him tightened, her nostrils flared as her lips twitched. Wetness welled in her green eyes. He couldn't do tears.

No fucking way.

Not right then.

Not from his *ma*.

Roman was not the man mentally wired to handle his mother's sentimentality at the same time when he was ready to spontaneously combust from rage. He didn't want to be an asshole, but he was quickly running out of solutions to keep that from happening.

He tugged at his arm in an effort to pull away from her, but Claire held on tight.

"Yes, I knew. He told me. I know you won't believe me because you think nothing about this family is worth your while, but I fought him on it. *I did*, Roman. I don't want you to go to Chicago. I love having you here ... even if you don't want to be most of the time."

As her voice trailed off, Claire finally released her son, making him step back.

"It doesn't fucking matter, does it?" he asked, letting out a clipped laugh. "The boss made his decision, and we all know what it means. Bratva before *blood*, Ma. Right?"

It was the brotherhood's way. A long time ago, he thought he knew what that meant; even believed he was born for it.

"*Roman.*"

Her chiding did little for him.

"I'm not wrong, though."

Claire stood a little stiffer. "Even so, your father has never made the wrong decision for this family."

She held her head high, because God knew even if it broke her heart to send her son away, her loyalty for Demyan would never waver. No matter what happened—*love means for always,* she told him once when he dared to ask how she could love a man like his father, *even if I don't always like who he sometimes is.*

Roman couldn't help but wonder what that would feel like, to have a woman by his side who was that devoted— someone who blindly loved him, and would sacrifice anything asked if it meant being with him.

He couldn't imagine it.

Or maybe he didn't want to.

"Yeah, well, he is right about one thing," Roman told his mother, refusing to meet her burning gaze. He didn't want to watch as she fought conflicting emotions—he didn't want to be one side of the war she had to fight. In the end, she would never defy her husband, and a part of him understood why. "A change of scenery will do me some good. I can't wait to get the fuck out of here, and stay gone."

"Don't say that, you don't mean—"

He simply walked away from his mother, feeling her stare follow him the whole way down the corridor. He didn't look back.

FIVE

The one thing Roman knew for sure about Josef Pavlov was that he was nothing like Marky. Older, tattooed from head to toe in the symbolisms of the bratva life like everyone else in Chicago affiliated to the Yazov organization, he wasn't exactly Roman's first pick as a partner.

If one wanted to call him that.

Even though the two men were spending a lot of time together in close quarters—the way Roman did with Marky back in New York—Josef was being paid to do it here. And that wasn't something he could afford to forget.

Standing side by side, the two smoked their cigarettes, Roman eyed the different rings that had been tattooed to the man's fingers; an interesting take on a spider had been added to peek out of his sleeve at his wrist, too. He hadn't realized how different it would be to work with men who were more *traditional* in a sense when it came to the Russian mob. It took him very little time in Chicago to realize his lack of decoration—by way of tattoos he should have earned over his life as a *vor*—was simply something that would cause suspicion for men who didn't know him upon sight.

Josef was the only one brave enough to point it out.

He and Josef surveyed the workers in construction hats milling around the building in silence. It was a way they had found to start the day that didn't include too much conversation usually.

Fun.

In the two weeks since he first landed in Chicago, there weren't a lot of things Roman found he liked about the city. He wasn't a real *look-on-the-brightside* type, either. He didn't care to look for silver linings just to make his current existence better. However, he did have his own setup here getting off the ground, and even though he was well aware of the Yazov eyes constantly watching him, for the most part, they left him alone.

Except for Josef.

The bull assigned to him by Maxim Yazov didn't fool Roman for a second. His job there wasn't purely for protection. Josef wouldn't have hesitated to pump a few bullets into him, and deliver him dead to the Yazov Bratva if that was his order.

Shit.

Maybe someday it would be.

For the moment, though, he shared a conversation with Josef like any guys working together would. What other choice did Roman have? It wasn't like he knew anyone else in the city. And he couldn't say he was keen on changing that, either.

Now that he was starting to kick things off with the chop shop, he'd already planned to bring in some of the crew from New York. The men who had worked with him for years while he built his business were as crucial to its success as his own instincts. They knew what to do, and how Roman liked to run the show.

Which was the only thing that mattered.

His circus—*his* fucking monkeys.

"So you literally chop the cars down, yeah?" Josef asked.

ᵀᴴᴱAGREEMENT

He was sucking in his cheeks to draw in a long drag of the cigarette, pulling the smoke straight into his lungs, and then releasing the gray cloud in curls around his face. The smoke almost formed a halo, making Roman grin because there was nothing holy about this man. Nothing holy about any of them.

"Yeah, it's way easier to ship parts of a car than the whole fucking thing. Gets through ports faster, too. They never know what the fuck they're looking at, you know? The guys I work with overseas—they put it all back together," Roman explained.

Josef nodded his head along like the fog was finally clearing, and things were beginning to make sense to him. "And these contacts, you trust them?"

"Never had a reason not to. I've been fucked over in the past, and it took me a long time to build a trustworthy team of guys I work with, in New York and overseas. I mean, we are who we are—gotta be real, man. It still comes down to a goddamn word. A man's word still counts for something here."

"They said you did it yourself, I heard."

Roman's lips twitched with an urge to smirk, but he held it back. *Barely.* The whispers about him and his business—and the reason why he found himself in Chicago—were already making the rounds, it seemed. It was even getting back to him.

That was fast.

"My father traffics guns—I did better with cars," Roman offered with a shrug. "It's not really the same kind of business, if you know what I mean."

Josef pursed his lips, impressed, sending Roman's thoughts into a tizzy while he tried to figure out if this conversation was even genuine. Ever since that meeting between the bratvas—the day he tried to steal Dima's Bugatti—he felt like everyone around him was screwing him over. Or he was paranoid enough to think it might be happening.

Including his own father.

Roman was now beginning to understand why his grandfather had always told him that he should never trust anybody. Least of all, the guy who shaved his beard.

Think about it, Roman, if a man was untouchable—bulletproof—who would you pay to do the deed on an unkillable man? Then, Anton would grin and add, *His barber, of course.*

Just because Josef engaged him in a chat didn't mean they were suddenly friends. He was still a Yazov bull, and Roman was just the Avdonin Prince who had been chopped down and shipped to Chicago to pay his dues. Just like the cars that had brought him here in the first place.

Not a single day went by that he wasn't reminded he was walking a tightrope. The only reason he was here was to make money for the Yazovs, another check and balance that he wouldn't be free and out of prison if it wasn't for the friendship between Maxim and Demyan. They would have left him in there for as long as it took the Avdonins to get him out while Maxim's *people* kept pulling their goddamn strings.

All he was expected to do now was to stay out of trouble, keep his head down and set up the chop shop scene in Illinois. Once that was done, and Maxim was sufficiently satisfied, he would be able to return to New York. Roman didn't know if this would also redeem him in his father's eyes, but he also couldn't say he cared. It wasn't exactly a puzzle—this had worked out perfectly for both Maxim and Demyan. His father believed his son needed to be taught a lesson that forced him out of New York, and away from his privilege.

Away from bad influences, his familiar streets, and the power he could so easily extend because of who he was.

Maxim got a new business venture in return. One that would bring him in hundreds of millions of dollars in a matter of years.

"What are they building here—an apartment block?" he asked Josef.

The construction crew continued above them, hammering, sawing and cementing high walls. The premises belonged to the Yazov Bratva, and it was where Roman had been given a small shack as his own office. The construction sounds alone would have been enough to annoy the fuck out of anyone else. Roman had an ability to drown everything else out, barely even noticing the sounds around him.

Josef shrugged in response, muttering low, "Maybe apartments, maybe offices. It's none of your concern."

The reply was curt, but not unfriendly. It still reminded Roman that he needed to color inside the lines here—with *everyone*.

Roman shrugged, too, flicking his cigarette butt to the ground before he stepped down with his shoe and pressed it into the muddy gravel. "No, it fucking isn't."

Josef, pleased with that response if the tight smile he gave was any indication, gestured to the shack. They started walking in the direction of the room where Roman worked. At the moment, his hours revolved around making the right phone calls, gathering lists and contacts, and having his ear to the ground. He had to first formulate the team of people he trusted the most, so that when he was ready and had the opportunity for their first serious theft run, he would have a team that was capable, too. One he wouldn't need to worry about fucking up because they were too green to the business.

"Is the new project going well?" his mother had asked him on the phone two days ago. She wouldn't outright ask about his work, making it sound like it was a new corporate job because that was easier to swallow, he imagined.

"Fine, Ma."

"Aren't you going to ask about him?"

Roman had hesitated. They both knew she had meant his father. He asked instead, *"Does he ask about me?"*

"Don't be like that. He misses you, baby."

Roman had nearly cackled. *"Did he use those words?"*

Though he hadn't been looking at his mother's face—he knew she had to be smiling. Demyan Avdonin, usually emotionless on his best days, wasn't going to talk about his son in that way. Certainly not now when Roman was a grown ass man.

"So, maybe not," his mother had added at the end of their conversation with a laugh, *"but I know he does, Roman. He's missed you for a long time—longer than you realize. But how is he supposed to tell you that when you can't even stand to hear me say it to you?"*

He'd needed to get her off the phone after that.

"Don't worry, you'll like it here."

Josef's voice snapped him out of his thoughts. Roman wasn't paying attention, and hadn't realized the man was still talking.

"The only issue with that is I'm not sure I like it anywhere."

Josef lifted a brow indifferently. "It's not like there's a rulebook that says you have to fit in, no?"

At the door of Roman's new office, he stopped at the threshold and gave his new companion a twisted grin. Josef would remain at the door for as long as Roman stayed inside.

"No, I don't really care to fit in," Roman noted, giving the work around him one last look, "but nobody said anything about me not having a little fun."

Josef raised his brows in surprise. "Depends on your brand of fun, *Prince*."

Roman almost scoffed.

Almost.

"I'm sure you can find something for me to do, *and* keep me in line—it's far worse when I have to go and find it for myself."

Josef groaned, his cheeks working like he was chewing over his thoughts with every clench of his beefy jaws. Technically, it wasn't an outlandish request. Even the boss would agree that a man of Roman's age needed a bit of legroom to move and breathe if they wanted to avoid burning him out. Maxim had never specifically mentioned not being allowed to find other channels of entertainment.

He just knew to stay out of trouble.

Simple.

"I'm supposed to keep your nose clean, yeah," Josef commented after some thought.

"Who says I'm not doing that?"

ᴛʜᴇAGREEMENT

Josef considered that some more, and Roman could sense the weight shifting in his favor a little. "I'll think of something," the bull eventually replied.

"Yeah man, just think about it. I've got all the time in the world."

Technically.

Roman had a smile on his face as he walked into the office. Genuine fucking delight dared to creep up on him for the first time in two weeks. Finally, he might have the chance to live a little while he was here.

Shit.

He had to make it worth it.

Right?

• • •

"Igor Ivanov, you have heard of him, yes?" Josef spoke.

Roman was just about to get out of the car when the question stopped him. "He's a Yazov brigadier—why?"

"He owns this place."

Josef tipped his head towards the club behind them. Right smack in the middle of downtown Chicago, and there were people everywhere. This particular club seemed isolated, though. No long queues snaked out from the front entrance because it was as if everyone knew to stay away. Several bouncers stood at the door staring every passerby down, and that was enough to send any curious people on their way. *Fast.* Nobody was welcome—quite a vibe.

"Thanks, I'll keep it in mind," Roman replied.

"Yes, it *is* for your information so that if you decide you want to make it out of there alive tonight, you will behave yourself."

Josef's voice carried enough warning itself without the words, but they simply drove the point home for Roman. They walked together to the door, and the men guarding it stepped aside when they noticed the approaching bull. Without being ordered to do so. Well …

At least, they had assigned him a man who knew his way around, and would use it.

63

Roman could already feel the floor vibrating under his feet as they made their way to the inner door. Flashing neon lights first blinded him, and then brightened his vision all at once. The thumping music pulsed in his veins, and he was beginning to realize that when sober, *this* was as much of a drug as the cocaine. He had been craving … *something*. Maybe just a reminder he was still alive and well, and he didn't even know it.

Josef extended an arm past his shoulder, pushing the door which swung open ahead of Roman. The blast of the music and the shards of roaming neon lights were a punch to the gut. He had been in withdrawal of clubs like he had been of drugs, apparently. Adrenaline pumped through his veins as he stepped in further, and surveyed the place. Josef was right behind him, following his every step.

For its large space and the coveted location downtown, the club was fairly unpopulated. At the centre of the floor was a stage with a stripper pole, a runway that led to a wall of satiny, black curtains, and a suspended cage. There were girls on the stage everywhere, mostly naked, thrusting perky tits out while they stretched their legs up poles or twerked their round asses high in the air. The girls inside the cage were dressed like kittens, licking their paws and down on all four as they crawled around and touched themselves.

Roman ignored his cock that dared to thicken inside his jeans at the idea of a lap tease from a chick with kitten ears—*just because.*

The place was definitely a hard-on.

Josef put a hand on his shoulder, indicating the bar to him, and the two of them weaved their way through. He recognized the Yazov crowd straight away, and they did, too.

Suddenly, all eyes were on him while he asked for a vodka at the counter. Did anyone drink anything else here? Roman always wondered why they even bothered to fully stock these lavish bars when the only drink every member of the bratva wanted was vodka.

Josef spoke to the chick serving the drinks while Roman made note of the men who continued eyeing him from their position across the way. Traditionalists in their bratva lifestyle, Roman stuck out like a sore and bandaged thumb amongst the group. He wasn't even fucking inked like they were. The only tattoos he had were the on the back of his neck—an eagle; his definition of true freedom—and the black roses on his chest afforded to him by his father. The only sign of his bratva rank.

And by the standards of these men—who wore proud, eight-pointed stars on their clavicles to signify *their* vory status—not a proper sign of rank, either.

If these men had to judge a guy by his cover at first glance, they looked for the ink first to tell them the story they needed to know about a man, and apparently, Roman had none. It was one of the many places his father's bratva had separated from the traditionalists over the decades.

If this was their first impression of the New York Avdonins—Roman knew he was doing a piss poor job of it. He gave them the standard *fuck off* stare, hoping one *would* make a comment so he could make something of it, and then turned to speak to Josef.

Instead, he found a different man standing behind him. He recognized the scar across his right eye. Something a pirate might have earned himself and would have covered with a patch—the unsightly, puckered wound might have been long healed, but it was still damn uncomfortable to look at. But Igor Ivanov didn't have time for shit like making others comfortable with something stupid like *staring* at him.

"You are Roman Avdonin," Igor said, the words a grunted utter through a thick Russian accent that made Roman tip his chin up a bit in response.

Another weak spot for him.

He'd never cared to learn the language.

Roman eyed Josef standing at the far end of the counter, watching with careful amusement. Apparently, he wanted to keep his distance while Igor spoke with him. Wasn't he supposed to be by his side at all times?

"Yes, I am. And you are Igor Ivanov. Nice place, man."

Igor arched a thick brow, the one where the scar continued right up through to his forehead. "Demyan Avdonin's *pup*."

"Tell me something I don't know."

Igor bared his teeth like a rabid dog might when he was at the end of his chain, and already going insane. "Okay, how about we try this, no? The only reason you are still alive is because our boss and yours have shaken hands. *Comrades.*"

No. The only reason Roman was even in Chicago was because their bratva had screwed him over, but he kept that to himself.

The angry Russian at his side continued on, saying through clenched teeth, "You think you're some big boss now—calling the shots on my fucking side of town for that stupid little scheme of yours? You're nothing more than a piece of slimy shit stuck to my shoe, *pup.*"

Nice.

Some guys just had to go and make a big deal about people coming into their territory—they made a show out of it, even. Roman couldn't say he'd done what Igor accused, but it wasn't *impossible*, either. At the same time, if those Russians in the corner were men of Igor's specifically, then this show made a lot more sense.

Everyone had to make their lines clear.

Mark their territory *well*.

At the same time, Roman wouldn't be made to look like a dumb fuck for Igor's pleasure, either. "I'm just doing what I've been told to do, actually. If my business has intersected with yours since I've been here, my bad—nature of my work sometimes, you know?"

"And yet, you are *here*, making demands. They'll have to find another warehouse for you—I won't be giving up one of mine to add to whatever collection Maxim is building for your spoiled ass, *suka.*"

Ah.

Now he'd gone from calling Roman a *pup*, to taunting him with the Russian equivalent for *bitch*. Weak men *loved* the simplicity of name-calling; he'd always thought it was really just a sign of someone's lack of intelligence. They didn't have a better comeback than a name that might piss a man off, or hurt his ego.

To him?

That shit was *funny*.

ᴛʜᴇAGREEMENT

Roman breathed deeply, squaring his shoulders as a realization dawned on him. He was starting to see what this was really about. Igor was undoubtedly pissed off because Roman had turned away the list that was sent to him—a list of men Igor suggested for the new team at the chop shop gig.

"I am going to run the scheme my way," Roman said to the man, keeping his arms folded across the bar, and his position as relaxed as he could seem. He had a short fuse, sure, but he also saw bait when it was right in front of his face. He wouldn't be the idiot taking it here. "I'm sure Maxim will agree that I know what I'm doing. He wouldn't have gotten me here if he didn't already believe it to be true."

"You're just … just a fucking *kid*!"

Igor's yell carried over the thumping music, making men turn to stare their way. It was just another excuse to look, everyone already knew Igor and Roman were talking business. Now they simply didn't have to pretend *not* to pay attention.

Tension was a buzz electrifying the air while conversations dropped to a low hum. They were all trying to hear what might be said next, and the ball was in his court. Roman took it, happily.

"And yet, your pakhan has given me the final say on everything regarding *my* business," Roman said. "So if you don't like that, you know exactly the man to take it to. I encourage you to do so."

Igor's knuckles whitened as he gripped his drink tighter. He took a step closer to Roman, but he held his ground, not moving a single inch. The man wouldn't touch him, he knew that. He was here under Maxim's orders. As long as he didn't provoke the man in a purposeful way that would justify a response, Roman wasn't doing anything wrong.

Igor knew it, too. One hard breath from the man, and he muttered, "Enjoy yourself tonight, yes? Who knows how long it will last."

Igor turned away, and immediately the conversations resumed around them. Josef almost looked relieved when Roman caught his eye.

The second Igor had walked away, Josef replaced his
empty space.

"Didn't think I could do it, did you?" he asked, daring to
grin.

"Just keep your fucking head down. You're going to get
my ass in trouble for bringing you here."

"We were just having a chat, man, relax. It's all good."

Even though Roman was smiling, a tightness settled deep
in his abdomen. This was Chicago, he wasn't the prince of
the streets here. Little Odessa's Devil was not in Brighton
Beach anymore, and every fucking piece of shit here was
going to remind him of exactly that.

Over and over again.

He looked around, scanning the crowd that had spread
away now, each group pretending they didn't have their eye
on him. If this was the only way to survive this place, he
would have loved to do it with a little bit of help to give him
an edge. One that afforded him the ability to not care.
However, cocaine was off the table. He knew he couldn't get
back into that chaotic spiral, not now.

Not here.

Maybe when he finally had some money coming in and
had something to show for himself—maybe then he'd be
able to test Maxim's limits if life was as boring as it currently
happened to be. Until then, just like Josef said, the only way
to get through this was by keeping his head down. Which
meant he needed to stay clean.

"Where are you going?"

Josef's clipped and worried voice hit his back as Roman
left the counter, and headed away. He didn't want to be
stuck in the VIP section all night, mainly because he didn't
want to stare at the faces of the Yazov crew the whole time.
Besides, he liked the look of the pussycats in the cage up on
the stage.

He decided not to respond to Josef, knowing he would be
followed anyway.

At the edge of the stage, Roman stood staring up at the
girls who were dancing and swinging their bodies in the most
delicious way. He was already reaching for his wallet, fishing

crisp bills out to stick in their thongs when they came near enough for it.

Hey.

Talent deserved to be rewarded.

"The boss had a message for me to give to you, by the way," Josef said as he came up behind Roman.

"And when were you going to tell me about it?"

"I'm telling you now."

Roman should have probably been paying a little more attention to what Josef had to say, but one of the costumed girls had crawled over to the edge of the cage. She was on all fours, purring like a cat, and staring with her piercing, painted cat eyes directly at him.

He was distracted.

But goddamn.

It was a good distraction to have.

"He wants you to go see him by the end of this month—before tribute," Josef continued.

"Why?"

Roman slipped a fifty dollar bill out of his wallet, and waved it in front of his face as his tongue flicked out to touch the top of his teeth. The girl sat up on her knees and then turned, displaying her long, curling tail. Underneath the tail, she was in a thong which he barely noticed. All he had eyes for was her plump ass which she offered to him by thrusting it up for him to admire.

Roman stretched out his arm, tucking the bill into the strap of her thong. When she shook her ass, the tail swished, and she winked over her shoulder in gratitude. His mind wandered to the thought of pinning her to the bars of the cage, fucking her right there in front of everyone to watch.

Yeah.

He wasn't even a fan of strippers. Certainly not for anything more than their chosen job. He didn't get off on the idea of people watching the woman he was fucking as much as he just needed to get his dick wet. It had been too long.

"He's the boss," Josef said, making Roman's irritation notch higher simply by hearing the man's voice alone.

Couldn't he just watch a chick shake her ass so at least he had a vision to jack off to in the shower later? *Fuck.* Unfortunately, Josef continued on. "He makes the rules. I don't ask questions. He wants to see you, and you have to go."

Fuck Josef.

Fuck the entire conversation.

Roman looked over at the bull, hoping the man would see the warning in his eyes. "Fine. Whatever. I'll go."

"You're not listening to me. You need to have something to show when you meet him. Do you understand? If you've not made any money here this month, you better have something else to show instead."

Roman emptied the remainder of the vodka down his throat, relishing the way it spread a warmth in the pit of his stomach. "Or fucking what?"

At first, it seemed that Josef was going to just stay silent, but he really didn't seem like the type to play the mysterious angle. Straight to the point was more his style. It was one of the few things he did like about the man. He proved Roman right when he stared hard at him, and said frankly, "The last time a guy showed up empty-handed when the boss was expecting something—he left without his right hand."

Roman clenched his jaw until his molars ached. "And what the fuck is that supposed to mean?"

"The boss had it cut off—made him bring it to the following meetings just because, no? Fucking thing even started to stink. It means, you arrogant little shit, that you should be thankful you still have two hands to hold your cash in. Mind your manners, and you still will at the end of the month, too."

Well, then.

Fair enough.

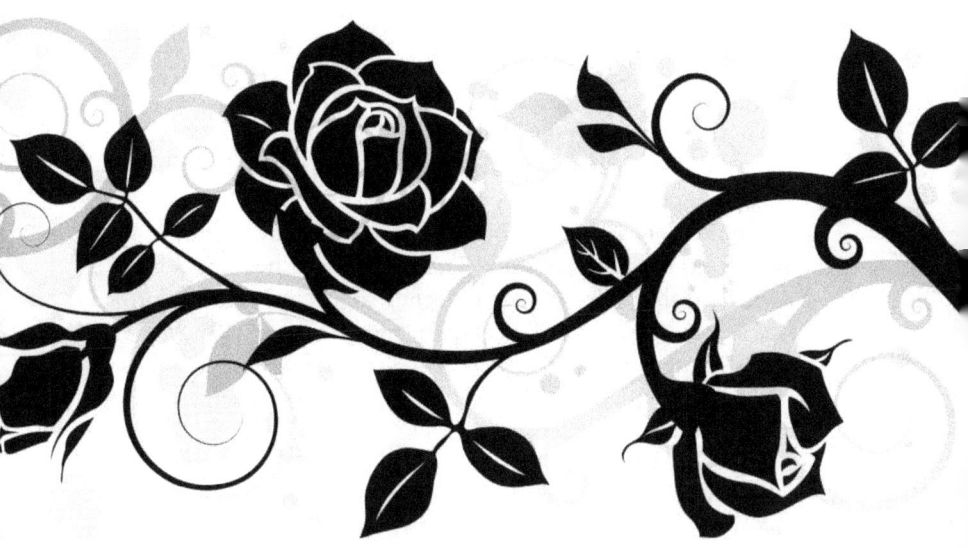

SIX

Karine Yazov's eyelids fluttered, her body's way of threatening to pull her from sleep, but she refused to open them yet. A silly part of her had always believed that if she just kept her eyes shut, pretended that she hadn't woken, then she would quickly fall back asleep. It never worked— she also didn't stop trying.

It was only the warmth of the sunlight on her face that made her decide maybe it wouldn't be such a bad thing to wake up. The brightness shining in through one of her bedroom windows kept her from turning her face directly into the light, but that was okay, too. With her eyelids still shut tight, she kept her dreams to herself.

Somehow, she'd managed to convince herself that if she didn't open her eyes, then those wonderful dreams she was seeing wouldn't leave. She would then belong to that world where she had both hands grazing the thick, sturdy trunk of a tree as she swung around it.

But it was good there.

In the dream.

Warm, soft moss at her feet. Shrill, but sweet, laughter curling into a summer day.

There was another girl there—a kid, actually. She had the same chestnut hair as Karine, long, pin-straight, and brushed neatly to spread around her shoulders. The little girl continued to watch her in silence while Karine swung and swung around the tree trunk. The laughter she heard was her own childish giggle—that very feeling of joy and exhilaration was something she had never quite known before. A feeling that she knew would disappear if she opened her eyes.

She had decided already—she was never going to open her eyes again.

Simple as that.

"Get up, get up. Stop playing foolish in your bed sheets because you don't want to deal with a hangover."

Masha's voice broke through the scene in her head—the sharp tone of her nanny ripping Karine back to reality before she was ready. She could still feel the twisted bark of the tree's trunk under her fingertips. The little girl watched on as Karine was yanked further away, but Masha's voice continued on like a loud echo in her brain that came from somewhere else entirely.

Somewhere that the place she dreamed of—with warm moss under the trunk of a tree a little girl who never talked—didn't exist. No matter how hard she tried to hold on to the false reality in her dreams, she couldn't. A life, one still cloaked in make-believe, waited for her.

Her eyelids fluttered again, and this time opened, just enough to let the sunlight filter in.

Too bright.

So bright.

"Don't be lazy, Karine," Masha scolded. "Must we do this *every* day?"

She still refused to crack her eyes open beyond what she already did as Masha walked around the bedroom, pulling curtains open and brightening the room further. Another day, Karine might have demanded to be allowed to sleep more, but she didn't have the energy to make those protests.

ᴛʜᴇAGREEMENT

The easiest route to a decent morning was for her to do as
Masha said.

When she did finally open her eyes to the full blast of
sunlight coming in through the window, the room was
ablaze. *And so was her fucking head.* She whimpered, and turned
her face away immediately, losing hope that she'd be able to
get herself out of bed today. Especially with the deep
throbbing that started somewhere in the back of her head
and reached all the way to her temples.

A hangover?

Right.

This felt like death.

"Here, have some water—you need it," Masha said.

Her voice was kind, but commanding at the same time.
Much like a *baba's* would be—no one knew how to be a
better caretaker and disciplinarian than a Russian
grandmother with a wooden rolling pin. Karine had never
known her own grandmother, so Masha was the closest
thing to it that she ever had. Even if the forty-year-old
woman was a bit young to claim her as a grandchild.

Blindly, she reached out toward Masha's voice, and found
a cold glass of water pressed back into her palm. She molded
her fingers around it, silently grateful for Masha's
attentiveness to Karine's constant plight—especially in the
mornings—even if she did hate the process of waking up.

Every single time.

Masha continued to hold the glass, guiding it to Karine's
lips, and helping her take the first sip. She smacked her lips
lightly as she drank more water, desperate to rid the dryness
that chapped her lips and made her tongue feel like
sandpaper against the roof of her mouth.

The water was *heaven.*

When was the last time she had something to drink?

Masha had to be right. She was too hungover to remember
or move. However, she couldn't recall a single memory of
how she found herself in this condition either. Walking
around with a glass of *something* in her hand—usually vodka,
maybe a bit of wine—was commonplace for her. What
began as a little something to make breakfast go down easier

ended up with mornings where she found a nightstand full
of empty glasses.

Only dribbles of liquor ever remained.

"Open your eyes now, dear."

Masha's voice came softer than ever, and a gentle hand
pressed to Karine's forehead. She recognized the touch well
since nobody else was affectionate with her—not like this.

Not any other member of her family, only Masha.

And Masha was *just* a slave.

Hers, sure.

Or that's what her father always said.

But a slave all the same.

Karine opened her eyes, then, testing the waters of her
hangover once more. The pain wasn't as bad—she didn't
think she was going to immediately puke all over the dark
hardwood floors. Bleary-eyed, she quietly watched while
Masha strode around the room, plumping pillows, dusting
surfaces, and chatting about the roses that were in bloom in
the garden.

White and red.

Pink was her favorite.

Yellow was hard to keep—*sometimes*. It depended on the
rain, apparently. She listened on, not really replying to joining
in on the conversation, but the older woman didn't mind.
Karine had never really thought about who Masha was
outside of the confines of her own life. Certainly not beyond
the walls of the place they called home.

A nanny—that was who she told herself Masha was to her.
The reality wasn't that straightforward. Masha certainly had
all of a nanny or caretaker's responsibility, and she possessed
these all through Karine's life. Ever since she was a child and
could remember, Masha was the one who tucked her in bed
at night.

She was always there.

Kind.

Soft-handed.

Promising better things.

Karine was twenty now, and Masha still helped her bathe
most days. Well, if one considered bringing her the things

she needed and running the water so that Karine didn't have to touch a thing was *bathing* her.

The difference between a nanny and Masha—was that she was not allowed to leave the Yazov mansion unless it was with Karine, or one of the bulls. Masha had no freedom and no other home. She would never be free of Karine, or the rest of the Yazov family. More importantly, she was not paid for her undying loyalty ... or her lifetime of services.

Masha earned her keep by serving Karine and anyone who called the Yazov mansion home with her every waking minute. She looked after Karine, ruling her life with a firm hand to get her through the day and yet, she had no power or control.

Even though Masha spoke to her as though Karine had no choice but to listen—all Karine needed to do was point at the door, and Masha would apologize and leave the room. Those were the rules that existed between them though they never actually acknowledged it.

The levels of power and expectations existed everywhere else in the Yazov household, except in Karine's bedroom. She also made it a point to never make Masha feel less than, or reminded her of her true position within these walls—that of a slave.

She meant *more* to Karine.

More than just that.

"It's time to get ready, yes? Your father and the others will be waiting for you." Masha stood at the entrance of her walk-in closet, speaking with her head tilted to the side. Like someone might do to a sleepy child. "What happens when we make them wait? You've already slept in too late."

Karine didn't need the reminder.

And yet ...

Masha still gave it.

"Why do I have to see him?" Karine asked, at least making an attempt to keep the whine out of her words. It was the most she could do. "Why now? I have a headache."

"Yes, that much is obvious, child. But here's the thing— you *constantly* have a headache because you have been drinking too much and having a good time, haven't you?"

Masha asked, amusement thick in her voice as it grew fainter when she disappeared into the closet, presumably to pick out Karine's outfit for the day. "Too good of a time, apparently. Something to consider, Karine."

On mornings when she woke up feeling like this, which was more often than not lately, Masha was the one who took the responsibility of making all her daily administrative decisions. She emerged with a cream lace dress that would show off her figure, and tan pumps that had a way of making her legs look longer than they actually were.

At least, her nanny had good taste.

"How about this?" Masha asked, smiling eagerly as she waited for Karine's approval.

"Isn't that too much for a morning visit with family?"

Masha's smile stretched wider as she brought the items over to the bed. "You're being silly again. You must always look your best, no? Especially for the family."

The throbbing ache at the back of Karine's skull sent pain dancing down her spine in punishing steps. She put the glass down on the bedside table, and leaned further into the high-piled pillows, pinning her eyelids shut again.

If only she could feel that delirious joy again—what she felt in her dream when she was circling the tree.

Masha's hand was back on her cheek in an instant, the back of her palm gently stroking Karine to wake up and face the day.

"Why does my father want to see me?" she asked.

Maxim *never* wanted to see her.

That was the whole point.

A part of her even liked it this way.

Karine forced her eyes open while Masha stepped away from her, replying softly, "I get directions—not details. You know this. Now, come over here, let's get you out of those clothes and into this." She picked up the dress and pumps, swinging them from her fingertips as she added, "I have some makeup laid out on the vanity. I think it would suit the look."

"I don't want to wear makeup. I don't even want to wear that dress."

THE AGREEMENT

Don't you care?

Karine couldn't bring herself to ask.

Even her protests came out as barely a whisper. She wasn't sure if Masha had heard her—she'd not quite learned how to be *loud*. She watched others do it, but the idea of drawing attention, especially unwanted, frightened her more than she could explain.

She could already predict what the rest of the morning and subsequent day was going to look like. One of those where Masha would have to supply her with a few *pick-me-ups*. Pills for her to swallow—quickly and discreetly. It helped her get through the day, at least.

If she made any more complaints, Masha would quickly offer her the pills and Karine knew she would readily accept. It was the only way for her to feel remotely human— someone capable of a conversation and a smile, even if it was a little too loose—and then everyone would be happy.

She wouldn't feel like such a lost cause. Everyone else would pretend they didn't know the truth.

See?

Simple.

"What beautiful skin you have—women spend thousands to make their skin as soft and pale as yours," Masha said.

Karine, out of bed now and positioned in front of Masha who was slowly helping her out of her clothes and into the lace dress, mumbled back a non-reply under her breath. She hoped the woman was too distracted to sense how her cheeks blushed in response to the compliment even if she wanted to also act like it didn't exist in the first place.

She never knew how to react to something like that.

Compliments …

Attention.

Affection?

"And this will make you look even more beautiful," Masha continued. "The color compliments your skin and hair—and those *eyes*."

Karine blinked up, meeting the gaze of her caretaker through the sweeping veil of her inky lashes. "What about my eyes?"

77

"The prettiest blue."

"The sky is pretty. So is the ocean."

And both were blue.

Karine didn't think she was anymore spectacular or amazing than those things—and certainly not her *eyes*. Hell, those were the things that the people around her often found the hardest to meet. Staring at her meant *seeing* her.

Actually fucking seeing her.

No one liked to do that.

She just wasn't sure *why*.

Masha nodded once, saying only, "And they don't compare—nothing compares. Remember it, yes?"

She zipped the dress up neatly and smoothed down the front, running her palms gently over the fabric until she was satisfied with the way it sat on Karine's body. Next, she picked up the tube of stick foundation and a concealer that worked magic on the ever-present dark circles under Karine's eyes.

Behind Masha stood a tall mirror—the one Karine was avoiding looking into. She never really understood the unsettling feeling that came to cloak her in anxiety when faced with her reflection, but she knew she couldn't look at it for long. It was only a reminder of how she didn't recognize the person who stared back at her.

Masha's hands flitted over her face tenderly while she stood there for her, unmoving. Despite her care with the makeup brushes blending color and life into Karine's cheeks, she was hurrying. It was apparent that Masha had received her orders, and was trying to get her ready to go as quickly as possible.

Karine wouldn't make her job harder.

"There, all done, and now we'll put some color to your pretty lips," Masha muttered.

This time when the older lady moved, Karine couldn't look away fast enough. Her eyes fell on the reflection staring back. She held her face as still as possible while the pale coral lipstick was being applied to the small bow-shaped mouth that matched the rest of a face full of equally delicate features.

₮AGREEMENT

The dark circles she had inevitably woken up with were gone now—hidden away under the magic touch of Masha's concealer. Her face looked bright and fresh in the mirror, alive again. But Karine knew as well as Masha—it was all a facade.

A mask.

The emptiness she felt inside was clearly reflected in her eyes. Those same ones that Masha called incomparable to the sky and ocean—they were empty.

Big, and blue ...

And empty.

Masha had moved on to her hair now, brushing it gently and over and over again till her limp dark tresses radiated with a bit of natural shine. She pinned it back out of Karine's face neatly, and then, hooked a finger under Karine's chin. Turning her head slowly, side to side to admire her work, she said with another smile, "Beautiful, yes? You look beautiful, child."

Then it was time to go.

She was accustomed to this by now—coming and going when and how she was told. For as far back as she could remember, Karine was transported from one location to the next, herded along like cattle without an explanation. The reason, she was told, being that her place wasn't to *know* things, but to do them.

Things she was told, of course.

Not things she wanted to do.

She had always simply accepted it as part of her life. What it meant to be a Yazov girl—the forgotten daughter of a mere man made into a king.

A very cold king.

Besides, there was nobody she could pose a question to. Masha certainly wouldn't have the answers.

They stepped out of her bedroom together into what was an attached living area to her section of rooms. This wing of the Yazov mansion was just *hers*, an ecosystem for Masha and Karine to live in together, surrounded by a handful of housekeepers and the men who kept watch from a respectable distance as to not intrude more than they needed to.

It wasn't like they worried about her running.

Who would she run *to*?

On the table near the kitchen counter, where Karine usually had her meals, she spotted some drawings strewn everywhere. She didn't recognize them and stopped to look. At first they appeared to be violent scribbles, like something a child would draw if given some crayons and color pencils to go wild with.

"Where did these come from?" Karine asked, her hand trembling from the after-effects of too much alcohol and mixed medications, as she held the drawings closer. "Isn't that ..."

Vaguely, she recognized the hastily drawn faces of the people on the page—the rage twisting expressions dark between the men made her blink to take in the image again. On one of the drawings, the name *Katee* had been written on the top-right corner like a signature—the signature of a child if the loopy writing could be trusted.

Katee.

Masha was at her side before she could ask again, already plucking the drawings from her hand and pulling her away from the table toward the door. "Your father is *waiting*— today isn't the day to be late, Karine."

She spoke sweetly.

The words said it all, though.

Masha acted like nothing was amiss.

Nothing new to see.

Karine glanced back at the trashcan where Masha stuffed the drawings as they passed. "But—"

"Your eyes look a little cloudy," Masha interjected, bringing her attention right back in an instant.

Weren't eyes supposed to be the windows to the soul? Did the emptiness in hers mean she didn't have one of those left, either?

"Maybe I can help with that—something to perk you up before you start your day?"

ᴛʜᴇAGREEMENT

Even though there was a part of Karine that wondered what the rest of her day would look like if she didn't take the pill—the present, more prevalent part of her instinctively brightened at the possibility of Prozac. One of her caretaker's favorite medications to keep on hand because Karine preferred it in the daytime.

Masha made one appear seemingly out of nowhere, offering it without a second thought. Karine popped one in her mouth and gulped it back dry, enjoying the chalky bitterness it brought to the back of her tongue.

It really shouldn't be mixed with liquor.

Or a hangover.

And yet …

Karine had never once questioned where the medication came from or how it was available in such great quantity seeing as how Masha never ran out.

Why did it have to matter?

Life was better this way.

Easier.

The world owed her it.

At the very least.

By the time Masha led Karine out of the mansion's wing and down the long corridor leading to the doors that separated into her father's living quarters, her mind was already lighter; breathing wasn't such a burden.

Prozac was good for that.

• • •

Standing in her father's massive kitchen—a space she was sure he had never once put to use to make a meal—Karine understood why Masha had gone to such an effort to dress and try to make her look presentable. She tried not to be bitter about said reason.

That was easier said than done.

Dima's voice droned on, too loud—and way too close—in her ears while he spoke on the phone. He hadn't got off the call even when she walked in with Masha, acknowledging her with merely a grunt under his breath and a nod of his square chin.

She stood in the middle of the kitchen, clueless about how he wanted her to act while he proceeded to ignore her at the same time. Although, it wasn't anything new for the two.

"Here, eat something, you'll feel better."

Masha to the rescue.

As per usual.

She had a plate with a cream cheese bagel ready, holding it out for Karine to take whether she wanted it or not. Karine had to do everything in her power not to go running out of the room—even the growling of her stomach that belied her disinterest in the food wasn't enough to quell the urge.

To be anywhere but there …

Away from the man she was supposed to marry.

Yeah.

Dima Kuznetsov was her fiancé. A decision delivered upon Karine with little fanfare, and a total expectation of *compliance.*

"Well, get the motherfucker on the phone, then, yeah? Let me hear him say it," Dima growled into the phone, making Karine's skin crawl. It was his voice, and the way he spoke that did it, but most importantly—the words he used. He enjoyed the vicious way his words could terrify people, including her sometimes. Then, he let out a dark laugh that sent shivers racing down her spine when he muttered, "He won't, though. He knows I'll have his balls cut off, and shoved down his throat first."

At least, one good thing was coming from Dima's distraction with his phone call. *Two* things, actually. He didn't care to pay attention to her, for one. And for two, the passing seconds gave her cloudy mind the chance to remember what she was doing here, and why Masha had been asked to deliver her *on time.*

Dima hated being made to wait on her, and they were supposed to be making wedding plans. As if they planned for her to actually take part.

Unlikely.

ᴛʜᴇAGREEMENT

Karine took one small bite of the bagel, giving in to her need for some sustenance, and immediately regretted the choice. Her gag reflex was still as strong as ever, but at least she managed to avoid Dima seeing her hold back the bagel by turning away. It wasn't her stomach that refused the bagel, but the strange taste that accompanied it. It took her more than a few chews to decide whether or not it was the bagel, or just her own body refusing the food.

She kept eating, though.

It did make her feel better.

After handing her the bagel, Masha had merged into the background of the kitchen to remain out of the couple's way. It was a part of her role—to be present without being seen, to predict what her mistress's needs were without being commanded. She was certainly not permitted to make her presence known when Dima was around. He didn't care to deal with the likes of people he considered lesser than him.

Like a slave.

Karine was envious of Masha—she would give anything to be truly invisible. Especially now when, more often than not, she wondered if she might prefer a slave's life to one where she was going to be bound to Dima forever.

That was a horrifying reality.

It stared her right in the face.

As she watched Dima continue his abusive phone call, a silly little thought fluttered through the back of her mind. It dared to be hopeful, which only made it all the more painful.

What if she told her father how she truly felt, her mind whispered, *would he even be willing to listen?*

Maybe she could try—just one time. Maybe she was wrong about him all along. As soon as the ridiculous thoughts filled her mind, she knew they were nothing more than idiotic notions to have, considering. Her father despised her, without ever having explained why or explicitly said it, she *knew it*; felt it deep in her heart whenever she gained the courage to look the man in his face.

She was well aware of the fact that he shunned her to a separate wing of the mansion because he couldn't bear to have her around more than he requested. It suited him best that she existed in the periphery of his life where he didn't have to look at her, or speak to her. But this had been her entire life with the man, too.

A shame he wouldn't explain.

She was more than a burden.

Karine didn't understand it because she couldn't recall what she had ever done to defy or upset him. When had she ever been a bad daughter? Nothing she tried pleased him enough to earn his attention or affection.

Not that she suspected her father's attachment to her would make a difference to whether or not she had a choice of refusal when Dima declared that he had chosen her to be his wife. If anything, that created a solution for Maxim. He had a viable excuse to finally wipe his hands of his problematic daughter.

Nonetheless, a part of Karine had hoped the news might please her father. Dima and Maxim were close associates— he was someone who was trusted by the family, and respected by the bratva. Everyone else congratulated Karine on an excellent match, like she had really been given a choice, and some even sounded envious.

When Dima delivered the news to Maxim, it was the first time Karine noticed something akin to a smile on her father's face when he turned to her. She had thought he would be proud—for a moment, she allowed herself the vulnerability of expecting something rare from her father.

Kindness.

She shouldn't have bothered.

"It's the best thing you can do for yourself."

That was his only comment.

What else had she been hoping for?

"You're late," Dima snapped.

Karine's mind was elsewhere—her constant distractions from her thoughts and the world around her never left—but he brought her rudely back to the room. He never hesitated to remind her that she needed to be on her best behavior when he was within earshot of her very presence.

The man demanded a lot.

But he gave very little.

⅋AGREEMENT

"Sorry, I slept in," Karine said dimly, barely managing to look up and meet his eyes.

A cold anger stared back.

"You were supposed to be here fifteen minutes ago. Do you not know how to read a clock?" Dima turned to Masha who still remained at the back of the room. A fear that accompanied her more often than not when she was in his vicinity welled in her throat when he asked Masha, "*Well—* you're not a fucking idiot, yeah? You can tell me why she's late, can't you?"

Karine wanted nothing more than to shrink away from Dima, and disappear. Except she couldn't bear the idea that he would take out his anger on Masha simply because he knew he could get away with it easier than he could when it came to Karine.

"It wasn't her fault, it was all me," Karine rushed to say, bringing his attention back to her. Even though it ached in her chest to be in his line of fire, she still breathed a silent sigh of relief that she'd managed to distract him from Masha. "I spent too long in the shower—I always do. I'm sorry. I wanted to look pretty for you."

All it took was a smile, and a bat of her drug-heavy lashes.

Dima was a dangerous man, sure, but he was still just a *man.* His eyes traveled over her body, taking in the plunging neckline of her lace dress, the rise and fall of her breasts. His gaze lingered a little too long on her legs, and finally, he glanced back up at her.

Satisfied.

He arched a brow, sucked air through his teeth, and nodded once in reply to whether or not she had succeeded in her task of *looking pretty.*

Masha had done a good job of selecting her outfit for today. Karine wasn't even sure how she managed to put on this act for him. It was almost like muscle memory. As long as she kept Dima pleased at all times, and made sure he had no complaints in between, then everything was easier.

She tried not to forget it.

"I had to send the wedding planner away, but she'll be back in a few hours," Dima said, taking a few steps towards

Karine, and she flinched. Just his proximity could provoke that reaction. She hoped he hadn't noticed it, so she forced on a smile instead. He touched her hair, tucking in a few stray strands behind her ears. Her skin still crawled from the feeling his touch left behind, and she didn't even have an explanation for it.

Yes, she knew he could be hurtful.

Violent, too.

Cruel, even.

But she couldn't recall a single incident where he had been violent with her—he didn't dare. She was still who she was, after all. Her last name meant something, of course. It still wasn't enough to make Karine feel safe with Dima. He was a man she had known all her life because of his proximity and work with her father, but she still had to wonder if he was also just biding his time until she didn't mean anything to anyone at all.

What would happen then?

"I promise I will be on schedule the next time," Karine told him, still smiling demurely.

He liked that.

Her fake innocence.

All that naivety.

She couldn't say it quite came off the same when her head wasn't stuck in a cloud of pharmaceutical-making. Then again, if Dima knew her at all, he would have seen right through the bullshit.

Another huge red flag that this entire engagement was going to end horribly for Karine. Was she expected to play this dumb, airheaded, constantly *high* housewife that Dima could use and abuse to his will forever?

It made her sick.

And she still didn't get a say.

"I have a meeting to get to—your father doesn't like to wait," Dima said, his fingers trailing from her hair until he was stroking her cheek with his thumb. She forced down the bile that rose up from her churning stomach. Maybe the cream cheese and bagel hadn't settled quite right after all.

ᵀᴴᴱAGREEMENT

"And then, we will talk to the wedding planner together. Hmm?"

"Sure, whatever you like," she repeated, trying her best to sound pleasant.

Grateful, even.

Definitely compliant.

Karine kept balancing on a very tight rope—every interaction she had with Dima only served to show her how hard it was going to be for her to keep it up.

"It won't be long now until you're officially mine." Dima's eyes narrowed on her while his mouth twisted in a smile that felt anything but comforting. "Three months."

She wished the prospect of getting married on the day she turned twenty-one filled her with joy. Instead, the dread became an ever-present, constantly growing weight that she couldn't escape.

Planning a wedding was supposed to be a happy and momentous time. The proper beginning of two people starting a life. Or that was certainly how marriage and love was presented to her from the people she dared to ask, and the few books and movies she'd been exposed to. She was vaguely aware of the idea of romance, love and a happy marriage, despite never having actually witnessed any of those things in people around her. In fact, there were *no* couples in her life to act as a reflection for her to consider.

Either way, even if there weren't any butterflies in her stomach when she looked into Dima's face—was there supposed to be a pit there, too?

That deep, sinking sensation.

It just wouldn't leave.

Dima's phone buzzed in his pocket, and he fished it out to check the screen before saying, "I've gotta go, but *you* don't go anywhere."

Karine froze that smile on her face as he left her side, and kept it firmly in place until he was finally gone from the room. Just like that, finally, she felt like she could breathe again. She continued to stare ahead at the empty space he had left behind, more unsteady and confused than ever.

Masha was right there to save the day once more, and drag Karine from the darkening, spiral of her thoughts.

"Please, at least finish the bagel," Masha said.

She'd almost forgotten about it. Masha already had what remained of the bagel and cream cheese ready to hand it to her.

Karine didn't dare to speak—not even to refuse. If she tried eating anything now, she was definitely going to get sick. Dima had that unfortunate effect on her. She doubted she was the only one.

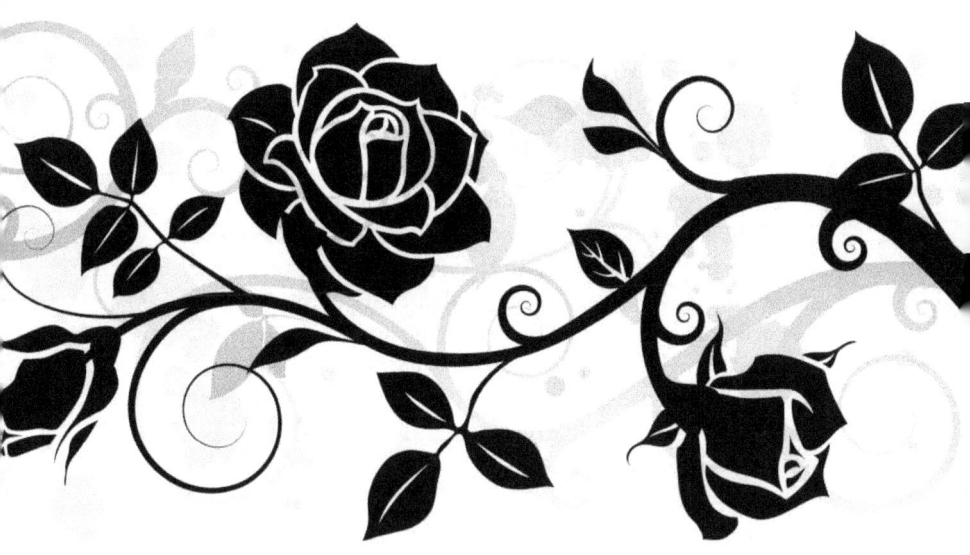

SEVEN

Roman stood at the doorway of Maxim Yazov's office,
looking in. The two bulls that had led him through the maze
of the mansion since he parked his car outside were gone,
now, too. They'd done their job. Josef had driven to the
mansion with him, of course, but he wasn't allowed this far
inside Maxim's lair.

Apparently.

So, why was Roman?

Was he supposed to feel special or something? He didn't
want that kind of treatment, but certainly not from a boss
with an organization of men who were only trying to find a
problem with Roman.

The call for the meeting came in the morning, or rather,
Josef's did. Maxim let the bull know that he wanted to meet
with Roman—no excuses—and to keep the day free of other
duties. He knew better than to demand an explanation from
Josef. It wasn't like anyone explained anything of significance
to him, either.

The guy was just doing his job.

Standing in the entry of the room with its tall oakwood doors and windows, all stained a dark chocolate brown like the inside of an old church, he surveyed the walls of bookshelves lined with books. The furniture was all upholstered in similar dark leather, shiny with recently polished cream. He could smell it mixing with the scent of leather in the air. That, and thick cigar smoke, wafting from the ashtrays on a massive desk that took up much more space than was needed for the man sitting behind it.

He wished the smoke made the scene harder to see because then at least it might have been easier to digest. Or shit, maybe it wouldn't have instantly pissed him off as much as it did to see Dima sitting in the chair across from Maxim.

Fucking Christ.

Wasn't that just his luck?

Somehow, in all the weeks that he'd been in Chicago, Roman hadn't been in a situation where he was face-to-face with the man. He clenched his hands into fists by his side, the veins popping out in his arms like a network of rivulets from the pressure he rhythmically applied over and over.

The anger came fast.

Faster than he could prepare.

What the fuck was *Dima* doing here?

The only thing that kept Roman from asking that exact question—and probably earning himself a punishment for it, too—was the expression on Dima's face. At first, when Roman entered, it seemed like he was in the middle of a sentence, convoluting his expression in a way that gave his irritation away. He had been directing that at Maxim over something, but snapped his mouth shut the moment Roman appeared in the doorway.

The irritation melted to anger just like that. Roman almost laughed—at least he could find some sick sense of retribution in the fact that his presence made Dima uncomfortable. That was worth something to him.

Maxim, however, offered him a smile as he leaned over his desk to get better access to the ashtray where his own cigar was resting. Dima stuck his between his lips, and puffed smoke out in a hazy, gray cloud that lifted toward the ceiling in dancing spirals.

"Come in, Roman, don't be shy, yeah." Maxim urged, grinning.

Shy was the last thing Roman felt, but he did what he was asked. Entering the room with confident, quick strides, he approached the desk where the two men were seated. He opted not to take a chair, refusing to lower himself to Dima's level even if it was only physically, unless he was made to do it.

"I'm afraid we haven't had a chance to give you a proper welcome to Chicago, have we, Dima?"

Across the desk from Maxim, Dima only shrugged at the question. The boss didn't seem offended, and Roman found his smile a little too jovial. Why the fuck was he this happy to see him?

"We've been busy," Maxim added.

That time, Dima nodded and smiled, slyly.

Roman had no interest in whatever they were hinting at. If Maxim hoped he would pry into the bait he was feeding out, the man would have to hold his breath forever.

"No welcome necessary," Roman replied, "I'm just here to get shit done."

Maxim wagged a finger his way. "And I hear you're already making good progress."

Dima shifted in his seat at that statement. It was clear to Roman that the man despised him. Almost as much as he hated Dima. Maybe the asshole was still sour about Anastasia, and the thought put him in a happy place for a moment.

The fact that Dima's paid whore gave *him* head wasn't something that could be taken from him. He got for free what Dima could only pay the woman for. That was a hard hit to the proverbial balls because he seriously doubted the man had any actual ones left.

"Like I said, I'm trying to get shit done," Roman repeated.

Maxim hummed his approval around another drag on his cigar, sitting back in his chair harder than before. He leaned so far into it that the legs creaked, and it swung a little, but he straightened up just as quickly to say to the two men, "I think it's time we buried the hatchet, yes? What do you think, boys?"

Was that why he was called here?

Roman could think of a million better things to do. Like spooning out his testicles with a rusty spork on a busy highway. Literally anything would be better than this.

Dima puffed on his cigar more, unconcerned with the heady clouds he sent Roman's way. All the while, he remained standing, unmoved by the subtle aggression.

"Okay, well, I wasn't fucking asking," Maxim said.

A narrowed gaze accompanied the growled order. The inflection and intent was clear: *do as you are told*.

"What do you want us to do?" Dima asked.

"Have a drink together, no? *Now*, even." Maxim's thin patience was on clear display as he waved his hand between the two. Dima had to know it as well as Roman that defying a bratva boss could have extreme consequences for them both. "*Well?*"

That last word was all it took.

Dima was the first to make a move. A tray on the desk carried a crystal decanter and matching glasses with gold bottoms. He poured the vodka out of the decanter into two glasses, and finally turned to offer one to Roman.

No smile.

Not even *here, asshole*.

When Roman didn't make a move to accept the drink, Maxim spoke up again.

"Maybe a part of your experience here can be … growing the fuck up," the boss told him with little inflection to his tone, and not an ounce of sympathy for the choice Roman was forced to make. He didn't want to make nice with Dima; he wouldn't piss on him to put him out if he was on fire. Too bad he wasn't, really. Maxim continued on saying, "You're here to pay off what you owe us in kind, and Dima has better things to do than hold a grudge. So, do act like a pair of grown men, get on with it, and *drink*."

On the verge of turning on his heels and walking straight out of there, Roman only hesitated to consider his options.

ᴛʜᴇAGREEMENT

This wasn't a part of the fucking deal. He wasn't told he'd have to make nice with Dima in order to live and work here.

And yet ...

He took the glass because he was on Yazov territory. He had no Avdonin support or protection around him. The only reason why he was still alive and considered a usable asset in Chicago was because he was keeping himself out of trouble, combined with his last name. He needed to down the drink, and move the fuck on.

Suck it up, so to speak.

The vodka traveled smoothly down Roman's throat, and Dima gave him one last glare before looking away when he handed the glass back over, turned upside down, and empty.

"There you two are—a proper do-over, no? You'll meet some of my brigadiers later tonight over dinner, Roman," Maxim continued. "I expect the same kind of behavior at my dinner table. Is that understood?"

"Dinner?"

"Yes, here, in my house. Stick around, get to know the lay of my land, as they say. If you're going to be working for me, you will have to know how I like things to be done around here. The same as everyone else."

Maxim tapped his cigar against a crystal ashtray as he finished speaking. This was the first Roman had heard anything about a dinner. He didn't want to be included in any Yazov meetings, and had little to no use for the brigadiers in regards to his own side of business. He had every intention of working at the chop shop alone, other than his hand picked crew, just like he did back home.

What was he even supposed to do around the estate until dinner?

Play with my nuts?

Coke was still a no-go, too. So that was out of the question, and it was looking like he was going to have to suffer the formalities of the Yazov Bratva simply because he didn't have any excuse worthy enough to get out of it.

Fun.

Maxim continued staring at him, clearly waiting for the only acceptable response that he expected to come from Roman. One that he wanted to come without question.

And it did.

Unfortunately.

"It would be my pleasure," Roman said.

The only problem with that?

He was a bad fucking liar.

Always had been.

• • •

Maxim and Dima had to have known that Roman held no interest in breaking bread with the rest of the Yazov men. And yet, there was nothing they could say about it since Roman had accepted their invitation.

Once he'd walked out of Maxim's office, he decided to take the boss's suggestion of checking out the mansion and the rest of the estate. It wasn't like he had anything better to do, and any plans he might have had were fucked now. Nonetheless, he was under no disillusion. He understood good and well that he was always being watched. Men showed themselves in every corner of the mansion, and only a few cameras covered certain areas.

Maxim would be sure to get an exact report of Roman's every activity in his house. If this was New York, and his father had essentially forced him to stay until dinner, Roman would have gone up to every camera that was watching and given it some footage to remember.

This was a whole different ball game. He had to consistently remind himself to watch his ass—nobody else was going to do it for him.

Maxim Yazov's mansion was considerably large, and sat on a plot of private land that kept any curious neighbors far away. He passed more corridors and rooms than he would know what to do with if this was his home. Wealth covered every bare inch that it could. From the rich stains that glossed the hardwood floors to the heavy, silk drapes hanging from every window.

™AGREEMENT

It was much bigger than the Avdonins' family home. But then again, Roman's mother always insisted they didn't need to go overboard with the size of their home as long as it had everything they needed, and was easy to maintain. Clearly, the values of his parents differed from that of the Yazovs.

This house reminded him of jocks in a locker room bragging about the size of their cocks. Ultimately, none of it mattered if you didn't know what to do with it.

He had slipped out of the sliding doors at the end of one of the rear hallways to find himself inside what could be best described as a conservatory. A glass dome-shaped extension at the back of the house that was big enough to contain its own large swimming pool. A good thirty by forty feet with an apparent deep and shallow end. Perfectly maintained, green grass with a stone pathway leading to sitting areas at the edge of the pool, and the light inside this conservatory seemed to make everything magnificently brighter than it needed to be. Everything appeared magnified, and the sun's heat was trapped because of it, making the air hotter than it already was. Every breath he took was accompanied by the taste of chlorine.

Roman blinked, glancing up to stare at the sun through the curved glass roof. He was about to shade his eyes when he heard a splash. His first clue to the fact that he wasn't alone in the space.

He was too far away to see the pool clearly, thinking so far that he had been completely alone. Finally rid of the men who were milling about the place, and seemingly watching him from a safe distance, he moved toward the edge of the crystal clear, cerulean water. All he could see of his unknown companion in the pool was the flash of an arm—wet, cream-toned skin—and a dark head of hair bobbing below the surface.

The closer he got to the pool, the more certain he was that the person swimming in it was a woman. She sluiced through the water expertly, traveling with impressive speed from one end of the pool to the other without once showing any sign of fatigue. She only came up for air just quick enough to dip back down in the water, and not for long enough to notice that she was no longer alone.

One lap.

Then a second.

Roman came up to the edge of the pool, watching all the while. She still hadn't noticed him because she hadn't once looked up. Whatever was motivating her to keep swimming wasn't about to slow her down yet. He couldn't take his eyes off her even though he didn't know who she was, and if he was even supposed to be watching her in the first place.

There were definitely rules in the Yazov home he wasn't aware of, and he wasn't in a position to break them. All things considered …

But Roman knew he wasn't going anywhere. Not until he had seen this woman's face. At the end of the third lap, when she was on the other side of the pool, she finally stopped to reach up and grab the ledge, straightening herself slowly while she wiped her face with the crook of her elbow.

He hadn't seen her face yet, but her slender back was on display for him now, distracting his attention as his gaze traveled over the curves of her shoulders and the water dripping down her spine. She appeared to be wearing a bra instead of a proper bikini top. The semi-sheer, white lace was nearly the same color of her pale skin.

Finally, she looked over her shoulder, and the biggest, bluest eyes he had ever seen found his. At first, all that stared back from her was *distance*—or rather, it was like she saw right through him. As if he wasn't standing there at all.

But *goddamn*.

He had never seen eyes like hers before; shockingly beautiful from so far away and yet *entirely* blank at the same time. There was something striking—and haunting—about them.

Because he couldn't seem to look away. Even though she was in the water, he was the one drowning.

Only her voice broke the daze.

"Did they send you to come get me?"

She called out to him from the other end of the pool. Her voice had a slow and dreamy quality, like she was taking her time with each word before she let them escape her lips, a careful consideration of the things she chose to say. It made her voice all the more melodic because of it, too.

She turned to the side ledge of the pool then, and began to drift towards him. Her slender shoulders bobbed gently in the water, small waves kissing the column of her neck with each rise and lower.

A woman moving through water shouldn't be an entire *experience*, but there Roman was … fucking experiencing it. Whatever it was.

"Well, are you?" she asked him again.

"I don't know what you're talking about."

She paid no mind to what he said, almost as though his words passed right through her. Her mind was elsewhere entirely—he could still see that distance in her gaze as it drifted from him to the doorway, and then back again.

But when she finally did stay focused on him, though—she truly saw him. For a brief second, he watched those big eyes of hers open further, and her stare looked him up and down. She tipped her head to the side a bit, a small grin playing at the edges of a plump, but tiny, mouth.

She didn't know him.

Well, he didn't know *her*, anyway.

But she looked at him like they did—like they knew each other *very* well.

Had they met before—was he supposed to know her? He was damn sure he wouldn't have forgotten a face like hers, not even on his wildest of nights when his memories were left more fragmented than consistent. Even from this distance, he could see the tenderness of her small features, her sharp nose and bow-shaped lips. *Dainty* came to mind— she looked like delicate fragility come to life, but wrapped in the sensual package of the body of a woman.

The sunlight streaming harshly through the glass dome reflected brightly on her face, spilling over her shoulders and through the water as she passed through a thick ray. It bathed her in a golden hue, making her damp skin glisten and adding a bit more color to her porcelain tone.

She couldn't have been older than twenty, the smooth face that spoke of youth said life hadn't quite taken her that far, yet. Although, he couldn't forget that gleam he first saw in her eyes—that distance that spoke of an old soul.

They existed.

His grandfather swore it.

You have one, Anton told him once. *You can see it in others, too—so look.*

Apparently, he'd finally found another. Why didn't she look at him the way other women did? If they knew him, well … *Mob* Prince. Mutineer. Womanizer. A man who might be the greatest lay, but someone not to be trusted. The thief. But if they didn't know him, it wasn't like he gave off the safe, *kind* vibe, either.

But that didn't matter.

No, she was looking at him like she had never laid eyes on another man before, but as though she saw right through him at the same time.

Her stare did that.

Those blue, *blue* eyes.

It set Roman off balance. He bet that he wasn't the first man to wander into this woman's path and suddenly find himself entranced just by being in her presence. Some women held that appeal—or so he was told. This was the first time he'd ever actually experienced it.

Couldn't say he liked it.

Lies, his mind taunted.

"He told me to wait, but I had nothing else to do. I was bored," she explained as she continued to inch closer, drifting slowly in the water.

Her words didn't match the way she examined him. Roman still didn't know what she was referring to.

In that moment, he became painfully aware of how strange the scene truly was. A beautiful young woman whom he didn't recognize was swimming alone in this gigantic pool inside the Yazov home. One *he'd* been told to explore. Did she not own a bikini or just hadn't bothered with one? Was she even supposed to be here?

And shit.

Because she was in the pool, should *he* be there? The idea that she could maybe get in trouble for this—it bothered him. Roman stepped closer to the edge of the pool.

"Are you going to be okay?" he called out to her.

She was looking through him, too far away in her mind to meet his eyes, anymore. That small smile came back to tug at the corner of her mouth, as if he had just said something silly and should have known as much.

"Yes, I'm always just okay," she replied, monotone. "They make sure of it. Masha makes sure of it."

What the fuck was she talking about?

Roman was starting to get the feeling that if he asked her too many questions she would shut up, cut him off, even.

The closer she came to him, the more clearly he could assess her. *Admire* her, really. Honesty was the best policy, after all. She had the quality of a wildflower on the top of a hill being thrashed around by a strong wind.

Yeah.

Like a good gust might blow her right the fuck over. The very sight of her actually had his chest tightening with a protective urge he couldn't explain. No woman had struck him damn near speechless and simultaneously confused all at the same time without doing much at all.

Drops of water clung to her skin like beads. Her dark hair was slick and wet, pasted to the sides of her face. All that exercise had caused her cheeks to turn a deep pink, the tip of her nose, too. There was no denying the fact that this woman was extraordinarily beautiful.

So much so, she deserved a second look. And maybe the kind of husband who would kill a man for daring to take a third.

He realized she was watching him too when she spoke, snapping him out of his dazed admiration of her body. He couldn't find it in himself to be ashamed at being caught, but frankly, she was studying him just as closely.

Roman even considered asking if she liked what she could see.

"Is this about the planner?" she asked, arching one dark brow high. "Is she waiting to see us?"

Roman's own furrowed in confusion, his body responding to the fact that she was even closer to him, now. Close enough that he'd be able to touch her if she wanted. Because Lord knew he *wanted* to. He had a terrible habit of admiring beautiful things. And she certainly was that.

The woman continued to speak regardless of whether she got a response from him. Really, he just didn't know what she wanted him to say when she was still talking in riddles that he couldn't understand.

"What does it matter anyway? It's not like I'll actually be able to choose anything or make decisions. They'll do it all for me. *God.* They'll even pick my dress."

He opened his mouth to speak, feeling the irresistible urge to ask for an explanation. Or maybe just to keep her talking. There really was a musical quality to the way she spoke, and how her words streamed together in her rambling.

Who is planning what?

A dress for what?

Before he could say anything, though, her gaze shifted to something behind his shoulder. Without warning, she hauled herself quickly out of the pool.

Water splashed everywhere as she straightened up right beside him. She was a punch to his gut. In panties and a matching bra that did nothing to hide the definition of what was underneath, fully soaked through so he could see the stiffness of her nipples underneath the bra's fabric, she didn't think twice about her state. Her cleavage was deep, the bra had shifted in its soaking weight to the extent that another inch down and her full breasts would be on display. The slenderness of her body, from the milkiness of her legs and their length to the soft curves of her calves, and even how tiny her waist was, he couldn't look away from it all.

A part of him wanted to.

He should.

Not that she seemed to care.

Roman did his best to ignore the growing length in his slacks, and he cleared his throat in an effort to … fuck, who would know? It was a strange war to fight within himself—equally torn between the parts of himself that very much liked what he saw, and another that wanted to wrap her up in a towel and hide her from the rest of the world.

He didn't want to stop looking at her. At least, he managed to put his attention on her face. Dignity, and all.

Everybody deserved a little.

Right?

She rubbed her hand over her face in an attempt to wipe off what remained of the water dripping down from her hair. Giving him one last look, she stepped past him without another word exchanging between them.

He didn't know what made her get out of the water or why she was running away. Her departure would be just as unexplained as her appearance in the pool, it seemed

Roman still had questions.

Who wouldn't?

Most importantly—if she left now, would he see her again?

EIGHT

Karine was sure he had bewitched her somehow because the man who was standing there at the edge of the pool appeared out of nowhere when she looked up from the water. He had bewitched her with his eyes. Dark, despite the clear blue, and deep, hooded heavily with sharp brows that furrowed while he watched her.

Unlike most people she encountered in her daily life, this man didn't seem to want anything from her but to watch. She had to go towards him, *closer to him*—it was like the water was pushing her in his direction and yet she didn't know what he was doing there—unable to ignore the need to find out who he was.

The only explanation for his unusual presence was that he was one of her father's men running an errand. Karine hadn't been entirely aware of the words that spilled from her mouth as she went towards him. He didn't seem to be much of a talker, and so she kept rambling in hopes that he might finally say something back that made sense.

THE AGREEMENT

Whoever he was—she couldn't help herself.

He just stood there looking like the most beautiful man she had ever seen, seemingly curious enough to remain there the closer she came. His strong jaw—and a mouth with lips she wanted to watch move, so she talked so he would do the same—was framed by a thick, dark beard, trimmed neatly. She found herself wondering what his pillowy lips might feel like pressed to hers, how they might taste, even.

Then, she saw Masha.

Over the man's shoulder, Masha came running toward the glass door of the pool house, and Karine knew … once again, she had done something that could get her in trouble. It happened to her quite often. She just wandered away … distracted by a thought or something interesting that caught her wandering, wild eye. It was usually Masha who found her every time and brought her back to earth.

But the spell had broken.

Whatever trance the man had put her under faded fast at the idea she was going to have to explain her current state and situation. Pulling herself out of the water, Karine stood in front of him for a few moments, long enough for her to appreciate the sight of him that close, and then she headed away from him without a look back.

Masha made it through the door of the pool house before Karine could exit. A long fluffy towel was thrown over her one shoulder while she kept a tight grip on Karine's forgotten dress and shoes in her other hand.

It took one look of Masha's face to see the worry etched there. She almost felt bad.

"There you are," Masha said in a rush, meeting Karine halfway to the door. "I've been searching for you. I found your clothes in the spa next door."

The grass underneath her damp feet allowed Karine to imagine that she was free in a meadow somewhere far from here. Except Masha was there to drag her back into reality, and responsibility.

"You must stop disappearing on me like that, Karine," Masha continued, throwing the towel around her without warning. "You know what that does."

As the woman rubbed her gently up and down, trying to dry Karine's body and her wet hair, she stood stock-still, allowing Masha to do whatever needed to be done. She couldn't help but notice the way Masha threw a glance at the stranger over her shoulder.

"Who is—"

"No one," Karine said quickly. "He's fine."

Wasn't he?

For a second, she had thought she looked into the man's soul, and she trusted him. Even though she didn't know him—*she did.* Somehow.

"My God," Masha muttered, not at all satisfied with the job the towel was doing to clean up. "What were you thinking?"

The answer to that was easy, and it came rushing out of Karine just as such.

"I like the pool, no, I *love* swimming in this pool. I'm weightless ... suspended. Free of *everything*," she said.

Masha looked up at her, nodding her head lightly as though she understood Karine's rambling and eccentric ways, but still disapproved nonetheless. She was always so worried about Karine—her first priority was to keep her out of trouble. God knew the woman worked hard to diffuse the ups and downs that chased Karine throughout the day.

It was yet another thing to scare her—she knew all too well how much she needed Masha. How much she depended on her. And yet, she doubted that she would be allowed to bring Masha with her when she married Dima.

Masha had never truly belonged to Karine.

She was still just her father's slave.

"You were supposed to meet with the planner, and then Di—"

Just the prospect of hearing Dima's name was enough to send chills down Karine's spine. However, Masha's words were cut off by the door of the pool house opening, and her father stepping in.

All at once, Karine understood what Masha had been trying to avoid. Her father finding her in the pool house in nothing more than her underwear, soaking wet. She probably still looked like quite a sight. Even though she had managed to slip back in her dress, with some help from Masha, her father gave her the same look he always did—as if her mere existence dissatisfied him, and just being within visual distance left him unable to hide his displeasure about it.

His silent judgement had her staring anywhere but at him, even down at herself where she noticed how the lace dress clung to her body. Her bra and panties were still wet, shaping and molding the dress to her curves and crevices in a way that revealed everything.

Her father didn't pay her mind anymore—he had already lost interest. Instead, his attention went beyond her to the man who was still standing a few feet away. For some reason, she didn't want to turn and face him.

She was already a mess.

No need to make it worse.

"So, you found her, then," Maxim said.

Karine dared a peek over her shoulder. The man remained where he had come to stand with his legs spread wide, planted firmly on the marble path that surrounded the shape of the pool. His arms were crossed over his chest, the bulging biceps tugged at the material of the shirt that also hugged a broad, defined chest. He wasn't looking at her, either, just like her father didn't.

Surprise.

No one liked the sight of her.

As it appeared; the two men knew each other.

"Did you lose your way, Roman?" Maxim asked.

"It's a big place. I may have gotten lost."

Roman.

Hearing his name was enough to send gooseflesh prickling over her skin, everywhere it was exposed. Karine didn't know what to do about that.

Masha continued stroking her hair with the towel, not yet convinced that she couldn't still present Karine in a satisfactory state to her father. Neither men seemed to care that she was there now, so what was the point?

Maxim chuckled lightly at Roman's response, waving a single hand high. "Come with me, yes? I'll show you the rest of the place."

Her father all but ignored her presence, focused instead on Roman. Maxim's treatment of him was starkly different from how she witnessed him behave with other men in the bratva who worked under him. He acted like Roman was a guest in their home.

Dangerous excitement danced through her, as fleeting as it was. Did that mean he might be staying around? The hope flared through her again, especially when Roman threw her one last look before he followed after Maxim on his way out.

Karine remained there, returning his gaze while Masha worked away at her hair. It felt the same as when their eyes met the first time, in the water. That same sense of familiarity swelled in her chest, fast and furious.

He had his jaw clenched tight, square and chiseled, leaving her breathless at the thought of feeling the roughness of his beard against the smoothness of her cheek. The desire was as sudden as everything else, and just as unexplainable.

Then, just like that, he pulled his gaze away from her, and he disappeared through the pool house door.

Come back, she wanted to call out. *Look at me again. See me.*

Nobody had done that before.

She wanted to feel it again.

But if he was smart, then he would wipe her from his memory the moment he stepped out. And if she was lucky, she would never see him again in this life.

As it was, though, Karine had always been terribly unlucky.

• • •

Too many hours passed Karine by at a snail's pace since she last saw the stranger from the pool house. She really wasn't in the habit of keeping time. Someone—Masha, usually—always told her where she needed to be and when. It was the one thing she could do particularly well.

Taking orders, that was.

ᵀᴴᴱAGREEMENT

Tonight, however, nobody paid much attention to her. Maxim had organized a dinner party to which the cream of the bratva crop were invited to sit at the boss's table and feel ... who the fuck knew?

Important, maybe?

Karine never cared for the details.

Things usually took the same turn by the end of the night. Music turned up impossibly loud, and alcohol passed around to keep any of them that wanted to drink their weight in an upright position.

Karine only knew all this by observation from afar. It wasn't like she was invited to the table, or the after-party. Her father had no interest in involving her in these festivities—she served no purpose but distraction if she joined.

Not that it affected her one way or another. She had become adept at enjoying herself on nights like these. Nobody had any idea what they were drinking, or how much of it. Discarded bottles and glasses scattered all around the ground floor of her father's wing became a game for her to find and indulge when her constant shadow's back was turned. The other thing she was very good at was camouflaging herself in the background—never drawing attention her way because she didn't want it. Karine managed all of this while sipping on discarded drinks.

A cocktail of mixed alcoholic beverages along with the bottle of pills she found in Masha's bag were all she needed to start feeling good again.

A damn good night.

If she'd asked Masha for the pills, she wouldn't have been denied but usually on nights like these, things tended to get busy—and lost—with the party. Especially Karine, and her whereabouts. It was always all-hands-on-deck in these scenarios, and Masha needed to help the other household staff members to keep the party running smoothly.

Karine used that to her advantage, helping herself to the pills and gulping them down with the half-drinks she'd found. By the time she staggered out through the back of the house to the stony patio, it was like walking on clouds.

The sky might have been dark.

Not through her eyes, though.

The wicker chairs arranged to be cozy on the patio were usually left unused. The Yazov family, or whatever was left of it, wasn't exactly the type to lounge around all day. Certainly not *together*.

What even was family?

She had never known it.

Karine deposited herself in one of the chairs, sprawling out with her arms thrown wide. The night sky overhead was an inky blue with a smattering of stars like freckles on a happy child's face. She gazed at them for what felt like years while she tried to recall the happy dream she was having that morning.

Why couldn't she remember it anymore?

Was there a tree?

A little girl?

Yes.

She could still hear the laughter.

Pressing her eyes closed, Karine tried to bring back that feeling of absolute abandon—something had made her giggle like a child. What was it?

"Are you alive?"

The deep voice broke through her hazy, high thoughts, and even before she opened her eyes, she recognized who it belonged to.

It was him.

The man from the pool.

The one who sent chills running down her spine and straight to her toes with nothing more than a flick of his brow. Karine took her time to open her eyes and see him, dragging in a slow breath all the while. She wanted to savor the moment.

Standing, he loomed over her in the chair, shaded by the ornate lantern-style lamps that hung in the patio. He was mostly hidden in silhouette above her, but she could somehow still look straight into his eyes.

A smirk—sinful and sly—curved those lips of his that had so entranced her earlier in the day. All over again, they did the same, making her own part with another quick inhale while he stared back at her.

"I don't know how to," she replied softly.

He was standing so close to her that she got a whiff of his masculine scent in the light breeze. A combination of musky cologne and cigarettes. Heavy, and delicious. She pulled in another lungful of air just to taste it again on her tongue.

"What is that supposed to mean?" he asked, leaning a little closer.

Karine froze up. They were nearly close enough to touch, and she wasn't sure she could handle that. She still wasn't sure why he made her react the way he did.

His brows furrowed as he kneeled down, reaching out with his thick fingers. Their gazes stayed locked together when he found some stray hairs over her face and tucked them back behind her ear with the softest touch.

"What don't you know how to do?" he asked, the demand coming out smooth and unconcerned.

For a moment, she was almost completely honest and told him the truth—she didn't know how to be alive, or how to *live*, for that matter. This was her existence. He was looking right at it. Stolen liquor, fuzzy days and forgotten nights, a myriad of pills, and an entire world where she didn't belong, but everyone else seemed determined to keep her right there inside of it.

Despite the fog of the drinks and the pills that clogged up her mind, she knew better than to raise his suspicions any further. The truth had never helped her before.

"I meant," she whispered, "I don't know how to answer that question, of course, I'm alive."

Roman remained exactly where he was, just a mere inch away, and close enough for the scent of spiced liquor to dance on his every breath.

"My name is Karine."

"You just read my mind," he said, chuckling low. "That was my next question."

His laughter truly was a beautiful sound.

An echo in her mind, now.

When his lips curled in a smile, Karine sunk further into the chair, amazed at the very sight. Suddenly, there was nowhere else she wanted to be but right there.

With him.

NINE

The last time Roman saw Karine, her hair was damp—slick as it framed her face. Now, dried in soft waves with only a little frizz, he could appreciate how it was still as dark as the night. All he wanted to do was sink his fingers into her hair to feel the softness tease his roughened palms.

He was glad she told him her name because he hadn't stopped thinking about her all day. It would have been nice to have her name when they first met so he could have put a name to the face—and in his fantasies of her that had kept him company while he *attempted* to feign interest over the day and evening at the mansion.

Roman had enough sense than to go digging around, trying to uncover her identity in the Yazov household. If they wanted him to know who she was, he would eventually find out. So, he considered himself lucky that he'd found her again, even though the circumstances seemed less than ideal.

Again.

The universe had a funny way of working.

It wasn't difficult for him to figure out what was wrong with her—why she had that distant look in her eyes while she laid there seemingly having her own private conversation with the stars. In her own world.

The girl was fucked up.

High as a kite—probably drunk, too, considering everyone else there sure as hell was at the moment. Except for him. Roman didn't trust these people enough to get plastered around them.

Karine hadn't even taken the trouble to hide the pills in her medication-induced stupor. The fluorescent plastic bottle in her right hand with pills stuffed inside it rattled when she moved. The trouble was he couldn't figure out what those pills exactly were without trying to get a better look inside the bottle. Maybe then he could determine if she needed attention.

Medically.

"Do you want me to go get you some help?" he asked, leaning a bit over her and gazing between her and the remaining pills in the bottle.

Maybe he shouldn't have touched her hair like that, tucking it behind her ear. He still didn't know who she was and if he was even supposed to be talking to her, but his fingertips also couldn't forget how she almost leaned in to be touched again, either.

For some reason—she was in the house but hadn't been invited to Maxim's party. She wasn't working like the staff members, either. What was that about?

"Thank you, Roman. Nobody ever asks me that, you're very kind to … but no, I don't need anybody's help. In fact, I would prefer it if everyone left me alone."

She spoke in a low voice, barely meeting his eyes while her lashes fluttered as if she was falling into a dream. Even her words ended on a slow hum he had to carefully decipher. Yet, she remembered his name from back when Maxim said it in front of her at the pool house. He figured …

She's probably okay.

And since she wanted to be left alone, he started to stand, but she grabbed his hand before he could move away.

\text{\small THE}AGREEMENT

"Not you, I didn't mean you," she whispered, high-blue eyes with pupils blown small flying wide to meet his instantly.

Jesus.

Roman took in a sharp breath. The muscles in his abdomen tightened as she held his hand with a feather-light grip, almost as if she was scared to grab harder. He could have easily pulled away from her, but he didn't want to. Why would he? This was the best he'd felt in weeks, especially when she nudged his fingers towards her mouth.

He watched in amazement, before he truly understood what she was doing, as she brought his thumb to her lips. The warmth of her mouth pressed against the pad of his thumb, kissing it softly before she let go.

Roman wasn't even sure if it actually happened—he had to be dreaming. How high was this woman? There was no other explanation. Karine leaned back in the chair again, and looked up at the stars like she had forgotten already.

"At least tell me what you took so I can try and help you, it could be dangerous." That was what he chose to say, trying his best to snap her back into the moment again. He opted to ignore the kiss for now because he didn't want to embarrass her. Or he was just a fucking liar because *he* didn't know what to say about it. Except that maybe he liked it. That was problematic enough. "Did you mix anything, maybe?"

A smile creased the corners of Karine's perfectly pink lips as she asked him, "Why would you want to pull me out of this? That would be the opposite of helping me."

Maybe she was right.

Who was he to judge?

If anyone knew the powerful allure of substances that took you to another planet, even if only for a short time, it was Roman. However, her speech was starting to slur even more, and her eyes glazed over in a way that disturbed him. She was barely even able to keep her eyes open anymore as she spoke. Roman had already made up his mind to go find someone who would be able to help her. Maybe he needed to call an ambulance.

Have you taken this mix—whatever it is—before? It helps to know your limits, Karine."

She didn't respond.

"Karine ..." he said firmly when her eyes finally closed. Her head stayed tilted to the side while her limbs seemed to have gone entirely limp.

Fuck.

He hadn't come to this place to watch a girl OD right in front of his eyes.

"Please, go—*please*. She will be fine." The flustered voice of a woman came from behind him, and he turned to find the older woman from earlier. The same woman from the pool house who had interrupted their conversation then, too. She rushed onto the patio, but had carefully shut the door behind her first. As if she didn't want to draw attention. "Please just go."

Roman didn't think so.

"She needs help," he growled at her.

Once next to him, she knelt beside Karine, lifting up her wrists and seemingly checking her pulse. She came off more affected by Roman's presence than Karine's state. But the way she was quick and tender when she checked Karine over, placing palms against her cheeks and leaning in to listen for steady, even breaths, he had to wonder ...

Was this her grandmother? Although, the woman didn't quite look old enough for *that*. And the two women didn't look at all alike, so he figured a mother was out of the question.

A friend, maybe?

"She's just tired, but she is okay," the woman continued saying, her back still turned to Roman. "I know her, yes? She trusts me. Please, go now."

The woman seemed to get more agitated the longer he stood around. Even though he didn't know what her role here was, or even Karine's in this house—well, shit ... he knew well enough to stay out of it.

He had to remind himself once again that this *wasn't* Brighton Beach. Little Odessa's Devil wasn't king in the windy city. Roman didn't get to come into a man's home—

especially one like Maxim—and ask questions about *anything*.
He was the only one watching his own back.

Roman backed away from the two women, not at all
satisfied that Karine was okay but knowing he didn't have
much of a choice but to leave her with someone who seemed
… accustomed to the scene in front of her. So to speak.

Neither of the women noticed him leave as he made his
way around the back of the house. He didn't want to go to
the front of the house by walking through the party again.

It wasn't his scene. The music was shit. The men had no
fucking sense of humor. Hell, even the chicks who were
milling around the place—serving as decoration—weren't
doing anything for him.

That was probably Karine's fault. He was sure she had
spoiled him with that strange encounter earlier looking like
the very image of *sin*. That was, at least until he could
somehow get her out of his system. His interest never stayed
for very long; he tended to like that about it.

This shouldn't be any different.

Right?

As Roman walked, he thought about Karine's kiss. He
could still feel her lips on his thumb, the soft imprint had yet
to leave. He brushed his thumb against the palm of his hand,
and it still felt warm from her touch.

He needed to dash her from his mind and move on with
the rest of the night—he had enough shit to deal with
already. Yet, something told him he wasn't getting rid of
Karine anytime soon. At least not from within the confines
of his mind.

That place was a prison.

He planned to keep her captive in there just a little bit
longer.

• • •

He would have liked to just slip away without being
noticed. Too much had happened today, and he wanted to
be alone to process it.

The loft he managed to procure in the city wasn't nearly as big as the one he had in New York, but at least he had his own space and some sense of privacy. Although, with Josef hanging about to watch his every move, he wasn't ever really by himself.

However, even though Roman wanted to get back to the loft, knock back a few shots of vodka and fall into a dreamless sleep, hoping he wouldn't be dreaming of Karine—he knew he couldn't just disappear. Not without taking his leave from Maxim who would be expecting it as a mark of respect.

These fucking guys.

All their pomp and circumstance had a way of pissing Roman off like nobody knew. He just didn't see the point—or maybe he hadn't grown up loving the same bratva they had, in a way. The men around him seemed to respect one's ability to make their own way—and mark on a city. He didn't see how decades of *mob* tradition played in to how much money he could make in any given year.

He came from a different generation—or that's what Demyan preached whenever Roman tried to explain that he just didn't care to go through the same motions as every other man in their business. It just was what it was, he supposed. Did they want his dirty fucking money, or not? That's always what it came down to.

Nobody ever said no, either.

It wouldn't be the same for him in Chicago. In Maxim's mind, he had taken the trouble of giving a fuck about Roman today by inviting him to the party in the first place. Roman was expected to return the gesture.

Once he made his way to the front of the house, he gathered himself enough to go back in and seek out the boss. Karine was still heavy on his mind. A part of him had to wonder if she was truly going to be okay in the hands of the older woman; a nagging thought pricked at the back of his mind, refusing to let go—*she didn't seem surprised at Karine's state.* It wasn't the first time.

More concerning—did that mean it wouldn't be the last?

THE AGREEMENT

Roman didn't have a chance to consider it longer—the boss had noticed he had come to linger in the entry of the sitting room. He simply intended to wave a polite goodbye, but that didn't seem like it was going to do.

"I'll walk you out," Maxim declared, jumping up from his seat in the middle of the room.

Instantly, all eyes turned to him as they walked out together.

This was definitely going to get people talking. Nothing good came from that shit. The bastards would bitch and moan about how their pakhan was giving the Avdonin *suka* undue attention.

They walked in silence together to the front foyer of the mansion where two great winding staircases grandly climbed the walls. Identical chandeliers hung all over the ceiling, casting the space in a glittering glow. Oil paintings hung in gold gilded frames. None of it really impressed Roman.

Disposable wealth being strewn around by a rich criminal boss who didn't know what to do with all the money he had. Exactly the kind of lifestyle his mother was so adamant against leading. He could still remember the day his father learned Claire regularly donated hundreds of thousands of dollars every month to any charity she felt was worthy—she *dared* Demyan to order her to stop.

His father never did.

Maxim came to a stop at the front door, and turned to Roman with a small smile. "You did good by drinking with Dima earlier today, and I appreciate the effort, yes? I know the two of you had a rough start."

Roman nearly laughed out loud at that.

A rough start was one way to put it.

He shrugged in response—what else could he do? He didn't give a fuck about Dima and frankly, didn't give a single shit about Maxim, either. He just needed to return to New York in one piece, get back to *his* life, and this was the only way to do it.

Maxim continued watching him with narrowed eyes, like he was waiting to see if Roman would slip up. So, he met the older man's gaze and remained calm. Let him look—there was nothing there to see.

"Anyway, it's been a good night, but I'm going to call it for now," Roman said, making his intention clear.

He wasn't interested in another chat—certainly not one of Maxim's lessons like the one earlier with Dima and the drinks. He could do without that business again.

Maxim grunted under his breath and as Roman was about to head for the door, he grabbed his arm. Thick fingers dug into the bands of muscles that made up Roman's forearm, yanking him closer to the boss.

He barely controlled the knee-jerk reaction of retaliating— clamping his molars down hard enough that he was sure they cracked under the pressure of his clenching jaw. It would be a mistake to pull away or even flinch. A show of weakness for Maxim to grab hold of. Roman had to show he was willing to be respectful, but at the same time—he wasn't willing to be kicked around.

It was a difficult line to walk.

"I want you to understand that this morning was the first and the last time you will be speaking to my daughter," Maxim explained, his smile gone entirely. His eyes, beady and blue in their intensity, nailed into Roman's, as cold as could be.

His daughter?

Karine was Maxim's daughter?

For fuck's sake.

Shit started to make sense, then.

Now that Roman looked more closely, he could see the similarity in their eyes. Where Maxim's were deep and icy, Karine's were large and empty. However, they were the same shade of electric-blue.

Roman said nothing. He wasn't sure yet if Maxim knew where Karine was at currently, or whether he was aware of their second encounter from just fifteen minutes ago.

"Karine spends most of her time in the background of my house, and my life, because that is where she belongs and where I want her to be," Maxim explained, his voice dropping much lower than usual. Careful to make sure no one else might overhear. "What happened today was a mistake, and it won't happen again."

Talking about his daughter had an adverse effect on Maxim that Roman couldn't understand. The words he used for and about her were unsettling, in a way.

Was he afraid of her, or did he just despise her?

Was he overprotective, or *disinterested?*

Roman couldn't tell.

"If you're smart, you won't find yourself alone with her again," he added, the threatening edge to his tone becoming unmistakable in Roman's ear.

Maxim's grip on his arm loosened a little, and Roman pulled away, slowly, almost too gently. He didn't want to make any sudden movements, like a hunter wouldn't want to startle his prey as he closed in on it.

The only problem with that?

Roman didn't know if he was the hunter ... or the prey.

"I have no intention of turning that into a habit," Roman told the man.

"Good. That is exactly what I want to fucking hear, hmm?"

Maxim dusted his hands, and took a step away from Roman, gesturing for the door as if he was free to go now, if he wanted. The conversation about his daughter was over even though Roman couldn't shake it off as easily as he should.

Shit.

Like he needed yet another giant red flag that something was wrong with that woman, and this entire goddamn *place.* Something left him with a bad taste in his mouth, and it wasn't from the liquor he hadn't been allowed to refuse earlier. He was quickly starting to think that this was not a man who was just being protective of a beloved daughter. A darkness clouded over Maxim's voice when he spoke about Karine, and Roman didn't like it.

He didn't like it one fucking bit.

"I'm sure you've already been reminded of tribute coming up in a few weeks, I'm expecting big things from you, Roman. Show them you're supposed to be here, yes?"

Roman stuck his hands deep into the pockets of his slacks, inside which, his palms clenched into fists. He really didn't need another fucking reminder of the upcoming tribute, or the story Josef had narrated to him earlier on the topic.

People thought he was stupid, or something.

What a joke.

Roman still didn't have a crew set up for the chop shop gig. He didn't have a client list that was ready to take cars from Chicago, either. He barely had the fucking resources to get it going currently. How was he going to make enough by the end of the month to make a monetary offering to the bratva?

"No worries—I've got it handled." Maxim smiled and nodded, satisfied. "And I'm sure you don't need the reminder that you're not here to make friends either, only money."

"I'm just here to pay my dues."

"Exactly. The day you stop being useful is the day you pay us some other way. Keep it in mind, young man."

The friendly, fatherly tone that Maxim usually spoke to him with was gone. *Fast.* The one in its place was that of a ruthless pakhan—the boss. His seat had to be unquestioned; his authority would be crystal clear to everyone.

"I understand my position here," he reiterated to Maxim.

He didn't get a reply before the boss walked away.

Frankly, Roman didn't really need one.

TEN

The relatively pleasant summer gave way to the wet weeks of end-July. Which only meant one unfortunate fucking thing—Chicago had started to remind Roman of New York. It was humid and messy, coloring the days gray and making him nostalgic for home in a way he hadn't expected.

Given the fact that he didn't know when he might be back in New York again, he should have been glad to be reminded of home. Hell, he might have been if today wasn't such a crucial day.

Pacing up and down the warehouse, Roman debated whether to call Josef, and ask the man to join him inside. Even though Josef hadn't explicitly admitted it, he waited outside in his car, watching and noting Roman's every movement. Today was definitely the kind of day he could use some company—even if it was from a Yazov man who was being paid to spy on him, if only to keep him from talking himself crazy inside his head.

But he didn't call.

He planned to keep as few people involved with his business in Chicago as was possible while he was forced to be here to work. Back home, he at least had a bit of a leg up where officials and cops were concerned—or he used to.

Here, though?

Here, he had shit.

Nothing.

He had to be careful. In every single aspect.

Still pacing along the bay doors inside the warehouse, Roman waited for part of the crew to return, driving the three, million-dollar cars they were supposed to hit.

The preparation and planning came together as the deadline loomed to the point where it was a *now-or-never* type of deal. He put together a team of people made up mostly of his old crew from back in New York, and a few new recruits directly from Chicago who came *highly* recommended in the car boosting scene from contacts he had in the business.

No fucking lie—Roman's standards were high. They kind of had to be, though. He didn't really have the time to mess around with people who needed him to hold their hand through how to follow an order, and definitely not with someone who didn't know what to do with a wrench. The plan needed to be executed with perfection and precision. Roman was kind of banking his life on it. *Literally.* Considering he knew his whole future in Chicago and with the Yazovs depended on it.

Behind him—while he continued focusing on the forty steps it took him to cross from one door to the third at the other end—were neatly arranged portable car jacks, boxes of tools, and all other equipment they needed to breakdown the cars once they arrived. Part of the procedure was also to ensure everything was set up in such a way that it could all be packed and cleared out in under ten minutes if necessary.

Roman had learned the hard way, through past experiences, that he needed to make sure nothing could be traced back to them. It was possible that they may not even have those ten minutes to pack everything up. Every precaution was taken to ensure no serial number could be traced back to him or the bratva.

⟨THE⟩AGREEMENT

This wasn't Brighton Beach.

The Yazovs would gladly throw him under the bus if they got busted, and step back while he landed his ass in prison.

Three luxury vehicles his crew had targeted today—each worth over a million dollars—would sell for triple that amount in auctions overseas. Roman also had a long list of contacts who would be able to get him in touch with exactly the people interested in the particular makes of cars he would have chopped up and ready to ship before the sun broke over the morning horizon.

Once Roman had the cars in his possession, moving them and selling them wouldn't be a problem. That was the least of his concerns. The crew just needed to do their job, arrive safe and sound, and things had gone according to plan.

If they didn't, he would have heard something by now from one of his people. It was relatively safe to say Roman could breathe easy—knowing the time on the clock across the warehouse assured him it was so—but he didn't want to get ahead of himself just yet.

There weren't too many perks of being fresh-faced in Chicago, honestly. Either way, he appreciated the ones that were sparsely available. One being that nobody knew him here, and no chop shop gig had been executed in a similar fashion in the recent past. Both things worked to his favor at the moment.

So, technically, the world was his oyster.

He didn't have to worry about watching his back *too much*, at least not for the moment … where the police were concerned. Nobody was here watching him expecting him to be doing what he was because his presence wasn't a big thing in the area. He had the upper hand of taking the scene by surprise. Once the same cars were repeatedly stolen, once a pattern was established—the job would get tougher. He, and the team, would have to work a different game. One similar to the tricks they pulled back home.

For now, it was all *cake*.

With a cherry on top.

A shitload of money for three neatly packed vehicles that would be every collector's dream. And it didn't take them very much effort to nab the cars, either. It wasn't just about having the right plan. Roman also needed to find the right team—to create the perfect combination of muscle and brain.

He achieved that task by building a crew of hackers, booster specialists, mechanics, and connected people who wouldn't shy away from a high-stakes chase ... should it come to that.

Not only did the heist have to be executed perfectly, but the cars would then have to be dismantled and hacked in a way that would make transportation easier with minimal—if any—damage. Then, there was the process of putting everything back together, so one had to make sure the team it was delivered to overseas had a decent reputation for doing what they did. The last thing collectors wanted to see on their cars was wear and tear, or even any minor imperfections. They didn't want to see a hint of the journey their prized possessions had undertaken to reach them. The more damage there was to fix, the less a car made when delivered and auctioned.

All in all, Roman had a good feeling about the job. He looked at the clock again, and then double-checked the time he knew was right with what it showed on his watch, the diamond bezel on the Rolex winking under the warehouse's bare bulbs overhead.

Ten more minutes, and the crew would be arriving at the warehouse. So, when the phone in his back pocket rang, Roman about jumped out of his skin.

A low *fuck* fell from his mouth after he'd fished the phone out, and checked the screen to see his father's number flashing.

Perfect timing.

Roman had a hundred reasons not to answer the call, starting with the fact he wasn't in the mood to talk with Demyan and ending with his current situation. But because he knew he had probably pushed his father's patience far enough, he swiped the green phone icon across the screen. He didn't even put the device to his ear, instead opting to keep it on speakerphone.

ᴛʜᴇAGREEMENT

Demyan didn't wait for a greeting before saying, "Son."

"I'm kinda in the middle of something, I'll call you back."

"Hmm, *nyet.* You've ignored my calls all week. And look, I finally have you on the phone. Let's talk."

Roman glanced at the warehouse shutters, and then his watch again. *Nine minutes.* He was terribly good at keeping track of time, but that didn't stop the urge to keep checking. He barely focused on what his father was saying.

Demyan didn't miss it. "See, and you're not even listening now. Why the distraction?"

Roman sighed, raking a hand through his hair. This was not the time to have a deep discussion with his father, however, he welcomed the distraction.

"My first job is taking place—yeah, as we speak."

Even though Demyan did a good job of keeping his curiosity—and probably excitement, though he wouldn't admit it—under control, Roman thought he could hear his father's pitch heighten just a smidge. "Is it in the bank? You think you're going to secure this?"

Roman went from feeling a sense of pride because he managed to excite his father—to something else entirely because Demyan had to follow it up by questioning the success of the job.

"Of course, I'm securing it. The plan is airtight. I've had this set for—"

"Shit can go wrong at the last minute.," Demyan interjected frankly. "Maxim is expecting results. *Monetary* results."

"You don't have to remind me. I know tribute is coming up. I've spent the whole month preparing for it."

"Maxim doesn't take disappointment well, and I heard he prefers—"

"*Cash.*"

Demyan stayed quiet.

Roman continued, unfazed. "I have it—seventy percent owed to the Yazovs from what I expect to make from the cars boosted today. He wanted it in cash, and that is what I have. *In cash.* Mine is still wired to an offshore account."

"Yeah?" Demyan asked, sounding a little surprised at first. "Maxim is a traditionalist—I'm sure you did your research on the man. Forgive me for making sure."

Roman remained silent while his father continued to speak, although Demyan muttered more to himself rather than his son.

"He likes to feel the paper between his fingers. Physically feeling it ... seeing the cash holds value for him. If he can't smell the ink, it means nothing."

Well, damn.

Roman wished he cared.

That shit all spent the same.

Still, he told his father, "I know. I think I've gotten a bit of an understanding about Maxim by now."

His father remained silent, which urged Roman to continue speaking. If only because he hated the stretching silence, and the unanswered questions that kept poking at the back of his mind like invisible insecurities that only he knew existed. Something he would tell *no one*.

"I know what you're trying to do here," Roman said, still keeping an eye on the bay doors and the view he had outside. "You're testing me with this—waiting to see how I perform under this kind of pressure in Chicago, making sure I've cleaned up my act enough to be *stable* for you. Maybe then, you can decide whether I'll be worthy of taking over. You have to justify it, don't you?"

He waited for his father to say something—a part of him really wanted an answer. Even if it was one he wouldn't like. At the same time, Roman wanted Demyan to know that he'd figured out this little pact—or whatever bullshit they'd conspired—between him and Maxim. His father had as much of a role to play in his new circumstances as Maxim did. He just didn't have the details as to what extent.

"You're wrong about that, son. Partly. I can't give you any more than what I already have—and if you ask anyone, they'll all happily say I gave you too much. You've had free reign over everything here. Little Odessa is your kingdom. *Still*, and I think you know that. I think you still wouldn't appreciate what it means, though. Either way, you are my son, and this is not a *test*."

"Then, what *is* it?"

"Time," Demyan said simply.

That told him little. There were a dozen other questions Roman had in mind, but the returning silence on his father's end kept him quiet. Moreover, he already seemed to have issues believing that Roman could actually succeed at this job, so why bother.

He decided to change the subject. The topic of going home and making changes—well, that would have to wait.

"I met Maxim's daughter. *Karine*, she's ... *strange*," he settled on saying. Although, his mind was quick to add *and interesting*. Except he couldn't say it was for an innocent reason. Roman added to his father, "I mean, they're all a little fucking different here as far as that goes."

Demyan's reply took longer than his son expected. "Met her where—*he* introduced you to his daughter?"

"Not exactly. I bumped into her accidentally." *Sort of.* "She lives with him, I think."

When his father grew quiet again, Roman was growing tired with the lack of conversation happening from Demyan's end of the call. He considered cutting it and going back to obsessively checking the time.

Demyan spoke before he could. "I heard he had a daughter, but that is all I know about the situation. That isn't the sort of question you ask a man like Maxim Yazov."

"Why wouldn't you ask him about his family?"

Had he missed something?

Probably.

Roman should have paid attention every time his father or grandfather tried to educate him on the bratvas ways outside of their own organization. Except he really hadn't cared to learn because those traditions made no difference to what he was capable of. Not to mention, the amount of influence he had inside his own family that *wasn't* culturally Russian—like his grandmother and ma—kept him from being too attached to the same kind of pride other men around him had about their heritage.

It just didn't matter to him.

Never had.

"Men like Maxim Yazov—traditionalists in this ... *life*—are stuck in a different world. They don't believe in family because they don't want to be saddled with the liability. They rarely lay a public claim to their children unless it serves them some purpose to do so. I guess the fact that he has a daughter who lives in his house, well, knowing the way his mind works like I do, sounds a bit like a target on his back to me."

That was a lot to unpack.

Roman didn't have the time.

The roar of an engine outside the warehouse, the echo growing down the road leading to his location, took his mind off the information his father had just given him.

He had business to do.

"I gotta go," he said abruptly, and ended the call.

Without warning.

Maybe he'd apologize later.

Roman checked the time again—they were early. By only two minutes, but still ... that only meant one thing.

A good thing.

Everything went exactly as planned.

Roman pressed the button attached to a steel pillar, and held his breath at what waited for him when the south side bay doors of the warehouse lifted up.

Yeah.

There was nothing quite like stealing a beautiful car.

ELEVEN

Hide and Go Seek isn't a game for girls your age, Maria liked to tell nine-year old Katee Yazov, but she disagreed. She may have been a little tall for her age, which made it difficult for her to hide well sometimes, but it was still her favorite game. And even if Maria did say she was too old for it, her nanny never refused to play whenever Katee asked.

It was why she cared for the woman as much as she did. In fact, Katee couldn't remember a time when she was without Maria. A mother was a concept that she didn't understand, and couldn't remember having one of her own, but Maria was the closest thing to it for her.

She didn't quite know what having a family meant, either.

The closest thing to it was the bratva. The men who came and went from her home whom she watched from afar but never approached. Even the housekeeping staff, the people who maintained the grounds—people she saw everyday, the ones she was familiar with, but didn't engage.

Maria warned her not to.

They don't want to talk to a child, Katee. They have better things to do than indulge a girl's fantasies.

But nobody felt much like family to her, really.

Maria came close.

She knew her nanny liked to keep a close eye on her. Always watching—constantly *attentive*. It was yet another reason why the woman liked to try to convince Katee not to play hide and go seek. Maria worried Katee would hide herself too well, and for good reason.

But when she was hiding, it was the most fun she ever had. Heart racing, she wanted to feel that giddy excitement that accompanied possibly getting found. She'd hide somewhere, and listen for Maria's footsteps, waiting to be caught.

Today was no different.

Maria insisted that Katee should stay close—in case she needed to find her quick. Something about an important day for the family ... she shouldn't do anything to get herself in trouble.

Well ...

She didn't want trouble.

Katee wanted to hide.

She slipped out of the kitchen when Maria had her back turned while she prepared lunch of freshly cut fruit and sandwiches made with soft, white bread. She could still hear her nanny's voice in the background, chattering on about things Katee didn't deem important, as she skipped down the hallway, out through the glass doors to the side ... and just like that, she was outside.

Free to hide.

Katee only had a few minutes before Maria would come looking for her. She needed to find a hiding place before time ran out.

The stone wall that ran along the edges of the driveway continued all the way around the property, keeping everyone else out, and Katee *in*. Shaded with hedges and shrubs, the wall was covered with creeping ivy. All those plants and trees created a camouflage Katee could use to hide between without needing to worry about being too tall.

THE AGREEMENT

It would take Maria at least ten minutes to find her if she managed to hide really well—longer if Katee could manage to keep herself quiet. That was always the hardest part.

Proud of her find, she ran over to crouch near the hedges, a giggle bubbling in her throat already. The minutes ticked by, calming her nervous laughter so she could be as quiet as she was still between the hedges and the stone wall. Since she hadn't heard Maria calling for her, and had yet to run out of the house, Katee figured she might get longer than ten minutes, after all.

It was only the sound of cars roaring down the driveway that drew in Katee's attention, taking it away from her intent to stay out of sight. The vehicles headed to the front entrance of the mansion—a part of the house she was strictly forbidden from visiting. Katee's curiosity rooted her in place where she watched the guests arrive from one of the few breaks in the stone wall that acted as a pathway between the driveway and front grounds.

The cars came to park side by side, men pouring out from all four corners almost to the second the engines stopped running. Duffle bags followed, being pulled from the rear seats and popped-open trunks. They carried the bags into the house, each of them, and she wondered what was inside.

It had to be something important.

Another car joined the rank at the very end, close enough to her that she could hear the lyrics being belted by a singer through the speakers. That was, until the driver killed the engine and the music cut off abruptly.

The man who jumped out of the driver's seat was ... different. Katee could tell straight away that he wasn't the same as the other men he seemed to be following behind. It took her a moment to figure out *why*.

He had a kind face.

It was hard to look away.

One she didn't recognize.

Even if it felt like she did.

His dark hair slicked back under a large palm, and piercing blue eyes roamed around the driveway. He examined his surroundings as though he needed to take it all in again.

Because he hadn't seen it before—or maybe he just didn't know it well enough to be comfortable.

Katee leaned further to the side, beyond the hedges and the safety of the stone. She wanted to be able to see him more clearly, and what he was doing. He, too, pulled out matching duffle bags from the rear of his car. He threw them both over his left shoulder, the handles gripped tightly in one fist, and slammed the trunk shut.

It was then when Katee creeped along the wall a few inches more with her eyes wide and lips parted in silent question, that the handsome young man looked over his shoulder.

His eyes met hers instantly. She hadn't expected him to see her considering the rest of the men barely hesitated outside of their vehicles before heading for the house. They hadn't been concerned with their surroundings, or who might be watching.

This man wasn't the same.

She expected anger or surprise from the stranger about her spying—anyone else who was heading to the mansion's front entrance—would have reacted with exactly that. As they usually did whenever she got in their way.

From this man, she got a smile.

A *big* one.

Warm, and bright.

Like a silent hello.

Handsome, she thought. He looked like what Maria said about the men that played in the movies her nanny enjoyed watching. Strong features, and a smile that was impossible not to notice.

Katee's heart raced in her chest when he didn't immediately look away and go back about his business, and his smile didn't falter. *You're going to get in trouble,* a voice in her head hissed. She just didn't care to listen. That familiar feeling she had about the man only intensified when he seemed to recognize her, too, and wasn't bothered by her presence.

Except they didn't know each other.

At all.

AGREEMENT

"Hey," he called out.

And waved.

He raised his voice a little to make himself heard as she was still quite a distance away from where he had parked. All she could do was smile back, not daring to offer anything more. Her gaze drifted over him, taking in the navy silk shirt with the buttons undone near his throat, his dark slacks and leather shoes. He had his thick, black hair styled back slick, and his beard neatly trimmed along his jaw and uninked throat—another thing that made him different from the other men.

He looked *presentable.*

Ready ... for something.

She just didn't know what.

Katee resisted the sudden urge to wave back—to tell him her name, and introduce herself because that was respectful, even though she knew she wasn't allowed to. Maria's warnings were never far from her mind. She was never to say her name to anybody, especially not the men who sometimes wandered the halls of her home.

But the man looked so ... *kind.*

He had eyes that said so, and his smile made her think he might say hello. Would he let her talk, too? Would someone finally want to know what she was thinking—and oh, what a relief that would be.

The dream was quickly ripped away.

As she dared to raise her hand, and open her mouth to reply, she heard the monster's voice. Loud, domineering, and entirely *overwhelming.*

"Roman! We weren't expecting to see you until much later. Come on inside."

She no longer wanted to hide for fun.

Katee had to hide *for real.*

She didn't wait to see or hear anything else, let alone find out if she had been noticed by anyone else in the driveway. That voice was enough to send her running, whimpering for Maria under her breath as she stayed close to the stone wall, going back in the direction that she had come from earlier.

Her only hope was that Maria would be waiting there for her, ready to take her into her arms and keep her safe from the monster. And not at all angry that she had snuck out when her back was turned one more time.

If only she would protect her …

Katee wouldn't hide again.

Ever.

By the time the girl had made it back to her rooms, chest heaving with sobs, Maria was already in a state of frenzy about her disappearance. It didn't really seem like her reappearance made it better, either.

"Where have you been?" the woman demanded, her words hard and fast even though she kept her tone hushed and soft. "I told you today is an important day. We have to be on our *best* behavior, don't we?"

Katee whimpered again, the sound reminding her of a wounded kitten she had once found in the back yard—the poor thing had fallen from the stone fence, and broke a leg. Falling into her nanny's arms, it was only then that Maria noticed she was in a state. The carefully contained anger at her game was gone when she wrapped her tight, in arms that felt oh, so safe, and whispered, "It'll be okay. You must have got a fright, that's all."

Maria let her slide down to the floor in a messy heap of too-long-limbs and a trembling form, helpless while the sobs came louder. Katee hugged her legs until the woman bent over to meet her down there, soft promises and assurances at the ready.

"Come on, now, don't you want your food—I made your favorite?" She rubbed Katee's trembling back with soothing strokes, murmuring the same thing she had told her time and time again, *"Tvoya Masha tebya lyubit."*

She didn't know what it meant.

She also didn't need to for it to help, and before long, her nanny had coaxed her into the kitchen where buckwheat kasha cooked with mushrooms and sweetcorn waited. *Her favorite.*

Katee wanted to tell Maria about what happened outside. About the kind man with the blue eyes who might have wanted to talk to her … but the monster. She never spoke about the monster.

Not to anyone.

Instead, she ate her food. Like Maria said—maybe she would have a nap and forget about everything.

About the voice.

• • •

"All you have to do, sweet girl, is lie down in your bed and close your eyes."

Maria spoke tenderly, stroking Katee's hair as she tried to convince her into a nap. At least, with her belly full, Katee thought the food had helped, but she wasn't so sure about falling asleep.

That voice was still taunting her.

It always did.

"Here, I'll even pull the curtains—a dark room will help you sleep better," Maria insisted. Katee climbed into the bed while her nanny worked to pull the curtains closed throughout the room. Shrouded in darkness, even the blankets drawn up to her chin wasn't enough to warm the cold fear still settled in her heart.

"Will you try and get some rest?" she heard Maria ask. Katee's eyes adjusted to the lack of light easily enough, but the black shadows had her pressing deeper in the mattress. "You've had a busy morning."

Katee nodded, if only to make Maria happy, even though it wasn't true.

Her nanny gave her a happy smile and then stepped out of the room, closing the door behind her without a sound. That left Katee alone in the darkness that she feared the most.

She spent a handful of minutes in the bed, unmoving, *eyes peeled*, but willing them to close for sleep. Dreams were better than being awake in the dark. Bad things happened in the dark—she knew that all too well. But as the fear started to crawl over her skin, even under the thick, heaviness of her blankets, she jumped out like she'd been burned. Katee tried.

She did.

But she just couldn't do it.

Rushing to the windows, she yanked the curtains open again, panting when the light flooded in. Air sucked into her lungs, one giant gulp after another. She forgot how to even breathe in the dark.

Her mind buzzed while her fingers itched. The way they did when she felt that urge to draw. She needed to find something to draw on. It was how she remembered what she had seen.

Trying to keep quiet, Katee searched the room, pulling down books from the shelves and opening drawers. They always moved her things—she *hated* that. Nothing was ever in the same place twice, even when she asked.

It was okay, though. There were notebooks and sketch pads everywhere. Picking one that satisfied her, she moved onto her next task. Pulling sheets and pillows off the bed, and even the ones on the chaise near the window. They piled high on the floor, but Katee didn't care.

It wasn't until she found a pen stuck inside a book on one of the shelves that she stopped rummaging—also satisfied with the drawing nest she had made on the floor—knowing Maria wouldn't come knocking for a while. At least an hour.

Katee crawled into the makeshift bed of sheets and pillows, putting pen to paper with focused determination of the fast swipes of the pen's tip against a bone white background. She *needed* to start drawing—when she did that, it was all her mind could see. Just the image on the paper, the picture she was trying to show. The face of the man she had seen today. Then, she wouldn't have to see the other things waiting in her mind, lingering until she almost forgot …

Thankfully, the pen was so blue that she could color his eyes the same shade. *The right shade.*

She scratched the pen wildly to the paper, not stopping once to examine if she was doing a good job or if the side of her hand was smearing the ink. It was always perfect. Only her handwriting needed a little work.

Or so Maria said.

The door creaked open before Katee had a chance to hide the paper behind her, making her lose the image in her mind as her head snapped up to see who came to her room. *Maria*, she thought, ready to scold her for getting out of bed before smiling because she was drawing and mostly behaving.

Except it wasn't her nanny.

Katee's air caught sharply in her throat, aching as the words she wanted to use to call for Maria caught in her throat. All it took was the sight of *him* to do that to her.

The monster.

It wasn't often that he caught her by surprise. Twice in one day was too much for her to handle.

"What have you done?" he growled at her, stepping further into the room and widening the door on his way. His face scrunched up, and every bitter word that poured from his mouth had her recoiling more. *Already*. "Look at this fucking mess."

"I … I'm s-sorry. I won't do it again."

Katee's apology was instant.

And *meek*.

She wasn't even sure what she was apologizing for, only that she needed to appease him somehow. *Quickly*.

Katee thought to call for Maria when the expression on his face changed—the moment he heard her voice. It was a brief second of distraction, but fleeting. Her chance was gone before she even really realized it was there. His eyes grew wider, the anger melting away into a sinister smile that curled the corners of his mouth.

He drew in a deep breath like he was … *pleased*.

With what?

She was always asking him that.

Are you happy?

Is this what you want?

Will you leave me alone now?

The answer was always the same. He kept coming back, after all.

He turned away from her only long enough to close the bedroom door, and lock it. Katee was already shrinking back, away, curling herself into a ball. That wouldn't stop him from doing what he was going to do.

It never did.

TWELVE

Roman had been made to wait an entire hour before he finally got to meet with the boss. Tribute meant a lot of things to different men in their life, but the money was the one thing that never changed. He sensed everybody around him waited on tenterhooks, careful with their every word or request because no one wanted to piss off the pakhan today. It seemed like Maxim was in the kind of mood where he could randomly lose his shit over nothing.

When Roman was finally shown into Maxim's den, he walked into a cloud of smoke the second his feet passed the office's threshold. Thick and gray, created by the cigar that Maxim was smoking where he sat behind his desk, the smoke stuck in the back of Roman's lungs when he sucked in a breath.

Only one other man remained in the room with the boss—Leonid. Dima's father, he knew, and one of Maxim's *spies*. The closest hand to the boss who made sure every brigadier in the bratva was toeing the line.

ᴛʜᴇAGREEMENT

Whatever line that was.

Roman rarely cared to learn them.

Dropping the two duffle bags on the floor, Roman said nothing while Maxim and Leonid glanced at it, and then toward him again.

"What are your thoughts on your job so far?" Maxim asked, that cigar bouncing from the corner of his mouth with every word.

Leonid stood up and walked over to grab the bags without being ordered to do so. Roman remained still in place, unmoving. He knew how this worked. It was not his first tribute day—the ritual had been with him while he grew up, reminding him monthly of where he would eventually be expected to be in one way or another.

The only difference?

His father didn't expect the money delivered in cash anymore.

All it would take for the money to disappear was Maxim's ashtray catching fire. The whole place would burn down, and take the cash with it. Roman never really understood the value of having cold, hard cash by the millions just lying around. It was harder to hide—harder to keep.

Then again, nobody asked his opinion.

"Well?" Maxim demanded.

"I did the job, as best it could be done, under the circumstances and given the resources I have. *Currently.* Having said that—I'm just getting started."

"So, you're saying you'll have more for me next month?"

Roman only shrugged in response. Let the man make of that whatever he wanted. He wasn't the type to make promises he couldn't keep, but he also knew what was expected of him at the end of the day. More was always *better.* To an extreme. Greed knew no bounds.

Especially in their world.

Maxim would never stop wanting more and more … and *more.* Frankly, Roman had to respect it. As much as he could manage, anyhow.

Beside him, but closer to the boss's desk, Leonid sat at a table with an electronic counting machine. Sliding wads of cash into the machine, the man never looked away from the dancing money while a loud whirring sound resounded through the room with each one. The slow smile and subtle nod told him Leonid was happy with the results he was seeing. He even grunted his approval toward Maxim, a signal for the boss to turn back on Roman.

"And what about your cut—have you paid yourself?" Maxim asked.

"Last night. The money came through to one of my offshore accounts. Not that I expected anything different."

"And the … cars?"

Did he care, or was the man just curious? What did it matter how Roman was paid, or the details of the overall job as long as Maxim was paid?

Roman indulged the question because he didn't have much of a choice. "They're already on a boat, all taken apart in a thousand different pieces, but there. That's my part of the deal, they'll deal with the rest."

Maxim nodded, impressed.

Silence reigned in the den as Leonid continued his business at the table. Maxim seemed fine to let that be the case while he worked on the cigar still filling the room with smoke. He toyed with the glass of vodka on ice at the edge of his desk, sipping on the drink, and watching his spy pile up stack after stack of dirty money.

Roman counted the minutes.

A good thirty of them.

Finally, Leonid muttered, "And the money is all here, yeah? Every last dollar."

Maxim gestured to Roman once more, saying, "You've done good work here. I'll make sure your father hears about it, too."

That was all Roman needed. He wasn't here for more. Having gone through the expectations of tribute and the charade of the event, he no longer needed to remain there once his offering to the boss was counted as right and *good*. Turning to walk away, Maxim stopped him again.

"And I want to thank you for not speaking about my daughter," Maxim said, the low words still managing to crawl across the room and slam into Roman's tense back like a punch. "Not mentioning her to anyone, no?"

Roman stopped in his tracks, careful to control the surprise daring to spark in his eyes when he pivoted on the spot, facing Maxim.

What the fuck was this about?

He raised his brow higher, and Maxim continued.

"It's a delicate time for her ..."

"And us," Leonid murmured to himself while he stuffed the money back into the bags.

Roman kept his confusion under the surface—but only because one thing was clear. The fact that the Yazov Bratva clearly had some kind of problem with Karine. Even though she was Maxim's daughter, something strange surrounded her.

Especially here.

It bothered Roman.

He opened his mouth to ask for an explanation; he hadn't even mentioned Karine. Maxim's willingness to offer conversation about her—even if it was only to thank him again—struck Roman as odd. Considering the way the man had acted the first time.

Roman hadn't forgotten that threat.

Maxim was quick to keep talking, forcing Roman to stay quiet and listen. "I was just curious to see if you would speak to someone about her. It'd be natural, you know? Human nature. Anyone would want to find out more about my daughter, but certainly when they're new to my world. Ask questions about her, even. But you didn't, and that's a good sign, Roman. Another testament to your loyalty, I think."

Roman flexed his jaw with every clench of his teeth, uneasy with the man's tone that didn't fill him with confidence, despite the words Maxim used. He offered the remark about loyalty like it was a compliment, yet it landed more backhanded than perhaps he intended. Or maybe that was exactly what Maxim wanted.

There was only one thing Roman trusted in Chicago—that he was watched and reported on constantly. Who was it? Josef, likely. One of the many bulls that came and went, lingering a little too long whenever Roman showed his face at the business of a Yazov affiliated man. Or were there others keeping a close eye on him? Some even he hadn't caught on to yet? Reporting back to the pakhan when Roman had done something or nothing.

Probably.

But the thing was—the more Maxim talked about his daughter, bringing her back to Roman's attention for no other reason than he apparently could, the more he fixated on her. He certainly wouldn't forget about Karine that easily. Certainly not when everything about and around her seemed ... not quite right. He found that interesting even if it was a problem.

At least, Roman knew *that*.

One thing to his benefit, anyway.

"If that's all, then I should go," Roman said, offering nothing in return about Karine or Maxim's random statements that felt way too much like bait. "I have calls to make."

Since the boss didn't interrupt him that time, he made a beeline for the door.

If only it could be that easy.

Just as he was about to step out, Dima appeared.

Roman's blood ran cold the moment the two came face to face. It wasn't just him who stiffened with a narrowed stare. Dima matched his demeanor and posture. Vodka be damned—that grudge was alive and well.

The guy still despised Roman.

Well, shit.

The sentiment was mutual.

"Where have you been?" Leonid snapped behind Roman, interrupting the hatred swelling silently between the two men in the doorway. "Today's not the day to be fucking off, Dima."

Dima openly glared at his father, making Roman clear his throat and avert his own stare. Awkward was a fucking understatement. No matter what issues existed between Roman and Demyan, his father would never talk to him that way. Not in front of other people.

He was grateful for that.

Maybe, instead of the unsettling, constant irritation that accompanied him whenever the guy was within breathing distance, Roman should have felt sorry for Dima.

Or not.

"I was busy," Dima replied shortly.

"Nothing is that important. You're missing *business*."

Leonid's response hit its mark. Dima tore his glare away from his father, and fixed his bloodshot eyes on Roman. The two returned to their defensive postures and cold expressions without blinking.

"Don't linger in the driveway this time."

Dima had spoken through clenched teeth, and Roman wasn't sure if the others even heard him.

"You should come. Shouldn't he, Maxim? You should come, Roman," Leonid said, bringing him back to a conversation he hadn't paid attention to in the first damn place. Roman was regretting that now.

Roman spun on his heels to face the room again. "What?"

"I'm sure the boss will agree that you've earned an invite," Leonid continued.

Maxim nodded as he sucked on his cigar while his right-hand man grinned, and looked to Roman for a reply. Maybe a *thank you*, who the fuck knew? But for what?

Roman wasn't exactly sure what he was agreeing to, but he mumbled a sort of non-committal response, anyway. Whatever got him out of that office. He didn't want to stick around a moment longer. Not when Dima was around.

Nonetheless, it worked.

Satisfied with his reply, Roman was dismissed without another word. He waved a hand over his shoulder, and left the room, forcing Dima to take a step aside to let him pass. Briefly, he might catch one glimpse of Karine. He should have known she would be nowhere to be seen—Roman was starting to believe certain people didn't want her to be.

At all.

· · ·

Maybe it was because Dima told him not to linger, but Roman decided to do just that. Even though the asshole remained in Maxim's office, he took pleasure in defying Dima's demands.

It was the simple things.

The little stuff.

A part of him hoped Dima might be waiting at the entrance when he made his way back around, but no such luck.

Apparently, the two weren't going to get another run-in. That was unfortunate considering with tribute done and over, Roman had a whole month to find ways to piss Dima off just because he could. *As long as he could get away with it.* He was sure he could find a few different ways to make that happen.

Roman milled around the foyer and lobby area of the mansion for a bit, sharing easy conversation with a few of the men waiting. The bulls were familiar with him by now, and despite the day, they didn't mind the distraction he offered for a while.

Everybody had shit to do.

Didn't mean they wanted to do it.

After a while, nobody seemed to care that Roman was admiring the oil paintings hanging on the walls. His mother's appreciation for art kept him standing there admiring the brushwork that had gone into a particular painting with a plaque underneath dated only *Fall, 1930.* Roman tried to picture it, but he couldn't quite imagine Maxim picking out the art himself. He had to have a collector on his payroll who made the purchases on his behalf—*investments,* likely. Much like the rest of the material wealth in the estate.

All of it was just to prove a point to the rest of the world—Maxim was king of Chicago. He had the most, *the best.* What everyone else didn't.

Roman knew, in some ways, he was a disappointment to his father and grandfather. His less than savory habits and wild ways, to start with, left them feeling like he was constantly walking on unsteady ground. Even if they never explicitly said it, it didn't have to be. And yet, he didn't want it to be like that. He also didn't want to be *this*, either.

The man Maxim was ...

A boss hiding in a big house, really. Trusting that just his presence and name was enough to ensure the men on the streets were all doing as they should—because his yes men said so.

What good did that do?

Useless.

The show of material-wealth and paid-for taste wasn't something that impressed him. Instead, it annoyed him, leaving him with heaviness in his stomach that was unsettling and uncomfortable. Pretty things usually hid ugly truths, and even he was a good example of that.

What was hiding here?

The more time he spent in Chicago, the clearer it became to him that Maxim was making errors with his people. In little ways, sure, but he caught it all the same.

Roman smiled to himself as he surveyed another painting. The last thing he had any right to do was offer advice to the pakhan of a successful bratva, and yet he couldn't help but consider how different things might be in Chicago if Maxim cared to run the streets, *on the streets.*

He wandered the halls until he found the guest toilets. He decided to go for a piss—even took extra long to do so, and washed his hands with a pearl-colored soap that smelled like vanilla and cream, before spending some time staring at himself in the mirror. Just to increase the chances of bumping into Dima again.

Roman was clearly bored if he was actively looking for trouble. For a man with his issues, nobody could say he wasn't self-aware. There was a method to his madness, though. He wanted the asshole to know he would continue doing exactly what he wanted, whenever he wanted.

It was a good lesson to learn.

Just when he was about to step outside the bathroom, he heard Leonid's voice echoing in the corridor. He wouldn't have stayed inside if he hadn't heard the tone of Leonid's voice—a shaky aggression that made Roman pause just long enough to actually hear what was being said.

"The day of the wedding. That is when you need to make it happen." Leonid's obvious growing frustration spilled out with impatient words for the person on the other end of the line. "No, of course it's not too soon, Katina. For fuck's sake—I'm starting to think *you* don't have it in you to see this through."

Through the crack in the door, Roman watched Leonid pace up and down the corridor. He'd never been the type to eavesdrop. That shit only led a man into trouble, and the truth was, Roman wasn't all that interested in other people's affairs.

This time, though, something stopped him from pulling away from the conversation in the corridor. He *wanted* to listen. Something about Leonid's voice compelled him to remain there, peering through the small crack in the opened door, even though he had no idea what was being discussed.

"August thirty-first. Do you get me? Maxim has to die by then or you're not getting what you want, Katina," Leonid added, the sharpness in his words feeling like the edge of a blade raking across Roman's skin.

And shit …

He wasn't even the person Leonid was directing his orders to in the first damn place.

Roman had to look away, even though that did nothing to erase the words that had already infiltrated his mind and wouldn't leave. Leonid, one of Maxim's most trusted men, was planning his boss's assassination. Or that was certainly how it sounded to him.

Despite the fact he was now privy to a plot against the boss, Roman wasn't truly shocked at the news that there was one to begin with. It was a lesson his father had given him long ago. He'd made Roman promise not to trust anybody. *Literally nobody.*

Roman was fourteen at the time when a plot was hatched to execute Demyan. Initiated by a man Demyan considered to be a friend, the plan was seen through until almost the end. Until it was almost too late.

⚘AGREEMENT

By someone they *trusted*.

His father had come out of it alive and well, of course. At the same time, he had armed himself with a life lesson which he imparted to his son.

As the boss of a large organization, Demyan expected to face criticism and disrespect from the outside, typically, even from friends and people he trusted, at times. A boss always had to remind people why he sat where he did compared to everyone else. Finding out a friend was plotting against you, on the other hand, was a whole other matter.

Roman would never forget the look on his father's face when he found out what was happening—rage, and *fear*.

Real, true fear.

Because they were never safe. No man in this life was, no matter how hard they tried to make it so. Reality was not as kind when it came back around to remind a man where he actually stood.

On shaky ground.

Roman tried to think back on that time as a young man, and how it all unfolded in the streets between the men when the truth started to leak out. It hadn't gone over well, really. It never did.

All the while, Leonid continued mumbling into the phone outside, but his body language hadn't changed. He still spoke to the woman he called *Katina*, threatening her without even taking a breath in between.

Roman's mind raced to catch up even though it might have been a smarter choice to turn away and pretend he hadn't heard a thing. Except ... he knew how significant this information was—even if he wasn't personally involved in the ploy to execute the pakhan of a bratva.

It could potentially start a war. If Maxim was assassinated tomorrow, the rest of Chicago would be running around like a flock of headless chickens. Men with too much control, entirely *out* of control. All vying to come out on top of an already bad situation, and probably willing to make it worse if that meant a better seat for them in the end.

It was just how this shit worked.

Something else made him pause, too. Roman didn't know where his own loyalties rested here. And he was pretty sure that simply overhearing what he assumed to be a plot against the boss wasn't enough to actually bring to the man and say it was fact—especially not against a man as high in the organization as Leonid.

What proof could Roman show for that? He had nothing to go on but the edges of an overheard conversation. And wasn't there a warning somewhere for messengers delivering bad news?

Yeah.

Nothing about this was good.

The information he now had was dangerous, and he was all too aware that he had a *very* short time in which to decide whether to tell it to someone, or not.

Outside, Leonid ended the call and through the crack, Roman waited as the man walked away. Until he was altogether out of sight.

He remained in the bathroom, not moving an inch until the echo of footsteps finally came to a stop ... or was too far away for him to still hear. Feeling too dazed to step out, Roman scrubbed a hand down his face, and tried to shake off the heavy questions banging around in his mind, and the weight now pressing down on his shoulders.

A sense of ... *responsibility.*

He hated that.

A part of him wished he hadn't lingered.

Hindsight was always twenty-twenty.

THIRTEEN

Karine tried to admire the sight of her reflection staring back, but she couldn't even do that considering the reason why she was even standing there looking like she did in the first place. She had been dressed and made-up for *him* … and everyone else. Before the night had even begun, she already knew she would look perfect tonight because Masha had one responsibility when it came to the evening ahead. To make sure Karine looked her very best because that was what was expected from them both.

The only thing that was expected, really.

Everything else was up in the air.

It was for the best, but she didn't even like the dress Masha stuck her in. The satin number, a shimmery, cream-colored cocktail dress, that stuck to every curve and crevice of her body with spaghetti-thin straps barely doing a decent job of holding the material up. When she looked at herself in the mirror, for a second, she thought she was nude.

Body on display.

A low dip in the front, and even deeper in the back.

There was no hiding the way the satin lay unforgiving against her frame, giving everything away with each turn of her body without truly *showing* it off. Not that it mattered. Karine wasn't one to show off anything.

However, Masha selected the dress for the evening because it *would* draw attention to Karine. Show off her beautiful figure. Make her father and Dima proud to claim her as their property.

A way to say *look at what is ours.* As if they didn't already say it enough.

Tonight was the night.

The night after which there would be no going back. Karine couldn't stop herself from hyperventilating the longer she was forced to stare at her reflection.

She didn't like her hair like it was, either. All neatly tied in a bun and pinned back from her face. She preferred it when it was left open and free flowing, then she could use it as a veil to hide behind, if needed. But they needed everything about her to be … *pure* tonight. Perfection.

It was only when Masha came over to touch up her makeup one last time before they left that she noticed the way Karine was breathing. Her chest rose and fell heavily, skin tightening around her collarbones with every fast breath, and her face had even started to pink from the stress. The bigger problem?

The tears in her eyes.

She couldn't hide those.

Masha searched for the pillbox she always kept within arm's reach, quickly pulling it from its hiding spot before popping it open, and offering one to Karine without even showing which pill she chose. "Here, have this. Take one and you'll feel better before you know it."

Karine grappled for the pill, and popped it back. Down her throat it went, and she closed her eyes tight, waiting a few moments for it to take effect. It wasn't that she would magically start seeing rainbows and unicorns everywhere—the edges simply became a little less sharp to her senses. Easier to deal with, maybe. If only she could forget the significance of what was going to happen tonight, then perhaps she might also stop panicking about the future.

Right—lying to yourself again, Karine.

What else could she do?

This was all she knew.

"You just have to get through the next few hours, and then it will all be over," Masha said, her whispery assurance adding to the way she stroked Karine's hair as she bent over. "Come on, now, isn't that enough of that?"

Not even close.

Vomit threatened to spill from her stomach before she could stop it. Karine was sure she was going to be sick, but nothing happened. That warm glow started to spread all over, traveling thick in her veins, promising the pill was taking effect. It wouldn't be long before she was going to be able to forget everything and go through the motions of the night's event.

When Karine finally opened her eyes and looked at herself again, she couldn't hide the way her hands trembled. Her hand was bare for the moment, but very soon, a big diamond ring would rest on one of those long, pale fingers.

A ring that would mark the beginning of her end, she knew.

"You look beautiful, Karine," Masha told her, soft hands flitting over Karine's face to brush away any stray tears or whatever else she might find that made her less than perfect. "So grown up, hmm? You'll be the most beautiful women at the party."

Masha's pride turned on her, making Karine suck in a stuttering breath. She would have loved for her father to look at her the same way and say those things.

The truth was cold, though.

And hard to accept.

No matter how strikingly perfect her dress was, or how gorgeous Masha made her look—to her father, she would always just be currency. Something to barter. A commodity to use for his benefit.

She wasn't *meaningful*. Karine meant nothing.

Not to him.

• • •

Masha gave Karine another pill on the way to the restaurant. Even though there weren't that many lights inside the place, Karine still squinted at the seemingly bright space, barely keeping her eyes open when they stepped inside. Not that it stopped her from seeing the scene that waited.

So many people.

The whole restaurant had been booked out for tonight at her father's request. Everyone was there who had been given an invitation—no one would turn it down when that would be disrespectful to the man who offered it in the first place.

Karine tried not to be unsettled by the number of guests she passed through to make her way to the table designated for her. One already filled with faces she didn't want to join. Dima. *Her father.* Others who were important enough to sit with the boss and his future son-in-law.

They all sat on one side of the table where she was made to sit between them. Masha disappeared somewhere in the shadows where she would remain unless called for by one of the men sitting with her at the table. The true extent of her role in Karine's life always made an appearance on nights like these.

She was there.

But she *wasn't.*

Seen, but not heard.

Known, but not acknowledged.

Before she had stepped away, though, Masha was quick to slip another pill into Karine's hand with a knowing glance— *this will help things go faster.* The pills usually did, so she was happy to take it.

Karine felt limbless without Masha there. Even if she did keep clutching at the small pill, shaped like a bar inside her palm, like it was a lifeline that might save her. What if she needed more? What if she started having those bad thoughts, or couldn't stop the trembling in her hands?

She didn't know how to do this—*any of it.*

Being normal, that was.

_{THE}_AGREEMENT

Or rather, pretending like she was.

Instead, she kept her head down and tried to focus on the pattern printed on the table cloth. There were mostly only men around her, all speaking in loud voices that made her want to shrink away. She was so physically close to her father for once, whom she wished would look at her or address her directly instead of talking *about* her to the room, that she could smell his cologne. Dima sat on her other side, smoking heavily. The smoke from his cigarette had her stomach rolling all over again, but she stayed quiet in her seat. Just his presence was enough to make her gag.

And yet, here you sit.

Her mind was a horrible place. One she lived inside more than anyone knew. A prison she couldn't escape, but not one of her own making.

The celebrations continued without much of her involvement or interest, and she passed through it all in a daze. It was the only way she could get through it. Without focusing on one particular voice or conversation, drawing in on herself and fading back against the rest of the people in the room … being present but silent.

She just hoped it would all glide through her, as most everything else in her life did, and then she could wake up in bed tomorrow morning. Maybe it would all turn out to be a bad dream.

The filled up shot glasses with vodka, spilling everywhere on the table in their raucous haste. Some of it even dribbled onto her dress, but she didn't care or even bother to clean up the spreading wet stain on her dress

A loud celebratory roar rang out around her, causing Karine to instinctively look up and seek out the need for all the noise. The others facing her across the table held up their glasses in a toast.

At her side, Maxim grinned. For a moment, Karine's heart dared to beat faster—*lighter*—but in the next, she felt a tug drawing her attention away. Right back to the man at her other side.

Dima, that was.

He had pulled on her to slip the ring on her finger. Large and glittery under the light, it took up her sole focus, draining color from her cheeks and making her stomach drop to her feet in an instant.

Karine chewed on the inside of her cheek, desperate to stop herself from screaming. Cold and heavy on her finger, the ring added the same weight and iciness to her heart. *This was happening.* The engagement was actually happening, and she had yet to come to terms with it.

Not that it made a difference now.

There it was.

On her finger.

Real.

That ring was a shackle being fixed around her very person. She was officially a prisoner to a man she had never chosen for herself. One without any escape.

Now that the ring was on, the whispers of her engagement to Dima was official along with the announcement—it seemed like the rest of the people around her didn't care anymore. The party was back in full swing, more drinks were poured until glasses overflowed and expensive vodka was drained from its bottles. They no longer cared to pay lip service to the girl in the pretty dress sitting with the men who had all of the guests' attention.

She was forgotten.

Again.

Karine simply hoped that meant she would be left alone for the rest of the evening, too. After all, she had done her part. Showed up. Stayed calm—*pleasant.* She thought she might have even smiled for the watching guests, but did it really matter?

What more did they want?

Apparently, nothing.

Fine.

Slowly, Karine stood from her chair. Nobody noticed, even though she was sitting right between the two most important men at the table.

Karine couldn't see Masha anywhere. All she knew was that she needed to be outside, away from this—far from these people who made her feel like a circus act one minute, and then meaningless in the next. She wanted to hide somewhere alone where nobody would find her.

Even if only for a minute. Maybe then, she could breathe.

Somehow, Karine doubted it.

• • •

Karine stumbled out into the alleyway in the dark of night with a shaky inhale of icy rain that chilled her down to the bone. She didn't think she would make it this far without being stopped or caught by somebody from the bratva. Behind her, the emergency exit door of the restaurant swung shut and *finally*, she heard nothing but the soft drizzle of rain falling on the loose gravel by her feet.

And those deep breaths of hers.

One after another.

She'd been right.

Breathing was easier like this.

Despite it being the first week of August, the rain was cold in the warm air, making the droplets warm on her bare arms. It at least made the temperature bearable, even if she did barely consider it before coming out.

It was another thing that didn't matter much in the grand scheme of things. Like how her dress was going to be soaked, her makeup smudged and ruined by the drizzle from above. What would her father say? What would Dima do if he saw her like that?

Who cared?

She should.

She should care.

God.

Karine wished she did.

The heaviness of that ring on her finger hadn't left. She opened her mouth to suck in more big gulps of fresh air, hoping it would calm her. Except the effects of the pills were fading, and *fast*. She wasn't in that glazed daze anymore—life didn't have the same bright, shiny appeal that came with a medically-induced happiness—and that was what made her run out of there like she had caught on fire.

"Seems we keep running into each other like this, huh?"

The deep velvety voice came out of nowhere. Karine gasped into the darkness, instinct making her hand fly up to her throat even though her racing heart dared to slow down at the same time. She knew who it was before she even turned to look.

She couldn't forget that voice.

Roman.

The handsome stranger with those striking soul-blue eyes. She had no idea he was supposed to be at the engagement announcement tonight. Either way, he had missed the announcement if he had been outside.

"Or maybe it's not an accident at all," he added as she turned to see the handsome grin curving at the edges of his gorgeous mouth. Something about the sight of his pleasure at seeing her made Karine's stomach do the strangest things. *Dangerous* things. "Maybe one of us is spying on the other."

With hands thrust deep into the pockets of his slacks, he had his head tilted to the side as he studied her. Waiting for her reply.

Karine was surprised to find she had to remind herself to actually speak. "Well, if one of us is the spy, it has to be you."

His smile grew wider, clearly amused at her answer, and he took a few steps towards her. Careful steps, she noticed. And with the way he kept his head cocked to the side like that, she thought he seemed ... wary of himself.

Or maybe her.

What was she going to do?

Bite him?

"You look like you don't know what to do with yourself," he noted.

Karine swallowed hard, replying only, "I rarely do."

He inched closer still.

She eyed him up and down, wondering what he might do when he finally reached her. A part of her welcomed the idea—good or bad. At this point, what did Karine really have to fucking lose?

Then, he said, "You're getting wet, babe."

The endearment came easily.

Slipped out fast, too.

And yet, the wave of emotions that crashed into Karine told the truth. She absorbed the impact of his concern wrapped in a pretty package all too well. It made her body ache with desire—for a man who looked at her like he did right then, and *cared.* Urgency followed fast behind, ready to remind her of reality. It was the panic that really clawed at her, though.

Deep.

And entirely unforgiving.

The same desperate need to escape that had sent her running from the party slammed into her all over again. Before Karine understood the implications of her actions, she lunged at him.

Roman worked at lightning speed to catch her. She fell on his chest as his muscular arms wrapped around her like a cage, the hardness of his lines somehow feeling soft to her the tighter he held her. For a second, everything was ... quiet.

Different.

Better.

She didn't care what he thought of her—the spectacle she made of herself was just one of many that made up her life. It was the fact that this man was the one person who showed up in her sheltered circle that offered her something no one else did. An opportunity she could *use.* Tonight, she just needed to forget. He might well be able to help her do exactly that.

But that wasn't even the strangest part. Rain continued to drizzle, the warm droplets sliding over Karine's eyelashes and falling on her cheeks. He stared at her with a look that said he expected this—her in his arms, that was.

How?

Their gazes met, his holding hers strong even though a voice in the back of her mind hissed for her to look away.

She didn't really want to. There was something enthralling about the way he watched her, how his stare swept down to her mouth when her tongue peeked out to lick away the raindrops from her lips, and then jumped back up to her eyes when she blinked away the droplets from her lashes.

He drank her in.

Held her *safe*.

And she craved that.

More than he knew.

"You're incredibly ... *beautiful*, Karine," he murmured, the edge to his voice making her shiver when he added quickly, "I wanted to say something else, but it didn't feel like enough. *Hot* wasn't enough. Beautiful isn't that impressive, but it's better. More fitting."

She blinked again, still silent.

Not because she didn't want to speak, though. Oh, She *did*. Karine just didn't know what to say.

Usually, a compliment like that would make her self-conscious. Maybe because she had never believed it, not if it came from a man. For one, there weren't very many men who were in a position to say that to her in the first place. Not unless they wanted to answer for it, too. It was yet another reminder that Roman wasn't quite the same as the men who surrounded her constantly. Something made him different, and she almost wanted to know *what*. And perhaps even why.

So, Karine, on the flipside of the same coin, left her surprised by her own body's reaction to Roman, she also wasn't shocked at all. She was accustomed to curling away, to feeling frightened and small in the view of others. Not with him. Instead, there was something about the way that he looked at her—it made her hold her head up higher, and stare back unashamed. She straightened her shoulders, daring him to keep *looking*.

She liked it.

And his words.

Returning the compliment to him in kind would be too much. Karine didn't know how to formulate the words needed to thank him, let alone the ones to say how she perceived him. Either way, the fact that she didn't pull away, and instead let her fingertips dance over the broadness of his chest, seemed to be enough for him because he leaned into her.

Impossibly closer.

Just like she wanted him.

Their hips grazed, and she pushed herself further into him, his grip on her loosening just enough to let her swing lightly in his arms. That didn't last long before he pinned her close to himself again, engulfing her in the warmth of his body. She got a whiff of his scent when his hand came up to catch her under her jaw, tipping her head back to make her gaze stay locked on his.

Leather. Pine. And something sweet along the edges. She could taste him on the tip of her tongue, and while his fingers pressed into her jaw firmly enough to make her breath catch, it was the scent of him soaking into her senses that kept her still and calm.

Unafraid.

"Are you playing a game with me?" he asked.

The question was a fair one.

She had to admit it.

Still, she told him, "No."

A girl like her ...

What games could she play?

Roman arched one dark brow. "I'm not sure if I should believe you."

"So, don't."

Seemed simple enough to her.

What did it matter?

Easier said than done, she knew. Just standing there with his hands on her was enough to get Roman in a lot of trouble. He'd already taken one risk with her tonight, and Karine was feeling bold enough to push for *two*.

Maybe her stare urged him on.

Or her silence.

Whatever it was, Roman's throat jumped with a swallow before he said, "Tell me what you want, Karine. I need to know what you want here."

His words came out in heady whispers, right there, dark at her ear penetrating her oh, so deep whiles knots tightened in her gut. An intense desire washed over her; something she had never experienced before.

There was a lot she couldn't pretend to understand about men. She wouldn't even begin to try. There were a few things, however, that she could never forget, either. Men were supposed to be feared. Men hurt her. They took away everything and made her feel small and inferior. There hadn't been one man in her life who didn't take the time in one way or another to remind her that she was insignificant, and *unwanted*.

But not this man.

He asked her what *she* wanted. Karine wasn't sure if he did that because of who her father was, or something else. Whatever the reason, it was the first time she had been given a real choice.

"Karine," he pressed, voice softer than time.

It was that softness he offered her—again without her prompting—that urged her to answer him back. To *find those words*. The ones that she hadn't really known how to use.

"Would you kiss me?" she asked, but he didn't move. More words slipped out before she became too scared to say the truth. "I wonder what you taste like—your kiss on mine. Do you want to taste me, too?"

Even in the darkness with nothing but a streetlight at the far end of the alley—illuminating their faces dimly—she could see the way he reveled at that, pleasure lighting up in his eyes in the smirk of his tempting mouth. Maybe at the frankness of her words, or how she said them ... either way, it was clear he liked it.

His hand traveled up the side of her body until his palm found her left breast hard over the damp material of her dress. Under the trimmed, dark thickness of his beard, she enjoyed the way his jaw clenched, like he could barely control himself. She knew he was hard—the ridged length of his cock pushed into her thigh as they remained close together.

"Well?" she asked again. "Do you?"

The rumbling hum that answered her back was delicious. It started a fire inside her body that she hadn't expected. But then he had to go ahead and speak, too.

That only made it worse.

"Are you fucking kidding me? I've wanted to taste you from the second you came out of that swimming pool."

Oh?

Good.

Karine let her hands travel down, too. Her mouth fell open hungrily as her hand wedged between them until she had cupped his crotch. Brazenly, she stroked him through his pants when he squeezed her breast even harder. His thumb found her nipple through the dress, erect and sensitive to his touch.

Karine loved it—that *sensation.*

The way he was careful when he touched her, like she was a piece of art worthy of being worshipped and cherished, but still held her tight enough that it could hurt if he wanted it to. She threw her head back a bit, delighting in his touch, and the way the rain fell on her face now. His free hand traveled to her ass, grasping hard and strong. Making her suck in a hissed breath when his hands flexed against her body.

All the while, she stroked him more.

Harder.

Then that hand at her throat reached for her nape, guiding her head back so she faced him fully again.

"I know better than this," he groaned.

She might have laughed. If only because he said it like he was mad at the world about the situation he found himself in with her. But she didn't believe he was mad at all, and it wasn't very funny.

Mostly because he wasn't wrong.

She knew better, too.

Then, he dipped down to take a kiss, their mouths met with lips already opened for the taste they'd both wanted, and Karine was sure she was going to explode into a million pieces.

Or maybe her heart would. The organ certainly raced like it might, the thundering beats slamming into her ribcage one after another as Roman's tongue tangled with hers. Every swipe of his lips over hers urged Karine to kiss back, wanting more. He pulled the breath out of her lungs with his kiss, but goddammit, she didn't mind.

She was right, too—there had been something sweet about the man, and she found it in the way his bruising kiss teased and lulled her into a slower rhythm. How he explored her mouth with every dart of his tongue and hint of his teeth grazing her lower lip.

The kiss turned into gentle sweeps of their mouths until both were pulling back for air. She would have gone back for more the second her lungs ached with fresh air, but his next words sent her spinning in a whole new way.

"Your mouth isn't the only thing I want to taste," he told her.

Roman shoved a hand between her thighs, and managed to push her dress up higher at the same time. Or it could have been the fact she widened her stance for him to do it. His fingers found the dampness and warmth seeping through the lace of her panties, two of them rubbing hard against her until she moved back against his hand for more. Her body sought what it wanted from him, the sparks of lust dancing over her skin with dangerous intent.

Only the rain kept her from sizzling into a plume of smoke because the fire inside of Karine raged hotter than ever. Devastatingly so. She'd never wanted a man.

Not like she wanted this one.

She stroked him back, too, feeling his thick cock throb hard inside his pants when she angled her rocking body into his to let him feel more of her. Pushed against the brick wall behind her, Karine couldn't take her eyes off Roman when he lifted her leg up, and his palm cupped her knee. That mouth of his came back for more, his tongue thrusting beyond her parted lips to slam into her own while his cock pushed in between her thighs.

She loved how he encompassed her—how he surrounded her with his size and strength. His presence loomed over hers, and yet he couldn't look away. Or maybe he just didn't want to. She wasn't diminished in front of him ... *not at all.*

THE AGREEMENT

Karine was all he seemed to see.

In a way, that was terrifying.

Even if she did want it.

"What else do you want to taste?" she asked, breathless.

She shouldn't ask, or want to know. Karine still did, and there wasn't a single part of her that regretted it at the moment, either.

Roman's fingers ghosted over her swollen clit through the flimsy fabric of her panties, doing nothing to offer a semblance of a barrier between them. "I think you know exactly what, babe."

God, yes.

Her pleased sighs even came out raspy as he touched her everywhere. From the hand between her thighs to the one working her body higher. He traced the curve of her neck before he tugged at her earlobe with his teeth, and then those lips of his trailed down the slick skin of her trembling jaw.

What were they even doing like this?

She didn't know, but ... she wanted more. She wanted to give him everything he liked, anything he might think to ask her for in that second, she'd happily hand it over. However he wanted it, too. Even if that meant spreading her legs for him in a dark, dirty alley on the night of her engagement dinner.

Really, she wasn't thinking about Dima, or her father. Or anything else except the man touching her, for that matter. Even if that meant she was stupid to do so. All he had to do was say the words for Karine to agree, but Roman held back.

He hesitated, and she saw it.

Felt it, too.

"Is it because of my father?" she whispered.

His jaw worked hard, tensing over and over while his hands stilled on her body before he finally replied, "Partly."

He didn't want to overstep—but the boundaries were already fading into the distance, right? That was long gone, now.

Although, Karine wasn't about to forget the fact that just seconds earlier, Roman touched her like he wasn't afraid of having to answer for it. She willed that boldness from earlier to come back—that piece of herself that wasn't afraid to ask him to taste her, *touch* her. If she asked now, would he fuck her, too?

She decided she would just *say it*, whether he said one thing and did another, but the sound of the door squeaking open to her side stopped Karine's words right in their tracks. The restaurant's emergency exit door.

Something snapped in her, dragging her back to a horrifying reality, and she forgot all about the courage building inside her. Roman came to the same conclusion she did, his reaction mirroring hers when Karine pulled away from him, and he didn't stop her.

"Karine, are you out here?" came the call from the opened doorway.

It was Masha. The older woman stood silhouetted by the shadows at the door, peering into the darkness because she probably couldn't see more than a couple of feet beyond her position.

Luckily.

Roman had slipped off to the side, further hidden in the shadows. She hoped Masha couldn't see him when she stepped up quickly towards her nanny whose gaze affixed to her emerging figure through the darkness.

Masha's brows furrowed—a mixture of worried and annoyance stared back. "What are you *doing?*"

The woman didn't even attempt to hide the way she looked her over, taking in every imperfection she could manage. Karine brought her fingers up to her face, reminding herself how her makeup and hair was likely ruined. So was her dress, now.

She almost apologized for her state.

Almost.

Karine couldn't find it in herself to care, though. Not after … everything else. She was still riding a high of her own making—as precarious as it was.

"Sorry, I lost track of time … and the rain," she tried to say, the excuse already forming on the tip of her tongue.

ᵀᴴᴱAGREEMENT

Masha's eyes grew narrower. "Just get inside—go to the bathrooms where you were supposed to be. I brought a bag of things in case we needed it. So we can fix all this. It's nothing to worry about. Go on, now."

Karine tried to smile, and at least appear grateful as she walked past in a hurry. She didn't dare look back for Roman, hoping he would have enough good sense to remain where he couldn't be seen until Masha had followed her inside.

She slipped beyond Masha in the open exit door, and once again, the sounds of the celebrations inside hit her. Apparently, that was what she needed to kill the high vibrating inside of her like the wings of a hummingbird.

Just like that.

It all vanished into thin air.

But it wasn't that simple, and just because the feeling was gone didn't mean her memories were. A shudder ran down Karine's spine as hot tears stung the backs of her eyelids. The kiss might be over, and it would likely never happen again, but she could still *feel it.*

And Roman.

If only that meant something.

Except it couldn't.

FOURTEEN

"She is spoken for."

Roman stiffened where he stood in the darkness, positive the woman couldn't see him. But that meant nothing if she still knew he was there. And as it seemed, she did.

Fuck.

"*Sir,*" she added, quieter.

And fast.

Like she wanted him to know she understood her place against him, and for a second, it took him by surprise. There was a difference between respecting someone's place, and making one *know* it.

The first statement would have been enough of a warning, but the second actually made him pause. Leaning forward a bit, and moving enough of a step to be seen in the shadows, the woman who had spoken to him—bold enough to warn him to stay away—also called him *sir* and wouldn't meet his eyes.

ᵗᵸᴇAGREEMENT

He hadn't bothered to get close enough to any man in Chicago that he'd been invited into one's home where a wife, daughter, mother or otherwise might be present. None except Maxim, and the few women he'd seen draped over the arms of men at parties and business meetings.

Docile women.

Quiet, *compliant* women.

He didn't come from that kind of world—his mother humbled his father daily as a form of foreplay that Roman *really* didn't enjoy knowing about in the first damn place. He wasn't accustomed to females that were to be seen, but not heard. And he couldn't particularly say he liked it, either.

It was that reason alone, and the fact that when the woman in the doorway did step outside, let the door close behind her with a loud *bang* that didn't even earn a flinch from her, she did dare to meet his eyes. He saw fear there, but she did it.

He respected that.

"*Please,*" she said, still staring at him, unmoving.

She was the same woman he saw with Karine that first time at the pool, and here she was, interrupting them again—he didn't think that was a coincidence. Roman never believed in those.

It was the strangest thing, but at her unwavering, knowing stare nailing him to the brick at his back, he almost felt the urge to *explain*. Or lie. He got the feeling she was daring him to say anything at all—*try it*—but the soft pleading of her expression even despite the fire in her eyes made him feel guilty.

Like somehow, he'd crossed some line. And not one he should feel particularly good about. What had she first said? Karine was ... *spoken for?*

Roman had no idea how it all happened. It took him by surprise. He didn't expect Karine to kiss him, but the way the woman behaved suggested he hadn't been doing anything wrong. She *liked* it.

Clearly.

"What are you talking about?" Roman asked then, foregoing the safety of the shadows altogether and stepping closer to the restaurant's door.

The woman was older—Roman's mother's age, or a little more—but the clothes she wore made it very clear she was not related to Maxim Yazov. The gray tunic, long-sleeve woven dress and comfortable, but practical, black ankle boots with the one inch heel was more of a uniform. Especially in comparison to the ten-thousand-dollar custom tailored suits worn by the men inside that restaurant. Even the servers had more expensive heels on their feet.

"I don't know what happened here," she told him when it appeared like Roman wasn't going to ask again. "And I don't want to know. I didn't see anything, but if you have a heart, you will leave the poor girl alone."

What?

"Poor girl?"

Roman chuckled.

The woman's eyes turned cold and harsh in a blink.

"You were in the restaurant earlier. I saw you. I'm sure you know what I'm talking about," she snapped back fast.

Not particularly.

It was true that Roman had turned up here because Josef reminded him again this morning that the boss expected him to be at this dinner. Despite the fact he couldn't seem to make it clear enough that he had no real interest in participating in the general semantics and theatrics of the bratva, everyone seemed determined to continue to require it from him regardless.

Apparently, Maxim and Leonid wanted him to be a part of the celebrations. So, *fine.* He showed up early, Roman kept to himself and didn't make like he cared to talk or stay long, once he'd showed his face to the boss and Leonid, he handed over five-k in cash stuffed inside an envelope. The standard gift from one made man to another for typical familial celebrations, which was what Josef assured he had heard this event would be. Thankfully, the man had been shadowing him a lot less lately—whatever the reason for the change, Roman couldn't say.

ᴛʜᴇAGREEMENT

Then, he was out of there. Roman didn't *care* what these people were celebrating. He didn't want to take part, or pretend to. The least he could do was not stick around and act like it mattered. It was none of his business. He figured he would find out eventually—what the celebrations were about if it was *actually* important or might make a difference to how he did business in Chicago.

He doubted it would.

Except he hadn't hightailed it out of the restaurant before he had the pleasure of seeing Karine walk into the restaurant. In a slinky, champagne-toned dress with a slit in the thigh and showing *so* much skin, that made her look like she belonged in the Playboy Mansion. The most intriguing part about Karine was she had no idea the effect she had on men.

On every man in the room.

In fact, he watched every head turn.

But she didn't.

It was at that point when Roman decided he had to get some air. He needed to catch his breath because seeing Karine was like being punched in the gut. The second gut punch came when he saw her sit between her father and Dima. Even though she didn't look at all like she wanted to be there, Dima stared at her like a hungry dog with a bone in his bowl. It made Roman's blood boil, and he couldn't explain why.

He had to get out of there, so he did, before the party even got started.

Roman had slipped into the alleyway, undetected, to have a smoke. He definitely wasn't expecting Karine to show up here a few minutes later, but she did and the rest was history.

"I missed the big announcement. Care to fill me in?" he asked the woman, though he was pretty sure he had already pieced together the entire shit show.

She sighed, and shook her head. "They are engaged. Dima and Karine. Everyone in the bratva has already decided she is his—he made his intentions clear months ago, and no one challenged him. Not even her father. And with that being said, Dima is the son of one of the boss's closest trustees. It doesn't matter what she wants or needs."

Roman stood stock still.

Why?

He didn't care to wonder what would make her agree—there was a good chance if there had ever been a choice for her where the engagement was concerned, it would be nothing more than an illusion. But that didn't explain why she would be out in the alley with him doing what she had.

What was it—regret, maybe?

"Huh," Roman said, more to himself than anyone else.

The woman didn't quite take it that way when she replied, "Yes, so if you want to make sure she doesn't get into any trouble, you will stay away."

"What is your name?" he asked.

The woman glanced at her feet, instantly reminded with one question of her place, it seemed. Roman didn't like what he assumed that to mean.

"Masha."

He pressed her more. "Last name?"

She shook her head.

Just as he figured—she was a slave.

One of the many that the Yazovs used and traded. There was an almost intermarket for that type of shit in the criminal underworld, especially when certain factions of an organization were already dealing in trafficking in one way or another. She had to truly care for Karine and her welfare to take the risk of speaking to a *vor* in the way she did to him.

She couldn't know he wasn't the violent type with women—Roman never got off on that, but it was still everywhere, too. Nonetheless, the fact she took the risk said a lot.

Her job definitely did not entail simply warning men against getting involved with the boss's daughter, and leaving it at that.

Masha apparently intended to make her point to Roman *very* clear, and for the first time since she stepped out into the alleyway, he decided to really listen. "I don't know what game you are playing with her, but you're putting her in danger. You know him—Dima. *Everyone does.* What he is really like. He's cruel and vicious. He can be unkind to her and … and … *violent.*"

Roman stiffened.

Masha continued on. "Even when not provoked, he just enjoys being mean. Imagine what it's like when he has a *reason.* I don't know what you want from her, but I don't want her to get hurt. I hope we want the same thing."

Roman stared at Masha, still absorbing her news. He couldn't come to terms with the fact that Karine—that beautiful creature who looked like the Devil's angel in her slinky dress—a woman who could have any man she wanted, and not just because of who her father was, had been given to Dima.

Fucking *Dima.*

Masha certainly hinted at the fact that Karine hadn't chosen him, and Roman could basically draw that conclusion himself, too, but that didn't change the end result.

The hot swell of rage that washed through Roman was the only thing that kept him silent. A part of him that he was trying to ignore was still attempting to piece together how the woman he had been thinking about since they first met—the one who occupied all his thoughts lately—was already spoken for by a man he despised.

The world was really laughing at him.

It had to be.

Unfortunately, it was the same anger that kept him quiet that also made him lash out at Masha when he told her, "And if you fucking cared about her so much, you would stop giving her those pills."

Masha snapped back, spine straightening.

"Don't act surprised," Roman said in a scoff. "I saw you slipping a pill into her hand before she sat down at the table. She might as well have already been reaching for it like she knew it was coming. Seeing that, it explained a lot of things to me. Like why she's always in such a fucking daze. This has nothing to do with who she is—it's what you're feeding her."

She shook her head frantically, the defiant fire back in her gaze in a flash. "Those pills are the least of her problems—

what makes you think she *doesn't* need them? You don't even know what they are."

Once again, he was reminded that Masha took a big risk speaking to him with such disrespect. His wounded pride wasn't so bad that he couldn't see the woman did actually care for Karine.

Masha seemed ready to end the conversation, though, when she glanced back over her shoulder. Keeping one hand on the door, she moved towards him a little before shoving a piece of folded up paper his way like she wanted him to take it. He looked down at it, and then back up at her again.

"Why don't you tell me what's really going on, and I can try and help."

"We don't need your help." Masha stuck the paper out towards him, saying sharply, "Well, take it. And let that be the last of it."

Roman did, but he wasn't sure he understood what the contents in or on the paper would do to change what had already happened.

"I really hope you will do the right thing and leave her alone," Masha added as she turned to head back inside the business. Tossing him one last look over her shoulder, she only offered a nod before she was gone.

Alone and *feeling like it*, Roman pulled a cigarette out of his pocket and lit it up. The rain had stopped falling by now, but the air was still wet with every breath, and he raked a hand through his hair, rubbing some of the water out. He had the piece of paper in one hand, the same one where he dangled the smoke between two fingers, but he waited while he took the first long drag of smoke. Filling his lungs, he exhaled, willing the gray cloud to take the hell in his mind with it, and then he opened up the folded paper.

It took a second.

And then *two*.

The darkness didn't help at first.

A sketch?

A man's face was etched into the paper with violent pen strokes. The style was like how a kid would draw, scribbling hastily, too fast, all over the page, but the art was actually still quite sophisticated. There was more than enough detail to discern that the face staring back at him was his own.

He was sure of it.

At the corner of the page was his name, too, written in a hand that was once again—very childlike. Slightly messy, shaky letters, still clear.

He couldn't understand it at all—not the sketch, why Masha gave it to him, or the entire night to begin with.

There were so many unanswered questions, and Roman wasn't sure what to do about them. The one thing he knew for sure—there was no way in hell he was going to apologize for putting his hands on Karine in the alleyway.

Having the information he did about Leonid and the plan on Maxim, and Karine's new place as Dima's fiancée, well …

Roman knew himself well enough to predict he wasn't going to drop it, either.

Taking one last drag from his cigarette, he tossed it into the darkness, watching the coal flicker as he blew out the smoke, and murmured, "Sorry, Masha."

FIFTEEN

"You're distracted."

The accusation from Marky hit Roman harder than he expected. Quickly, and without noise, he folded up the sketch—*his* likeness—and stuffed it back into his pocket before spinning around on the mechanic's stool to face his friend.

"I'm not," he replied.

They both knew he was lying. Marky didn't know what Roman was trying to hide to call him out on the lie, but there was obviously a noticeable change in him, and his friend pointed it out more than once. One negative of having the man working with him in Chicago considering Marky knew Roman better than most.

"Well, *you are*," Marky returned, but at the arch of Roman's brow, the man shrugged. "I can't help but say it when I see it."

Roman wished he wouldn't.

THE AGREEMENT

It had been a week since that night at the restaurant when Roman discovered what Karine's future was set to hold. The same night he learned that touching her was like catching the worst kind of addiction. It was all he kept thinking about, running those minutes over and over again in his head until the images were permanently imprinted behind the backs of his eyelids. He saw her, wet, in his arms, legs parted for him, ready to ask for more.

Why couldn't he get that out of his head?

Knowing what he did, *he should.*

The same night Masha had handed him the piece of paper with his sketch and name on it—clearly drawn by a child. Yet another thing that kept bringing in his attention when it was better spent literally *anywhere* else. Roman really was a sucker for punishment in more ways than one. His obsessive nature was going to get him into trouble.

That much was clear.

So, it had been a whole week of Roman being clueless about what the fuck was going on in the Yazov mansion. At the same time he tried to pretend like he didn't know anything was going on at all because what did it matter. Even if something was up—who was *he* to say so?

Yeah.

He was a little off his game.

People noticed.

Unfortunately.

"At least, you seem settled here, man," Marky said, breaking through his thoughts.

Roman had to admit that it was good to have a friendly face in the shop with him—the face of someone he could actually trust. Marky was going to be there for a week or a little more to help him with the next haul.

A fifteen-car gig that was coming up in the next twenty-four hours. Marky had it all planned out—to the very last detail—and they were supposed to be going over it. Except, Roman was off in lala land.

Like a useless *fuck.*

"I don't know about being *settled*," Roman answered, "but it's a decent scene. Work-wise."

"You been going out?" Marky asked.

"No. Obviously not. I've been careful with that."

"Staying out of trouble."

Roman nodded.

Marky's grin came out to play in a flash. "Shit, I'm here now. We could make good use of a bag of blow and a few pairs of tits."

Roman joined his friend's laughter, and took a swig from his can of beer. Thing was—his heart wasn't in it. Correction, his *cock* wasn't interested.

There was no use denying the fact that it had everything to do with Karine. She occupied his every waking thought. If it wasn't something less than innocent on his mind, then he was *worrying* about her for one reason or another. He was sure he was even seeing her in his sleep. And that damned dress with the slit down her leg so he couldn't take his eyes off her pale, smooth thigh.

Fucking hell.

There he went again … Roman grinded his molars in an effort to get his thoughts in another direction. She was what made up every red blooded man's wet dreams, though. No point in denying it.

"There something on your mind, or …?" Marky asked.

There were too many chunks of silence between them, and Roman was too stuck inside his head to keep up with his false pretenses.

"On some real shit?" Roman said to his friend.

That made Marky sit up straighter. "What about it?"

He considered what he wanted to say, and *how* to say it. Never was there a time in his life that Roman felt a need to be careful about the words he chose. It was a dangerous thing to be poking into the business of bratva men.

And still, there was something shady going on in the Yazov mansion. It was a good thing that the assholes had made a point of watching him and offering little to no trust, because he didn't trust them, either.

Chicago was a *mess.*

The men were all snakes.

ᴛʜᴇAGREEMENT

From plots on the boss, to a daughter he kept out of sight only long enough to be brought out in the open and paraded like a prize on the night of her engagement. And that was before he touched the topic of drugs—why was her slave feeding her pills?

"I need information on something related to the Yazovs," Roman finally settled on saying.

Marky instantly tilted his head to the side like a puppy might for a rolling ball in his owner's hand. "Like the men, or like *a* Yazov, because—"

"Marky."

Roman's sharp warning wasn't enough.

"You don't mean, Dima, right? That fuck is *worthless*, Roman. Don't get into another pissing contest with him—you'll *still* win it, but you already know you won't like the prize."

Goddammit.

He was seriously started to regret his previous take on having Marky in Chicago.

Roman scowled, saying, "I was actually talking about Karine Yazov. Maxim's daughter."

"He has a daughter?"

He almost laughed.

Except it wasn't funny.

Roman just nodded instead, not wanting to make Marky's shock into a big deal. He'd already figured out not a lot people knew about Karine. But why? That was the real question. There was no real reason to hide a beautiful woman who was clearly of age away from the rest of the world. Even the most controlled mafia daughters had lives outside of the confines of their father's homes.

But for Karine, it almost seemed like outside the circle of her father's closest people, no one knew she even existed.

And that didn't sit right with him.

Why?

Why do that?

"Yeah," Roman said, smirking his friend's way. "That's exactly the point. Nobody seems to know she's there. Even when she's standing in the damn room."

Marky squinted his eyes, considering the information. "If they are trying to hide her away, it's not going to be easy information to dig out."

"Which is why I can't do it myself—too many eyes on me currently."

Marky sucked in a deep breath, disapproval drawing his lips together in a grim line. He didn't need the man to say what was clear—Roman should stay out of trouble and not go digging around in a pile of shit. If only things were that easy.

At the same time, he knew better than to tell Roman anything—but especially what to do or not do. Roman wished he could explain everything to Marky, it would make a lot more sense. However, he had to watch what he said and what Marky might tell other people, too.

"There's a lot to unpack here," Marky said, twirling a finger in front of himself as if to magically conjure up a picture of Roman's mess. His friend wasn't dumb; he could put things together without actually asking. Like the fact he was *asking* about a boss's daughter. Something no man had any business doing. "And I'm thinking it's better if I don't ask, right?"

Yeah.

Definitely not stupid.

It was probably for the best if Marky knew as little as possible. Until Roman had all the facts, anyway. Whatever *they* were.

"Why did you bring up Dima?" he asked his friend. "Why did you think I would be interested in him?"

Marky gave him a look—an unspoken *wasn't it obvious?* Then, he laughed under his breath and said, "Honest to God, the fucker messed with you. He is the reason you got locked up—he fucking set you up. You're telling me you're not going to—at some point—make him answer for that? *You*, Roman. Little Odessa's Devil, never leaves a slight unanswered. Not going to happen. Besides, I didn't get a good vibe from him. It wasn't just the fact that he wanted to fuck around with your position and freedom, either. Some people just don't *vibe* right."

Roman's brow dipped. "Did you look into him?"

Marky lifted his shoulders quickly. "A little. Spoke to a few guys who've worked with the Yazovs here previously."

Roman damn near held his breath.

"Let's just say the motherfucker is bad news," Marky added after a second.

And there went Roman's good mood.

Bad news meant nothing.

The truth of the matter was they were all bad news. Marky, Roman, the Yazovs, and even his own family. The whole fucking bunch of them—it depended on which side of the fence you were on. They were branded as criminals by the majority of society. And yet, they were still family, friends, husbands, lovers, fathers, sons, and more to the people who lived their life with them.

Monsters?

They're not so scary when you love one.

Marky could see Roman's lack of interest clearly, because he was fast to say, "Well, you know he has a major role to play in the Yazov's trafficking operations."

"Yeah, that's common knowledge."

"But apparently it goes deeper than that. It's not just grown women he deals with. He has connections with groups that deal with a younger demographic. Real young. Pre-pubescent."

And then there was the scum of them all, he thought. The lowest of the low that would do the worst of the worst for greed and power. Dirty money couldn't get dirty enough. He understood he didn't have a lot of room to speak—being crime was crime, and sin was sin—but he didn't mess with that kind of shit.

In any way.

Fuck.

Child trafficking was something that could make the tiny hairs rise on the back of Roman's neck. Not a feeling he encountered very often. How far did his connections go with those groups—was he directly involved, as *hands-on* as he was with his working girls? Did Maxim know, or Leonid?

Likely.

Money was money, right.

They didn't have to *make* it.

Roman had one hand in the pocket of his leather jacket, and it grazed against the folded up piece of paper he carried around all the time now. The sketch seemingly drawn by a child. A child that lived in the Yazov mansion?

It was apparent they were trying to keep Karine hidden from the outside world for some reason. Frankly, it didn't seem like all that far of a jump to assume there were more secrets to uncover there.

"You understand what I'm saying?" Marky asked, bringing him back to the conversation.

Roman nodded, but absently. "I just need some intel on Karine."

The suspicious glint in Marky's eye said he wasn't entirely sure he believed his friend, but he didn't seem willing to push it. Roman drank another gulp of his beer. The more he thought about Dima, the worse his stomach churned. He needed something concrete first before he started digging anywhere near that asshole. Too many balls were now tossed up in the air, and he *had* to catch every single one of them.

And if Roman was really going to climb this hill, then Karine was where he would put his focus first. Like why she was being treated by the Yazovs the way she was. He had to make sense of her first, before he could look in to what was going on with Dima. If there was a connection that led Roman to the other issues he still had up in the air at the moment, well ... that's probably where he would have to move next.

If she was being forced to marry Dima, then Karine might have some answers he needed—but he had to get to her first.

Marky sighed, drawing Roman back again.

"I need you to act fast," he said. "I don't really think I have a lot of time to ... put a puzzle together, so to speak."

And he was missing *a lot* of pieces. That much was clear.

Then, Roman stood up and walked over to his desk to shuffle through some papers. An action that would tell Marky that the conversation ended there—he didn't need opinions, only action. Not when he knew his friend couldn't actually give him any insight. He needed facts first.

It was that kind of situation. Roman had to tread carefully. Behind him, Marky remained silent, telling him that his best friend understood.

Good enough for him.

SIXTEEN

Days melted into weeks, and for the first time, Karine felt acutely aware of it all. Every second, minute, and hour. Each one that made up a day. And then all seven in an entire week. She couldn't pinpoint why the change, but she knew exactly when it began.

The second she kissed Roman in that alleyway. She didn't like to think about that night—when her inevitable destiny was unashamedly announced to the rest of the world. She might as well have been officially branded as Dima's property.

Signed and sealed.

Being shipped off to a man who terrified her loomed ahead as her wedding day inched closer and closer. The day to end all her freedom. Even the little that she had now— still living in her own quarters in the Yazov mansion—would be gone altogether.

What would she do then?

ᴛʜᴇAGREEMENT

Once she was married to a man who would control every breath she took; every thought in her head. How was she going to make it through the rest of her life?

Karine blinked the tears threatening to blur her vision, still unsure of how her life had ended up the way it did. It wasn't a good thing to count down time—it could make a person *so* aware of how fast it was running out that they became obsessive about what they wanted to do with it. She was no exception to the rule.

Tonight could be the only night she had to *live*. In any real sense, as it were.

Standing in the veranda that could be accessed from her bedroom, she had a long-shot view of the front of the mansion. The section that was a part of her father's side where she was rarely allowed to visit, unless it served some purpose, especially not on a night like tonight.

Tribute, that was.

She knew the rules. That side of the mansion where she might be seen was off-limits unless otherwise said when she couldn't be monitored and wasn't needed. Meaning, *wanted*. Usually, Karine was very good at following the rules. She had spent her whole life living by them.

It made things easier.

That wasn't enough to make her wonder ...

For her to consider .... it could be her only chance to see Roman again. Before the wedding, of course. After that, she doubted the light of day would grace her life for a while. She didn't know if he would be here tonight, but given what she understood regarding tribute, it was likely he *would*.

A thrill ran down her spine at the idea—at the thought of seeing him again—because she hadn't once got the man out of her mind. All it took was a kiss; the way he looked at her when he touched her was too much.

And not enough.

She could almost taste his hot mouth against her own, demanding she give him another lick, and the imprint of his fingers digging into her hips to keep her pinned to him had remained for days.

She'd done something stupid, then.

Karine wanted to do it again.

Tipping her head back, she stared at the night sky—when was the last time she had seen so many stars? She blinked repeatedly, wondering if they might disappear if she stared at them hard enough. Except they didn't. The stars remained exactly where they were. The only constant in her life.

And sadly, she was only now starting to notice that fact. There was a reason for that, too.

Karine hadn't taken a single pill—one she stumbled upon on her own, or medication from Masha—in longer than she could remember. Was it that morning—yesterday? At first, she thought she was being crazy, but she wasn't imagining it.

Masha offered her less than she used to with no explanation. At first, Karine was confused and angry. That was the one way she made it through the day, something she almost *depended* on. It was a lot to constantly drown in her thoughts and emotions—no longer numbed to it all by a never-ending supply of this pill or that one to keep her perky and happy when needed.

It was a different kind of helplessness and fear. She fought through it—taking it one day at a time, one moment to the next. She might be so jittery she could barely sit still one second, and then she'd be lost to her mind in the next.

And then one morning, Karine wasn't so angry about it. Maybe that was the moment her mind started to clear of the haze, her random thoughts *weren't* just irrational. She started to consider what it would feel like if she didn't ask for the pills—Masha was still quick to give them when she thought Karine might make a scene, after all. What would happen if she stopped taking them altogether?

What would be left of herself or her mind when the surge of fake chemical happiness and nerve-numbing calm were suddenly missing from her life?

It was scary.

More than she wanted to admit.

Yet, Karine was determined. She could stick it out—*she would*. Especially now that she had the chance to be able to hold a single thought longer than a few moments at a time when Masha wasn't offering medication constantly to deal

AGREEMENT

with every little upset. More importantly, since this could be
her last chance to have any independent thought before her
impending marriage. She wasn't about to ruin her moment of
possible freedom for a couple hours of rose-tinted emotions.

Those few minutes in the alleyway had proved to her it
would be more than worth it. Just like that, Karine's mind
drifted to that night with Roman. Something changed in her,
then. She felt it click in her brain. Not that she even knew
how to begin to describe it.

No man had ever touched her the way he did—none made
her *want* it. Not like he did. She felt safe with him—he'd
made her brave and bold.

And she wanted to feel it again.

Be that again.

Masha wasn't there—on tribute nights, her services were
required by her father, more often than not. Or rather,
Maxim *preferred* her over others. Karine usually spent the
night by herself, as she was supposed to do.

Now that she stood at the veranda and heard the cars
driving to the front of the estate, she couldn't help the
shivering tingle of excitement. It crawled through her veins
slowly, with promise. Something she very rarely felt about
anything.

This could be it.

Her only chance at exercising her own thoughts and
wishes. For once, she could do something she wanted,
because *she* wanted to do it. Her life was about to change
drastically—she didn't want to regret what she hadn't done.

Besides, what more did she have to lose?

• • •

The big weeping willow tree at the side of the mansion by
the rocky wall that outlined the driveway became her newest
hiding spot. Karine knew the tree well. She had spent a lot of
time under it when she was younger and wanted to stay
hidden and unseen.

Tonight, she found herself under the tree again, sitting on
a large, exposed root at the back side. The branches and

185

leaves that surrounded her created the perfect canopy against prying eyes.

Besides, as much as her father liked to keep the mansion well lit and imposing, the driveway usually remained dark when the sun set. He preferred to keep his guests and arrivals secret from curious neighbors and cameras. Even Karine could figure that out.

She plucked wildflowers growing in the grass around her, brushing the soft petals along her cheeks. If she pressed her eyes closed hard enough, she could almost imagine Roman touching her again. For a man with a presence as imposing as his, including his size, he had a soft touch. Even in the hardness of his stare, she had found something kind, and *curious*.

Her eyes flew wide as more cars arrived, driving in and taking their positions at the entrance to the house. The spaces were quickly filling up and still, there was no sign of Roman.

Her heart fell at the possibility he wouldn't show up. She had no idea if he was even in Chicago anymore—she didn't really know anything about him at all. What was his life like outside of her world?

Then, she saw a car and there he was, sitting in it. Parked at the very end of the row, it had come in only seconds after the car ahead of it. She hadn't paid it much mind because it wasn't Roman driving. Someone else sat in the driver's seat, and the two men chatted with smiles on their faces. There was an unmistakable camaraderie between them. The way they shared easy laughter made Karine think they had to be friends.

That traitorous heart of hers skipped a beat when she saw Roman stepping out of the car. His friend did the same, except he went for the duffle bags in the backseat.

"*Roman!*"

Karine froze the second she spoke. She hadn't even meant to say his name, but it slipped from her lips before she could stop it. An urge she couldn't control.

THE AGREEMENT

Her voice, carried by the breeze, still reached him. She wasn't standing that close to him, but he still turned like she had reached out, and touched him on the shoulder.

Karine was so sure that nobody would be able to see her, but he looked at her directly. Through the swaying branches covered with thick leaves, he *saw her*. Like he had known the whole time exactly where she was hiding.

His friend followed his gaze, and she knew he could see her, too.

Roman looked back at the man before he took a few steps towards her. Karine tried to ignore the vibration at the base of her stomach—butterfly wings beat hard with every ounce of her anticipation. And *nerves*. She honestly hadn't thought they would be face to face again.

His first words to her were harsh, though.

"What games are you playing with me, Karine?"

Unexpected, really, from a man who hadn't hesitated to kiss her back that night—who was so quick to put his hands between her thighs with only a little encouragement, and then dared to tell her he wanted a taste.

Karine tilted her face toward him, asking, "*Am* I playing games?"

Roman stood at the edge of the driveway, careful not to take another step closer, and kept his voice low. Conscious about the people in the mansion who may have been watching them. "What you're doing, what you did before, it could get me fucking killed. Don't tell me you don't know that. You know who you are—the people you *belong* to."

"But do you care about that?" she returned fast.

Karine didn't know where these words were coming from—the braveness that raced from her mouth like it hadn't come from her own mind. It had to be the result of weaning away from relying so heavily on her medication, or maybe she was just finally growing a fucking spine for the first time in her life.

Whatever it was, she liked it.

Roman seemed like the type who might like it, too.

He remained silent at her question, unwilling to answer. Or maybe he wasn't a liar. Just what she thought.

He didn't give a fuck.

Not about the *rules*, anyway.

"I want to spend the night with you," she blurted out.

Or that's probably how it seemed. Instead, she'd carefully planned those words. She wanted to see the way he would react to them.

Roman's stare didn't move from hers, but his left eyebrow jumped higher. "You've gotta be kidding me."

"Which one of us is laughing?"

"Why would you even offer that to me knowing who you're marr—"

The words came tumbling out of her mouth to stop him from saying another thing. She only cared to make *one* thing clear about any of this to him. Boldness might get her what she wanted. "Because for once, I want a choice. I want to do exactly what I feel like doing tonight. Would you give me that … you were willing before? I don't think that's changed."

Again, he was silent.

That was all the answer she needed.

Tonight, Karine didn't care about the consequences of her actions. She cared about the *feasibility* of it. She just needed to figure out a way to make this happen. After that, she wouldn't ask for anything.

If she could just choose, for once, to have what she wanted if only for a night, then she would follow each rule, all their demands and orders. Their every command—like a good girl. Maybe, in the hell she was sure to find within her inevitable marriage to Dima, it might finally be the way she had never been able to find before to make her father proud. But all of that was past and future.

She only wanted the present.

Tonight, she was going to make the most of that, and what she desperately longed for was to feel like she did in that alleyway with this man. To be touched, and *love it*. For him to make her ask for more. She wanted to look into the eyes of a man who wanted her back just as much, who could use her the way she would like, and *need that*.

ᴛʜᴇAGREEMENT

Karine intended to be fucked by this man standing right in front of her.

Roman was staring at her, waiting for her to continue. The solution to her problem—how to make all of this happen—came to her out of the blue. Divine intervention, maybe. She bit down on her already-swollen lower lip, reddened and tender from the abuse of her top two front teeth. A habit she had picked up from anxiety and stress.

She met his stare courageously, trying to summon back that bold part of her. Somehow, it worked. "There's a veranda that leads directly into my bedroom. You can climb up to it."

A dark sound echoed from Roman before he muttered, "I am a twenty-seven-year-old man, I am not climbing up a girl's balcony like some ... *boy*."

However, that hint of grin on his mouth said what he didn't. The idea appealed to him, and that was all she needed to know.

"But won't you?" Karine asked.

That grin of his turned into a devilish smile.

Of course, he would.

She didn't actually need him to reply.

SEVENTEEN

Maxim sat in the same cigar smoke-filled den as he had the last time Roman visited with a duffle bag full of cash. Only on this evening, the dense cloud didn't irritate him in the same way. He had other shit on his mind, and that was never more apparent than while his heart pounded in his chest as he stepped into the den.

At least, he had more cash than Maxim was expecting. Even though tribute was being held earlier than usual this month—to accommodate the wedding plans and not clash the two events, or so he was told—Roman had been able to make the target cash, and then some.

A few hours ago, he'd been feeling good about *this*—the money, that was. He was confident Maxim would be impressed, and might have considered granting Roman the leave to go for a quick trip back to New York he had planned to ask for. In return for his good work, and behavior, of course.

ᴛʜᴇAGREEMENT

Roman needed the space—not that he was keen on admitting to himself *why*. But then he had to go ahead and indulge Karine outside, listening to the crazy proposition she made ... he wasn't sure how he was going to make it through the rest of the night without bursting a vein.

Dima and Leonid waited in the room, too.

As he expected.

Leonid counted the cash, as usual, and Dima at least had the decency to look busy on his phone. He didn't bother to glance up at Roman's arrival.

Good.

He didn't particularly want to look at the motherfucker, either.

"What do you have for me today, Roman?" Maxim asked, speaking jovially through the cigar that was clenched between his teeth. "Something good, yes? It better be."

Roman deposited the duffle bags by Leonid's feet so he could begin the count. Dima finally flicked a fleeting glance at him before turning to his father.

"We should test the vodka first," he said, offering the word like he was continuing a conversation they were having already. Leonid nodded his agreement for his son's idea, his hand waving at the liquor in question.

So, they were going to be drinking tonight.

Fun.

Like he needed another reason to loosen up his self-control.

Maxim had a few questions for Roman, and he posed them as Dima called for the servant in an attached section of the den to come ready the drinks. He tried not to show his surprise when Masha appeared between the doorway framed by old bookcases. Wasn't she always with Karine?

It certainly seemed that way.

Except there she was.

Roman found himself considering whether Masha's distraction with serving the boss during his tribute was another reason why Karine felt comfortable approaching him like she had earlier. Those thoughts ran wild in his head, the rebellious side of his nature lapping the idea up because it was yet another thing he wouldn't have to worry about if he actually took Karine up on her offer.

Gonna get yourself shot, Roman.

Right, right.

He ignored his inner voice.

Instead, Roman tried to focus on the boss's inquiries. The last thing he needed right now was to raise suspicions, but goddammit, he didn't know how to act casual, anymore. If the men in that den knew *any* of the things he had done thus far with Karine—the room would be his own personal deathtrap.

Fuck walking the line.

Roman pissed all over it.

Maxim probed him on details about how the chop shop was being run, who was on his crew, and other aspects of his business that Roman still didn't care to talk about with other people. Still, to keep that composure and facade up, he mechanically answered the questions—sipping on expensive vodka between each one while his mind was buzzing, trying to decide what he was going to do when he left that room.

The choice should be easy.

The right one *was.*

On the surface, yeah. Except the only problem with that was Roman had a feeling there was a lot at play in the Yazov household—*and* bratva. A lot of it was interconnected, and his selfish actions with Karine was only a small part of the bigger picture.

Until it wasn't.

The way Roman saw it, technically, he only had three options. And none of them were great.

The first was that he did what Maxim would expect him to do as his boss—divulge the conversation he overhead Leonid having during a phone call. There was very little information he actually had about the details, but it was enough to alert the boss something might be brewing amongst his closest people.

There was just one problem with doing that—Roman couldn't say Maxim was actually on his side. He demanded loyalty, but that didn't mean he offered it. Men in high, dangerous positions were known for shooting the messenger. What if the plot was a trap that Leonid had set?

Roman wasn't privy to *everything.*

Besides, did he really owe his loyalty to the Yazov Bratva? From personal experience, they were experts at manipulation and him being there in the first place was proof.

The second option was simply feeding his own selfish needs by taking the risk of spending the night with Karine. Even just the thought of that set his body on fire, the uncomfortable tightness of his pants being the proof that she only needed to be on his mind to capture all of his attention. He could still see her emerging from beneath the leafy tree outside, looking as sweet as sin and asking for him.

Spending the night with her possibly promised him two things—one was his dead heart in a box delivered to his mother, and the other was information. Karine could be his closest chance at finding out what was really happening inside the Yazov boss's mansion. What might explain the strange things that were keeping him up at night. It was possible that she wasn't even aware she might have answers, too, but he wouldn't know unless he asked. Or found where someone was hiding what he wanted to find.

Of course, the reality of that choice was painfully clear. If anyone even got a whiff of a hint that he'd spent the night with a spoken for woman like Karine, a boss's daughter promised to a high-ranking man in her father's organization, well ... nobody would hear from Roman again.

That early grave was calling.

The third and the most logical option was to fuck all that noise, and do the task he was sent to Chicago to do. Pay his dues, and beat feet to the pavement when the job was done. Nobody sent him there to solve mysteries, fuck their women, or uncover assassination plots. His sole purpose under the control of the Yazov boss was to earn *money.*

If his father was presented with the three choices—well, Roman knew exactly which one he would take. The only one that concerned his duty, and what was owed. Nothing more, and nothing less.

That was exactly why he hadn't been calling Demyan, or answering his calls. If he heard his father's voice—his choice would be inevitable, too.

"Good, it's all here," Leonid spoke up, interrupting the conversation between Maxim and Roman without apology. Two piles of cash sat high on the desk. One tower was the cash that was actually due—the second was just extra.

Bonus.

No boss refused that.

Maxim surveyed the money from all the way behind his desk, and nodded. *Pleased.*

"I'll make sure your father hears about this," he said to Roman, pointing the cigar in his hand to the stacks that waited for the boss's hands to appreciate them properly. "Gotta say—if you kept earning like that, I'd shut my mouth and mind my business about your private matters."

That backhanded statement nearly earned a response from Roman, if only because that was the first time Maxim had so obviously called out the reason why the younger man stood there. Never look a gift horse in the mouth, Roman knew.

He didn't plan to start now.

"Is there anything else?" Roman asked.

Only out of respect.

Maxim shook his head, murmuring a low, "*Nyet.*"

A hard no for a quiet answer.

Roman didn't want to look too deep into that, either.

That was that. With the meeting over, Dima still on his phone, and Leonid flicking through the cash again, like he couldn't keep his hands off it, Maxim said nothing more to suggest he wanted Roman to linger.

So, he didn't.

Roman walked out of the den without a glance back. Another month was over—he'd made it through a second tribute in a city that didn't belong to him under the thumb of a boss that never left him feeling quite … *settled.* Technically, they didn't even need to see his face for a month, maybe more, depending on how long Maxim waited before calling the next after the wedding and whatever celebrations had been planned for that mess.

THE AGREEMENT

It would have been so easy for Roman to simply walk out of there, and forget about Karine and the shady shit happening within the Yazov Bratva. Forget about the plot against Maxim—who gave a fuck about Chicago? This was not his home; he hadn't even wanted to be there in the first goddamn place.

More importantly, he had no plans of staying any longer than was necessary. If he got himself tangled up in other people's shit, more so than he already was, then he would have no choice but to see it through to the end.

He didn't have to feed into his selfishness—or his *worries*. Those little bastards that had never really been much of a concern for him before wouldn't leave him alone now.

Roman could take the easy way out of there—out of all of it, really. Simply by doing what he was there to do, and nothing more.

But he walked out of the mansion, and stepped into the cold air of an inky-black night. He could see Marky standing at the end of the driveway, leaning against his car while he smoked a cigarette, and waited for his friend.

Roman had always taken the easy way out. That was exactly why he had gotten away with so much shit for as long as he had. Maybe it was time he changed a few things in his life.

Particularly, *that*.

• • •

Marky threw a half-finished cigarette to the ground when he noticed Roman's approach.

"Good to go?" he asked.

Roman only nodded.

Marky had been there when Karine turned up in the driveway earlier, and heard most of the conversation. He was the one who had reminded Roman it was time to go meet the boss, redirecting his friend's attention back to what was important.

"Yeah, we're good to go," Roman said.

The two jumped into the car with Marky behind the wheel again—the only person Roman really cared to let drive him around.

"Did something happen in there? You came out looking mean, man."

Roman shrugged. "No, it was good. Maxim's happy. So was the accountant."

"So, we go celebrate now?"

Actually, that was a great way to describe what Roman was about to do.

"Yeah, I think I do want to celebrate," Roman replied.

Marky's brow furrowed as he started the engine—maybe it was the fact Roman said he was willing to have some fun when he'd been clearly, and *loudly*, refusing to do exactly that since his friend arrived in town. The car sped down the driveway to the gates, only the headlights cutting through the darkness of the estate. The exterior of the mansion was as dimly lit as the inside was bright.

"Stop here," Roman said without warning.

Marky crunched hard on the breaks, sending both unbuckled men flying forward in their seats. Roman was the only one to catch himself from smashing into the dashboard. He wasn't really sorry about the way his friend glared over at him from behind the wheel.

"What the fuck, Roman?"

Well …

Now or never, he figured.

"I'm getting out."

"Here? Why—where the fuck are you going?" Marky demanded, waving out with squinting eyes at the dark.

When he turned back to Roman, the answer seemed pretty obvious when he didn't reply and only lifted one shoulder. In fact, he thought Marky should have known this might happen from the start. He'd heard that conversation, after all.

Even if he did have motives behind it, who would turn a look like that down? A foolish man, that's who.

Roman swung the door open as Marky grabbed his arm, jerking hard to tug him back into the seat.

ᴛʜᴇ AGREEMENT

"Don't be a fucking moron," Marky hissed at him. "You're not seriously going to see her, are you? That could get you killed, man."

Roman arched a single brow at his best friend, dropping his stare to where Marky's hand was still on his arm. He didn't even have to speak for the man to let him go with a muttered *fuck, sorry.*

Not willing to argue, Roman stepped out of the car. He wasn't exactly sure where to go to find Karine, but he figured there would only be so many verandas he was capable of climbing up, right? He'd eventually find his way to her.

"Pick me up in the morning," he called to Marky, rounding the front of the car, his form creating a long shadow in front of the headlights when he passed. "Five AM, man."

Marky remained in the driver's seat, fuming as he drummed his fingers to the leather of the steering wheel and shook his head.

"You're making a big mistake," he said in a groan.

Roman was already walking away, gravel crunching under his shoes. Tossing a middle finger over his shoulder, he muttered, "Yeah, yeah. Fuck you, too."

EIGHTEEN

Roman scaled the stone wall surrounding the section of the mansion's drive easily. Despite his quickness and the darkness of the property, he was hyper aware of the comings-and-goings of the men around the estate. Tribute was still in full swing, and every *vor* of the Yazov Bratva from all over the state, and beyond, would be there to see Maxim.

And yet, Roman felt invisible—or maybe, *invincible*.

Either way, everyone else seemed to have too much of their own shit to deal with than worry about keeping an eye on the boss's daughter. Clearly, they all believed she was too placid and sidelined to misbehave. He didn't think anybody knew who Karine Yazov was under her drug-induced surface, whereas he couldn't wait to find out more. Shame on him for being willing to take advantage of that—except shame was the last thing he felt about it.

He found his way to the veranda she had told him about. The only one on the side of the mansion capable of being climbed. And even from the ground, he could see white curtains billowing at the doors. It had to lead to her. Metal posts for pillars, constructed from twisted, interwoven metal all the way up, made for perfect rungs.

Up until that point, he hadn't noticed many security cameras, and figured he probably wouldn't find any this deep into the property. A point he was well aware of because Maxim was like most other bratva bosses who didn't want any records of what went on inside their premises. They were also stubborn assholes—overconfident in their ability to keep their shit under control.

Maxim most likely believed nobody would dare wander his estate beyond where he allowed, and especially not directly under his nose.

Well.

Just like he didn't know his daughter, he obviously didn't know Roman, either.

Before he started climbing the metal rungs upward, he gave it one last thought. A final opportunity to find a reason why and change his mind. Roman didn't *have* to go up just because she invited him—he didn't owe her anything, and she couldn't expect something, either.

Roman was always real with himself, though. He wasn't doing this just in hopes of gaining information from her—there was a big chance she didn't know anything about the things that had come to his attention and wouldn't be able to help him to begin with. And yet, he couldn't convince himself to turn away and go.

So, being there wasn't just about splitting the Yazov Bratva open—he *wanted* to see Karine. Needed to see her, even. Maybe if he fucked her just once, then he'd be able to get her out of his system and move on.

From the first moment they met, she occupied his mind and with this invitation ... shit, there was no way he would forget about her, especially if he walked away from tonight alive. If he didn't do this, if he couldn't follow through, he had the distinct feeling he was going to regret it.

Truth was, he'd already made up his mind.

Roman was there, after all.

Dusting his hands, he took the metal poles like ladder rungs swiftly. He barely broke a sweat when he swung himself over the railing, and landed in the veranda with a soft *thud-thud* of the soles of his shoes to announce his arrival.

The moon, silvery and bright against the sky's black backdrop, somehow seemed to hang lower and closer to her room. Those curtains in the doorway, white in the shadows, rose and fell in the soft breeze, urging Roman toward them. French doors had been left wide open—like an invitation.

She *expected* him.

Made it easy.

Hell, he appreciated that, and a woman who knew what she wanted. If it hadn't already been obvious to him, it certainly was now.

The curtains in the doorway brushed along Roman gently—like a soft hug—when he was close enough to the billowing fabric. He didn't linger long between the flapping folds before he stepped just beyond the threshold. Doing so allowed him a good view inside the room.

And Karine.

Standing right there.

Waiting.

Wearing nothing but a white, silk nightdress with lace trim that reached her mid-thigh, Karine stared back at him with wide, bright eyes. A pleased smile pulled at the corners of her sensual mouth, but then it widened into something *sweeter.* Almost instantly.

Roman would be a fucking liar to say it didn't do something to him to know she was happy to see him.

"I knew you would come," she said in a whisper.

He thought, speaking to herself.

Roman replied anyway, though he didn't think her words had been meant for him. "I'm glad you have more faith in me than I have in myself."

Her forwardness took him by surprise when she reached for him, grabbing his hands in her own, and pulling him deeper into the bedroom. All without saying a thing. Two bedside lamps lit the room, and nothing else. It wasn't sufficient for him to clearly see the space, but the moonlight spilling in behind them illuminated Karine in a silvery glow.

On another night, if he were there for a different reason and not at her invitation, he might have thought it made her look angelic. Considering the growing need clawing its way through his bloodstream at the way she kept watching him, though, well ... he couldn't find anything innocent about this.

And he didn't mind.

With the doors of the veranda still open, the cool breeze filtering in through the room calmed Roman. Not a lot, of course, but enough to soothe the heat traveling over his body with every squeeze of Karine's hands inside his.

Her touch excited him like no other. Worse, it only made him want her more.

That was dangerous.

So far in his life, women made him feel a lot of predictable things. None of which he found worthy enough to risk his life, even if it was a good time in the end. Women rarely affected him beyond the usual lust and need for relief.

Karine wasn't quite the same.

He had a desire to taste her—but not with just a kiss. What would her sounds be like when she came for him? Hard, and then *harder*. Would she take her pleasure from him, or let him give it? Again and again, the thoughts and fantasies filled his mind until it was all he could see. Already, although she did nothing more than stare at him and hold his hand, he could hear his name on her lips.

Breathy, and begging.

Roman wanted to see her toes curl when he was inside her. Stretching out her pussy, and filling her full of him. Would she ask him to take her ass, too?

Goddamn.

He wouldn't refuse.

His mind even conjured up the picture of her on her knees, taking every last drop of him down her throat until he had had his fill of her completely. Before he'd even got her naked, Roman had already mentally taken her every single way he wanted.

It was crazy.

Completely.

Despite the boldness she had shown, Karines gaze shied away from him. Just long enough for him to notice, and hesitate.

"Are you sure you want to do this?" he asked. We don't have to—"

"No, it's not that."

The assurance rushed out of Karine's mouth before Roman could even finish his own sentence. She couldn't possibly know how painful it was for him to say those words. He was positive that if he didn't have her tonight, in all the ways he'd imagined, he might explode. Except he also wasn't a monster.

He'd never been the type to find pleasure in someone else's pain. There was a thin line between the two, sure, but he wouldn't push her. A sense of fragility clung all around her. He found it staring back in her blue gaze.

She had a soul that craved something—the feeling was visceral to him, so *real*—was she searching for it in him? He definitely wasn't the man who could provide it. He didn't even know how to care for himself.

"Then, what is it?" Roman asked, settling on the words that seemed right. Not that he could say *why*—it felt better than anything else he wanted to say, though. Didn't that count for something?

Karine's fingers tightened around his as she said softly, "It's nothing."

He didn't believe that.

Roman wondered if she was thinking the same thing as him. If he took her now, what would happen to her tomorrow? That diamond ring should be on her finger— there it was, *bare*. Where was it?

She'd taken it off, and didn't even bother to hide her naked finger from his pointed stare. Clearly, she didn't want any reminders of Dima tonight.

That should have bothered him. Or at the very least, given him some sense of guilt about the situation they found themselves in together.

ᴛʜᴇAGREEMENT

Except it didn't.

At all.

The only thing he thought about the missing engagement ring?

Good.

Roman didn't care to indulge the jealous side of his nature, nor did he intend to admit he felt it in the first place. He didn't own this woman—she wasn't his. There wasn't room for his possessiveness here regarding someone who wasn't even his.

Yet, there it was.

Burning in his heart.

All because of a missing fucking ring. *Yeah.* There was no way he was going to poke that monster and wake it up more than it already was. Hadn't he played with fire enough without adding *feelings* to the mix as well?

Roman sure as shit thought so.

Apparently, his silence didn't settle well with her because the next words out of Karine's mouth were sharp, and they *stung.* "I know what I want. Do you think I'm just a silly girl? That I don't know what I'm doing here?"

"That's not what I said."

Karine's brow dipped as she regarded him quietly before asking, "Then, what are you saying—or, *aren't* you saying?"

He figured, if she could ask, then she should know. "That you may have changed your mind about this, and if you have, that's fine. I'll leave now—if you want me to. Say the word, babe."

She pulled her hands away from him as if she'd been burned, her nostrils flaring with indignation, and even though it was dimly lit, he saw the color pink her cheeks. The very fact that she was offended because she thought he implied she didn't know her own mind said all he needed to know.

It still wasn't enough for Karine.

She wanted to make it clear, it seemed.

Very much so.

Instead of saying anything back to him, she simply slipped the straps of her nightdress over her shoulders. They fell down her arms, dragging the rest of the thin material with them until it fell beyond her pale, full breasts.

She stood with her chest on display, tipping her chin up at him almost defiantly. Still, she said nothing.

Fuck.

He'd probably seen hundreds of tits in his lifetime—fake and real—and somehow, the sight of Karine's bare torso made it hard to breathe. He struggled to keep his gaze from wandering, or worse, from physically reaching out and allowing himself to pull the nightdress down the rest of the way. It was like he had never seen a naked woman before.

Or maybe it was just because she *was* so beautiful. And even more so when she stared at him like she was willing him to deny that fact.

He wouldn't.

God.

He couldn't.

"You don't want to see me?" she asked in a low whisper, the words still feeling like a slap to his skin all the same.

It wasn't always *what* someone said, but how they said it that had the right impact. He wasn't even sure she knew the effect of her words on him in that moment.

Roman took a step closer to her, his heart slamming beneath his rib cage because, *no.* Hell no, he didn't want her to stop.

"No, I want to see all of you," he murmured. "Every inch—spread you *wide.* I've been dreaming about it. Too much, if I'm honest."

A faint smile curved her pink lips, and she pushed the nightdress down over her hips without hesitation. It fell to the floor, pooling around her ankles before she stepped out of it. Closer—*again*—to him.

No panties, he noticed. And the triangle patch of dark hair at the apex of her thighs was trimmed short.

She was prepared.

Waiting for him.

Fully naked in front of him, the moon shone like a spotlight on the soft curves of her slender body. He couldn't take his eyes off her, taking in the way her dark straight hair fell like a curtain covering her shoulders but wasn't quite long enough to hide the way her nipples had hardened into peaks standing like she did with the breeze still light in the room. With her arms at her sides, legs spread a little apart, she didn't look ashamed to put herself on display for him.

"My turn," he said, smirking just a little.

It only seemed fair.

Roman's hands flitted over his belt, pulling it out from the loops in his slacks with a woosh, and tossing it aside to the floor. Then, his pants came off. His shirt soon followed. All of the clothing made a forgotten pile on the floor because as soon as they were off his body, he didn't care. Mostly because she hadn't stopped staring at him, and with each article of clothing he removed, her eyes grew wider until they were big, blue saucers locked lower on his body.

On his cock, actually.

Already hard beneath his boxer-briefs, there was no hiding the thick ridge of his dick clearly visible against the white fabric. His thumbs hooked around the waistband on the last piece of clothing before he started to tug it down.

Her throat jumped with a swallow.

Roman arched a brow at the sight. She had to have done this before—there was no way the woman was a virgin. He didn't know one to be as bold as she had been in her demand for him to join her for the night, after all.

Still, it was enough for him to pause.

Only long enough to ask, "Karine, have you done this before?"

Not that he wanted to ask, but the better part of his judgement pushed the words out of his mind before he could really stop them. His cock throbbed painfully between his muscular thighs, the waistband of the boxer-briefs biting into the tender, swollen flesh at the base where he held it, not yet ready to drop the clothing completely.

There was only one thing he really wanted to do right then—be inside her. Except he had never been a gentleman before, but here he was, *trying*. Even if it was only by asking questions. It was the best he could do.

"*Karine.*"

She still didn't—or *wouldn't*—answer, instead opting to look away from him, her expression darkening.

"I never said I was offering my history for this," she muttered.

Roman nodded, saying only, "Fair enough."

That was fine. She didn't have to answer his question. He was going to take her however she wanted.

As long as she asked for it.

Roman couldn't remember a time when he had wanted someone this much—*so much*, that the need he felt thrummed deep in his bones, and made the blood thicken in his veins. Every breath she took was measured while she watched him, waiting for something he didn't know; each one left him a little hotter. It was a show of the self-control he liked to say he didn't have if there ever was one.

Seemed he was a liar.

Because it took everything in him to stand there, and let her look. All the while, those nerves that had shown in her wide eyes and jumping swallows were starting to fade. Instead, he found lust reflecting back the next time her eyes met his. He could touch her, *pull her tight to him*, and it was enough to drive him insane.

But he didn't.

"What are you waiting for?" she asked.

"For you to say the word—ask or tell me."

Karine wet her lower lip slowly. The action was enough to make Roman clear his throat when a lump formed there from the tightening of his stomach. *Christ*. Every little thing she did was mesmerizing to him.

And he didn't even know why.

"*Those* words?" Karine questioned.

Roman nodded, stepping closer to hook a finger under her chin so he could tip her face up toward his. For a reason he couldn't understand, she forced her stare away from him again. A part of him wanted to ask why, but he doubted she wanted him to. Instead, he stroked her cheek with his thumb.

"You don't know how beautiful you are, and that's a fucking shame," he said, finally urging her attention back on him. Only now, there was a different gleam in her eyes. The vulnerability hadn't left, but he found that same daring, unafraid woman that kissed him in an alley and approached him with an invitation to join her bed.

He could handle her fragility.

As long as she knew what she wanted, too.

"*Please*," she said, the word so soft he strained to hear. "This is what I want."

And that was all he needed.

Roman pressed his lips to her warm forehead, the silkiness of her skin only a tease for what was to come. He bet the rest of her would feel even better against his mouth, and wrapped around his dick. Her hands found his shoulders before she turned her face up so he could take her mouth in his for a kiss.

His tongue pushed beyond her parted lips, darting past hers that flicked against his for a quick taste. And then she sucked on the tip of his tongue when he almost dared to pull back. Her light purr while he kissed her vibrated straight through his fucking chest.

That sound was pleasure, and sin.

Perfection.

Roman's sense of gentleness fled the second Karine decided to take what she wanted by slipping her hands beneath the slightly lowered waistline of his boxer-briefs. The tight fist she made around his hard cock, stroking his tip fast, had the air catching in his throat.

"*I'm not glass*," she breathed against his mouth. "I promise not to break."

Roman nodded, still breathless. "Good to know."

He couldn't be gentle anymore, that patience and good will of his was gone. He wanted to go hard—possess her, even, if she would let him.

His hands moved down her body until he gripped a palmful of her ass. Round, and pert, he cupped and kneaded the flesh until her air came a little harder, and she whimpered against his cheek where her kiss had come to rest. She helped to shove his boxer-briefs down, and he let her, stepping out of them only once they'd fallen down to the floor below.

Roman could have taken more time to appreciate the curve and softness of her ass in his hands, but the grin she leveled on him had his mind going elsewhere. She stood up on tiptoes to kiss him once, and then twice. Quick and fleeting, it wasn't nearly enough, but he was fast to get more when he gripped her thighs, and pulled her up from the floor into his arms.

They fit together like a glove—like puzzle pieces, really. Her hands found his jaw, her fingernails scraping along his beard as he stole another kiss from her, refusing to give even an inch as the need for air burned in his lungs. His cock dug into her thigh while her breathy sighs were swallowed by his lips and tongue. Every single one she made, he wanted to taste.

Each one she made, *he owned*.

His mouth moved over her trembling chin, down her neck, and then he licked the soft fleshiness of her earlobe. Her giggle melted into a low, sexy moan when his teeth nipped into the spot behind her ear.

It was that sound coming out of her mouth that spurred him forward. Roman carried her to the edge of the four-poster bed, tossing her down to the sheets where he could watch as her perfect body laid bare.

Ready for him.

Open to him.

"God, look at you," he uttered.

Karine's shyness was long gone as a wicked smile played at the edges of her lips. She was all woman—one that tempted him more than he was willing to admit. On the bed with her hair spread around her face like a halo, she winked while she grabbed her breasts in both hands and squeezed.

She stretched herself along the bed for him, widening her legs until he salivated at the sight of her cunt on display for him. The sliver of wet, pink flesh was just one piece of the perfection that made up the creature below him. Her narrow waist melded into hips meant for riding a man, and he could already feel those legs of hers wrapped around him while he held her down.

ᵀᴴᴱAGREEMENT

Roman couldn't resist it any longer. He wanted to know if his fantasies were as good as the real thing—there was only one way to find that out.

Karine seemed to read his mind, murmuring, "Come on, then. *Fuck me.*"

What else did he need?

Nothing.

Roman grabbed her thighs, yanking her back to the edge of the bed and pushing her thighs wide apart until he felt her muscles shake. Widening her thighs opened her sex for him, too, pink and fleshly and *soaked.*

Already, she was wet.

He used the tip of his thumb to drag that wetness at her slit over the lips of her sex, spreading them apart as she trembled underneath him. Every soft *oh* and *please* at his soft touches while he felt her pussy tighten against the pressure of his thumb against her entrance had him dragging in hard breath after breath.

And then he replaced his thumb with the head of his cock—throbbing, growing harder, he was so close to getting what he wanted. Yet, he still held back. The tip of his cock swept through her slit, from the wet, clenching tightness of her slit to her swollen clit that he'd just been teasing with his thumb.

Hot against the bare skin of his dick, Roman told her, "Sorry—it's going to have to be raw."

He hadn't come there expecting to fuck—it wasn't like he had time to plan ahead for this. It was what it was, and it wasn't a careless mistake he'd made very often before. But he would tonight.

Happily.

Karine reached for him, dragging those fingernails down the path of muscles that made up his lower abdomen when she replied, "Lie, and tell me it's better this way, then."

He *could.*

Except ...

"It is better this way."

He took her then, a hard flex of his hips that buried his dick nine and half inches deep into the warm, wet heat of her pussy. He could have been slow—or *tried*—but just the feeling of her slick walls stretching open to accommodate him would have been enough to make him nut had he taken his time.

Nobody wanted that.

Karine's aching gasp echoed in the room when he'd filled her full, and she arched her body for him. Thrusting her hips up to pull him impossibly deeper, she watched him through lowered lashes when his hands came to rest on her hips, and he held her tight against him for a moment. She wanted him just as desperately as he did. It resounded in every tremor rocking through her tempting body.

But he wanted a second like this.

Deep in her.

Wet to his balls.

One hell of a view.

Roman stood at the edge of the bed with his legs spread wide apart. Hers remained open to him—*for* him. Pulling back until just the head of his cock had her tender pussy stretched for him, he pushed himself back inside with one quick thrust.

Not quite as hard as the first.

Still just as deep, though.

Their groans came in tandem when that second thrust was accompanied by a third, and then a fourth just as fast. He started the pace, and she answered him back with the music of her sweet sounds.

Her hiss sizzled with a low, drawn out, "*Yes* ..."

Roman wanted that voice of hers ringing in his ears by the time he was done. In that moment, all he wanted was to make her feel good. As good as he felt with tension licking up his spine as release teased the edges of his senses.

She was tight all around him.

Greedy in the way she moved on the bed, sliding up and down her sheets while he fucked her to get more of him.

Harder, came the first plea.

More, she demanded.

How could he not give her what she wanted? She raised herself a little, just enough to watch the sight of his cock sliding in and out of her pussy. One of her hands fisted into the sheets as her breaths came ragged and quick, the low whine building in the back of her throat the longer she watched him fuck her. Then, when his thrusts became even stronger, she collapsed back on the bed with a broken sigh.

He heard it, though.

That satisfaction.

She was getting exactly what she wanted.

He could go on forever. As long as it took to make her come, and then some.

Karine moaned his name, the sound pure bliss coming out of her mouth. She shook while he took control of her, rolling her hips into him with a hard grip on her waist at every thrust.

He wondered if they were battling each other to see who would cave first. Roman smirked at the idea—he could do this all night. Every time he felt that telltale tightening of his balls, he pulled himself back by focusing on her large eyes. *Still locked on him.* By reminding himself how much she needed this. *And how much he wanted it even more.*

They both tried to be quiet, but it was pointless. Her heady moans came in a crescendo, and he couldn't stop the groans of approval at the woman beneath him. She was good—knew how to work her body, and yet she still let him take what he wanted, how he wanted at the same time.

It was only when her lips parted into an O-shape, and her head tipped back for her eyes to fly wide at the ceiling above, that he felt it. Those tremors working their way through her body stilled as her spine curved high off the bed.

Her toes curled.

She breathed his name again.

She came *hard*—he fucked her through it, too. The milking contractions of her orgasm sent him over the edge as her moans started to soften. He barely managed to pull out of her in time to spill his release along her clenching stomach with the help of a couple jerks of his hand.

A fucking waste.

That should have been *in* her.

The very nature of his thoughts silenced him—from his mind, to any words he might have said. Nothing came out. He couldn't remember the last time he had paid so much attention to a woman's orgasm that he noticed how her lower lip trembled when she came, or how her eyelids fluttered as she came down from her high.

But he also didn't look away.

Couldn't.

Realizing he'd pulled out of her to come, Karine pressed her legs tightly together, and dared to put a hand over her face like she was embarrassed.

For what?

That she had allowed herself to feel good.

Because she took what she wanted?

Roman didn't care to see her shame, and wanted her to experience what she just had again instead. Before she'd said a thing, he was already down on his knees between her legs.

Her loud inhale reached his spot when he pulled her legs apart once more.

"What are you—"

Her words faded, but his mouth was already on her. That taste he'd been waiting for was everything he'd imagined, and then some. Tart and hot on his tongue, he lapped from her slit to her clit while he watched her from between her thighs. Karine had pulled herself up on her elbows, but soon fell back on the bed with a thump.

Roman pressed his mouth to the hot core of her pussy, sliding his tongue into her next as she whimpered and twisted against the sheets. While he sucked on her, his mouth flooding with the flavor of her juices, his thumb found her swollen clit.

Already sensitive from one orgasm, Karine cried out louder than ever, dark pleasure coating every sound. Her body arched up, and she grabbed his head, weaving her fingers in his dark hair until her fingernails scratched along his scalp.

She could leave marks.

There was no doubt he would be leaving some of his own, starting with a beard-burn around the insides of her thighs.

⸙AGREEMENT

And the thought of her feeling that tenderness tomorrow—
and maybe in the days beyond—did something terrible to
him.

Terribly wicked, that was.

He liked it too much.

All of it.

All of her.

His tongue and thumb flicked and stroked until he was
sure she was ready to fly again.

"*Roman* ... please ..." she begged. "Oh, my God."

He loved hearing her plea and when Karine came that
time, even her thighs quivered. Roman's face was stuck
between her legs, his tongue buried deep in her pussy, and
for a second, she tightened her legs around his head to keep
him that way. Another woman, and he might have shoved
her off—but not this one.

She was still hot on his tongue.

Wet in his mouth.

Christ.

A part of him thought ... *once won't be enough.* He already
wanted to see her like that again, staring down at him,
amazed and blissed.

He straightened up, but only to lean over her on the bed.
Still shaking, with her breaths coming fast one after another,
Karine watched him through half-lidded eyes that were dark
with her desire.

And there it was.

Her *smile.*

It was a victorious smile. Like she truly believed she had
won something.

"What?" he asked.

She shook her head, reaching for him. "You—just you.
Stay with me?"

Karine already had her hands wrapped around his
forearms like vise grips. He wasn't exactly in the mood to
pack up and go, though.

Wordlessly, Roman climbed into bed with her,
maneuvering them both until they were covered by the silver
bedspread. He pulled her against him, wrapping his arms

tight around her. She seemed content to lay like that, her back tucked tight along his chest. There was no hiding the racing beats of his heart.

She had to feel every single one.

Karine didn't say a thing.

Burying his face into her hair, he breathed in the scent of her. He wasn't the type to fall asleep with a woman in his arms, but he didn't want to let her go, either. At least, not yet.

Wasn't he supposed to get information out of her?

Hadn't he done this for a reason?

Yeah.

The thing was, Roman could already feel her muscles loosening with every steady, deep breath she took. She was drifting off to sleep right there in his arms, every soft curve of hers molded to each of his hard lines.

"This feels like a mistake—there's no going back from here," he murmured, hoping Karine would still hear him.

She didn't.

She was already asleep.

NINETEEN

It wasn't often that Karine woke up from a dreamless sleep—when she *knew* her consciousness was returning. It lapped softly against the edges of her brain, but no matter how much she tried, she couldn't remember if she'd dreamt through the night. She *must* have had one. Usually dark, and depressing, they left her with a bad feeling when she woke up.

Not something she could explain.

Something that just … *was*.

She was rarely able to make sense of the dreams when she had them, and almost always, they involved a little girl whose face she couldn't remember. A hazy, distorted image that wasn't at all *right*. But the voice of the little girl always sounded like her.

Like Karine.

Karine blinked fully awake, faced with the dark ceiling above her. The moonlight—so bright only a few hours ago when she fell asleep—had now faded. And the darkness wasn't so dark anymore, either.

For a moment, she was ignorant. Lost in the space between sleep and waking, waiting for it all to come back like it sometimes did. She couldn't remember where she was, if she was alone, or even what happened the previous night— but then it came rushing back to her. All at once.

Roman.

The willow tree.

She was daring enough to invite him to her room. The memories flooded in one after another. His hands on the veranda's railing, and the way his athletic, muscular body had easily swung over to land right in front of the curtains where she could see him through the sheer, billowing fabric.

Then, his mouth was all over her. That kiss—explosive, and *overwhelming*. Above all, it was the thing she remembered the most. It came back fast, and easy. She could still feel his lips devouring hers, even.

Karine had reached for him again, long after they had finished, but she couldn't remember actually falling asleep.

Feeling around her sheets in the dark, she already knew he wasn't there with her. Touching Roman had instigated a very specific warmth inside her—a sense of safety. Something she no longer had because the bed was cold.

On the bedside table, the small digital clock showcased numbers that read three-thirty-one.

In the morning?

Karine blinked at the time.

Rubbing her eyes with her knuckles, she tried to push out what remained of the sleep. Even though she couldn't have slept very long, she was still well-rested. Like she had been sleeping for days.

Given the state of her life lately, that wasn't entirely out of the realm of possibility.

Yet, she wondered …

Was it Roman—had it been his presence that let her sleep so well?

Movement in the doorway had Karine raising up to her elbows to see the figure standing at the bedroom door. A light had been switched on in the hallway, allowing a wash of color to spill over his wide shoulders, casting him in a dark silhouette. She couldn't actually see his face, but she knew it was Roman all the same.

Felt it in her soul.

He was naked but for his underwear. Karine, stretched out on the bed and covered flimsily by a sheet, shifted a bit to soothe the distinctive ache that settled between her legs. And the tingle spreading outward from her belly. Just his presence was enough to invoke a reaction she had never experienced for a man before.

Roman had taken her in a way that made her want more— she bet he knew exactly what to do to keep her wanting it, too.

She opened her mouth to ask him to return to bed, his name already on her lips, but he took one step in her direction and she fell silent.

What happened?

"What the fuck is this, Karine?" he growled.

Suspicion coated his every word, before she even had a chance to look into his eyes. There was so little light around them, and since she had no idea what he was talking about, she reached for the bedside lamp and flicked it on.

Roman came to stand at the foot of the bed with his bare feet planted wide apart. His shoulders, and every muscle of his body, seemed coiled and clenched. Ready to spring at any moment—another sign of his anger that she didn't understand.

It was the item in his hand that had her straightening higher in bed, pulling the sheet up around her to keep her breasts covered.

"What is it?" she asked, confused.

"That's what I'm asking you. *What is this?* What is it doing here, Karine?"

She eyed the item he held warily. "A notebook?"

"It's a *sketchbook.*"

That accusatory tone of his felt like a slap, especially when she didn't have the first clue why he was leveling it on *her.* What did a fucking sketchbook have anything to do with what happened last night, and why she woke up at three in the morning to find him gone from her bed.

Hell.

Karine should be the one asking questions. "I don't know. Where did you find it? I haven't seen it before."

Instead of answering her, he started flipping through the pages of the sketchbook. She couldn't see whatever was inside from where she still caught a few glimpses of colors on the pages despite how fast he went through it.

The whole time, Roman glared.

At each page.

He scrutinized the images closely—like they meant something to him, and he had a personal connection to what was staring back at him. She couldn't quite the same.

Still watching him in silence, an uneasiness settled deep inside her. It wasn't that she was afraid of him, or what he might do. For the first time, she wasn't afraid of a man.

Well …

This man, anyway.

He had looked at her in a way that said he would never hurt her. And yet, Karine couldn't put a finger on *why* all of this felt so wrong.

"You're telling me you don't know where I found it?" he snapped, the question raking over her skin. Like hot coals searing lines down her body. When he turned his eyes to her again, she found fire staring back. It burned from where she sat on the bed, still lost to what was happening.

"That's what I'm telling you," Karine replied, trying desperately to keep her voice level. She hadn't done anything to warrant the way he was treating her. "I don't know what it is, or why it matters."

"I found it under your bed, Karine. I almost tripped on it when I got up to go for a piss. *It was right there.*"

She looked at it again, her brow furrowing. He brandished the sketchbook in the air like a sword, daring her to deny what he was saying. Despite not *knowing* what the sketchbook was, what it held, or why it had been stuck under her bed, simply looking at it caused a swell of emotions that she couldn't explain.

ᴛʜᴇAGREEMENT

All bad.

It drowned her.

The confusion was heaviest, and most prominent. Except it was best friends with the disgust that filled up her stomach with nausea the longer she stared at the item he held. It was the fear climbing up her spine simply *because* he had the sketchbook that concerned her the most, though. All of those warring emotions—all at the same time, too.

Why did a sketchbook have that effect on her?

Karine didn't know, and she didn't care to find out. Not tonight, certainly not when everything else had been so perfect. Just like everything else in her life that didn't make sense and scared her, she wanted to hide it away and bury it as deep as it would go—*wherever* it would go.

Those details didn't matter.

It just needed to leave.

Now.

"Roman, *please*—can you put that away?"

Her tone remained calm.

She was anything but.

"Who is Katee?" he asked instead.

Karine shook her head. "I don't know."

"Come on. You need to trust me, and tell me the truth."

What was he talking about?

Stepping closer, Roman flipped through the pages—his hands a manic frenzy—until he seemed to find the one he was looking for.

"You don't know who this is?" Roman asked, turning the sketchbook around to force her to look at the image. Karine's stomach seemed to cave when she had no choice but to face the picture. Someone had drawn a young girl's face in angry strokes with a lot of different colors. However, there was no mistaking who it was—*her*. "A self portrait, maybe?"

His burning glare remained locked on her while she found that she couldn't look away from the drawing.

"That is *you*," he added firmly when she didn't reply.

She glanced up at him, water filling her eyes and her lips parting slightly, the urge to cry out for help welling within her. Somehow, she shoved it back down long enough to utter, "I don't know who drew that."

"*Karine.*"

"I don't!"

Roman shot her another stinging, fleeting look, muttering, "And this?"

He flipped over to the next page, and what she saw there made her wince. It was a picture of a man. Undeniably Dima, but with exaggerated facial features like a caricature from a cartoon, maybe. It was drawn in the same style as the previous portrait with varying colors, except this one had been violently scribbled and scratched over. Possibly with nails and crayons to the point that the page had torn in several places.

The anger and pain radiated from the page—bleeding into the lines and colors, evident in the wear and tear.

"There's no way you don't know who drew this, Karine. It was under your bed. You know who Katee is—you can tell me."

Roman's voice dripped with bitterness, but he still tried to soften it. He wanted her to trust him with the information he apparently had, except she didn't have the answers.

"I don't know," she insisted.

Again.

Roman sighed harshly, squaring his shoulders as he scrubbed a hand down his jaw. His patience was quickly running out, it seemed.

"What do you think will happen to her when you marry Dima, and you're no longer here to protect her?" he demanded.

What?

Karine shook her head violently, saying only "Protect who? I don't know that girl."

Her denials did nothing.

"Is she here? Do they keep her hidden—like you? Out of view?" Every question slammed into her harder than the last. Roman's tone grew deeper, and *darker*, unrelenting in a quest she hadn't known even started until it was too late. Her soul was stripped and exposed for him under his scrutiny, but she couldn't get away. He wasn't anywhere near finished, saying, "You're gambling with a child's life. That can't be who you are."

Roman wasn't the only one becoming desperate, though. Karine's mind raced to find a way to convince him she wasn't lying—her words spilled out in a rush before she could stop them, or consider what she said.

"No, she's *not* here ... I've never even heard that name before! I don't know *Katee*."

Yet, as she said the name, images from her past dreams ran through her mind at lightning speed. A movie reel she couldn't escape. A little girl's arms wrapped around a tree trunk as she spun and spun. Humming a nursery rhyme she didn't recognize. Karine continued to shake her head, rubbing at her mouth and face, even her forehead and into her hairline, with her fingertips to rid the sudden itch that seemed to crawl over her nerves.

"You're saying you've *never* seen these before?"

Karine blinked, not wanting to lie but also ... "Once, maybe twice. But only the drawings, and never—"

"*Bullshit.* That's bullshit, Karine. It's *you*, look at it."

"No, that's not ... it's not right. Stop ... just, *stop*," she muttered. And then, louder, "*Stop it!*"

Roman strode over to his pants that had been discarded on the floor in their earlier haste. He fished into the pocket, pulling out his wallet and then a folded piece of paper emerged from it. He came over, opening the paper and holding it up for her to see.

If anything, he seemed angry about it. *Angrier.* Defiant, even. Once again, daring her to deny the truth he put right in front of her face. Except she didn't understand.

"What about this?" he demanded, thrusting the paper toward her even as Karine inched back from him on the bed. "Are you going to deny this, too?"

Karine's breath stuck in her throat when she saw his profile drawn in the *same style*. The drawing was an uncannily likeness of Roman's face, with his name scribbled out in crayon in the corner. Just to drive home the final nail in the coffin.

Whoever made the drawings had done a good job—it was still clearly the work of someone who was young.

But *not* her.

"Where did you get this?" she asked, so unsure.

And cold.

Even as she reached to touch the image, seeing how careful the hand had been to shape the perfect cupid's bow of Roman's upper lip, Karine had to pull herself back. The comforting *familiarity* she felt to that particular drawing so strong that it scared her. She couldn't figure out if it was because she *liked* that she recognized something about the drawing, or not.

Hollow, she heard Roman say, "Masha. She gave it to me."

"Why would Masha—" Karine squeezed her eyes shut, and tried to process. "Where did she find it?"

"My bet, in this sketchbook."

Karine didn't need to open her eyes again to know he hadn't taken his off her, but she still did. Despite every reason she had not to, she couldn't look away from the drawing in his hand. The déjà vu was uncanny, but she couldn't explain why. She almost asked him to show it to her again when Roman slowly folded it up, and slipped it back into his wallet.

She didn't, though.

Roman scowled once the drawing was safely tucked away. "You won't convince me that you don't know anything about this, Karine. I saw you holding this sketchbook in your hand. You're lying, I just don't know why."

Karine stiffened.

No, he was the liar.

"I've never touched it before. Never seen it before."

Roman's fingers stilled where they rubbed at his jawline, confusion flitting over his face. "Tribute—last month. You were standing there by the stone walls when I got out of my car." He shoved the sketchbook her way, adding, "You had this in your hand."

Karine hadn't even noticed how the sheet had fallen away from her. With her back straight, she sat up in the cold air, uncaring that her nipples pebbled and she shivered. Roman didn't seem to notice her nakedness, only focusing on *her*.

She fidgeted under the pressure, refusing to admit yet another one of his lies that he demanded was true. "You're not making any sense. I didn't see you at the last tribute."

Roman's gaze flashed with a warning, his jaw clenching at her response—like she was pushing it, and he had enough. He wasn't getting what he wanted, but she didn't know what to tell him.

"I don't know what I'm doing wrong," she whispered, *wishing* he would believe her. If she could, she would have done everything in her power to please him, to go back to the way they were the night before. "Or what you want me to say, I'm sorry."

"What I want you to—" Roman's words cut off with a disgusted grunt, and his hand cut through the air as if to say *enough*. "You were standing right there," he replied hotly, barely tampering his tone now. "We spoke—well, no, *I* spoke. I don't remember if you even said anything. Dima was at the door of the mansion, calling for me. I didn't even get to turn back around, and you were running before I could stop you."

Karine shook her head back and forth fast—so much so that the room spun—and she was sure she looked crazed.

There was no way.

But how did he know?

She had seen that very scene in her dreams—remembered it distinctly. Near the weeping willow tree, she'd watched while Roman stepped out of his car. She wanted to speak to him, but couldn't get the words out. When she looked down, a little girl's hand waved back at him, hazy to her eye. That's how she knew she was dreaming. It was always a dream.

Then, Dima's voice had broken through the daze—she didn't want to be anywhere near him. Except it was *still* just a dream.

Wasn't it?

Roman kept talking, unaware of the fight happening inside Karine's mind. "Dima went looking for you—he ordered me inside, and to meet with Maxim. This happened, Karine. I stood there, and *looked at you.* You can't tell me I didn't see what I saw and expect me to just believe it. That's not how this shit works."

It was the disbelief coating his anger that brought her back to reality with a bang. And also told her that he truly believed he was telling the truth—why would he lie?

But that meant—

She didn't know what it meant.

Didn't *want* to know.

The sudden urge to protect herself from the things he was saying came on swift, and punishing. Her words came out in a hiss when she pointed at him and said, "You're lying."

That had Roman's brow dipping low—he watched again through heavy eyelids, careful and steady. If only that helped. If only it changed what he had already done.

When he came towards her again, a sound came out of Karine like she had never heard. The growl of a caged animal; the only warning she could muster for him to *back off.* Already, the tears tracked streaks down her cheeks. She couldn't bother to wipe them away or hide the wetness. Even as Roman stood there, wary with his hands lifting like he might reach out to her, because she *needed* it. She bet she looked like it, too.

She had managed to be so strong in front of him. His very presence helped pull Karine out of her shell, if only to make her take what she wanted, damn the risks. Nonetheless, the flickers of her true self came through when she was with him. Everything else was only pretend. And dreams didn't last forever.

The last thing she wanted was to break down in front of him, now.

Or ever, for that matter.

"Go," she told him.

Roman didn't move an inch. "Karine, I'm not lying. You have to know what I'm saying is true—why don't you remember any of this? Is it the meds, or—"

"No."

Her reply came out sharp, and high. Broken, too, because he dared to kneel down beside her on the floor. So close that she could reach out and hold him if she wanted to. A part of her *really* did. Another just wanted to shrink away. She knew he didn't want to hold her, not now. He wanted something from her that she couldn't give.

The flashing movie reel of images was back again, and worse than ever—the one she was convinced had only been a dream. Back in her room where she should be safe, but Dima followed her there.

It was *so real* that she could almost see him standing in the doorway when she glanced at it. The way her heart raced painfully, and she couldn't quite catch her breath only compounded the fear—the false image.

He had called her Katee.

Why?

Karine's mind stopped there.

Or the dream did.

She wasn't really sure.

"Karine, this could be our only chance to help each other—talk to me," Roman said gently, his palms turned up and open to her to take if she wanted. "I can't help if I don't know. What's going on, babe? *Tell me.*"

Tell him *what?*

God.

She didn't even know what to tell herself.

So all she said to him was, "*Leave.*"

Karine was convinced that soon enough, every cell of her body would disintegrate into nothingness. The edges of her vision had already started to blacken, and blur, but maybe that was just the tears. It didn't matter. She didn't want Roman here to watch it happen.

"I want to help you, I want to—"

"Leave, Roman. *Now.*"

She didn't even let him get the words out, screeching loud enough to make Roman stand with a jerk. The last straw for him.

Roman said nothing as he gathered his clothes, refusing to even look at her as he put on his pants, then reached for his shoes. His shirt came next, and still, he remained silent. So, why did it feel like she could hear him screaming with every movement he made?

Maybe that was just her own mind.

Karine remained on the bed, pulling the sheet up and around her trembling body. She wanted to shroud herself with it—*hide inside it*. He still wouldn't meet her eyes as he finished dressing.

Good.

Those tears came harder now—he wouldn't want to see those—stinging her skin as they rolled down.

She sucked in a deep breath, the air stuttering the whole way into her lungs, as Roman left through the open doors of the veranda. He didn't look back at her when he went, either. When she was sure he was gone, the footsteps from his retreat fading into the darkness, she let out a wail. A cry so loud, so *broken*, Karine was certain it shook the walls.

If only the house would crumble, too.

That's what it deserved.

Karine couldn't stop the heavy sobs that fought their way out of her chest, the force heaving her shoulders with each one. Not even when her bedroom door flew open, and Masha came running in soon after. She couldn't breathe— every gulp, it wasn't enough.

"It's not me. It's *not*," she wailed, shrieking the words through her trembling hands that she waved at an approaching Masha. "It's not me, Masha. I'm not Katee— I'm not. *I'm not!*"

The more she said it, the worse her darkening thoughts and reality fractured. Images and memories flooding in to prove that what she said might not be true—she didn't know her own *mind*. Couldn't trust it, but what was new?

That was her whole *life*.

Masha rushed over to her, throwing her arms around her in what should have been a comforting cage as she held her close. Except that safety was gone. The cold weight sinking in her stomach had chilled her to the bone. Her caretaker whispered soft words that she couldn't hear over the sound of her own crying.

"Please tell me I'm not Katee, Masha, *please*," she begged.

THE AGREEMENT

"Karine, *calm down*. You're going to—"

It was already too late. Karine knew what Masha was trying to warn—sensed it coming on, though she'd only experienced a handful of seizures in her lifetime. Sticky drool fell down the sides of her mouth, as she lost control of all her muscles and the violent spasms started.

Still, she managed to say, "Tell me I'm not."

"But you are, my dear," Masha said in a soft whisper.

Masha looked her straight in the face though Karine's vision had started to blacken at the edges. There was no mistaking the truth in her caretaker's words—or her eyes.

"You are."

TWENTY

"What?"

Roman might have had a second thought about the way he answered the door to his place at the sight of a Yazov vor standing on the other wise. Except he really didn't.

And then the man had to go and shove an envelope his way. The guy didn't move, making it clear just with his presence alone that he wouldn't until Roman opened it. So, he did.

The pearl-white invitation, designed on soft-to-the-touch cardstock with gold foil lettering, was for Karine and Dima's wedding. Only a mere week and some days away.

"Fuck."

The curse came under his breath, too low for the man standing in the hallway of his loft apartment to notice. But not Marky on the phone—Roman had his cellphone pressed between his ear and shoulder, trying to multitask as usual.

And failing.

ᴛʜᴇAGREEMENT

Marky only wanted to know what was going on. "What's happening?"

"It's the invitation."

"For?" his friend asked.

Roman's molars ached from how hard he clamped his jaws together, muttering only, "To the wedding."

Marky's answering silence was enough of an answer, but of course, it didn't last long. It never did where his friend was concerned. "You haven't seen her since that night, right?"

Yeah.

A night Roman didn't want to remember.

Jesus.

Roman slammed the door to his apartment without a word to the man waiting in the hallway. It didn't matter—the guy had done his job, there wasn't anything left for him to do there.

"It's been four days," he said to Marky. "Fuck."

"Roman—"

"*Fuck*, man. So, it's … it's actually going ahead. It's happening."

Really happening.

Roman didn't know how to process that. Or if he even wanted to.

He could hear Marky grinding his teeth through the phone. Back in New York for a few days on business—but apparently he had also been digging around matters concerning the Yazov Bratva—the man still wasn't keen on Roman fucking with Karine.

Literally.

Or figuratively.

"The thing is, there's nothing to be found," Marky said quietly. "Not about her. Literally nobody knows anything about her—it's like she doesn't exist to most of them. You can't keep asking about someone who isn't supposed to be found, Roman. Someone's going to start to notice."

Right.

But that also didn't seem like a good option to him, never mind one he cared to go with. If his next statement didn't make that clear to his friend, then nothing would.

"So, I have basically no time to figure this shit out," Roman muttered, pinching the bridge of his nose as he tried to focus his thoughts. "And nothing to go on is what you're telling me."

"When there's nothing to see, it usually means someone has tried very hard to keep it out of view, bro."

"I know that. I can feel it in my fucking bones. It's Karine. She is at the centre of everything going on with the Yazovs."

Whatever it is, he added silently.

Which was the biggest problem.

Marky started throwing together his own theories, none of which made sense, and Roman didn't want to encourage it.

Then, Marky said, "For my own peace of mind, I feel like I gotta tell you to leave it alone again, anyway."

And that was enough of that. There was no point in continuing the conversation, and besides, Roman had other things to deal with now. Like the fucking wedding invitation in his hand. He needed to think—he didn't need someone else's voice in his head while he did it.

"I've gotta go. Got a new gig lined up for tomorrow and I'm meeting the crew in fifteen," he said quickly.

Roman hung up the phone, and instantly turned on his heels, yanking open the front door and heading out of his apartment. He wasn't lying when he said he had to meet the crew. He just wasn't sure how he was going to keep his attention on that shit when all he could think about was Karine.

And that night …

Her breakdown.

Maybe she didn't want to be saved, but goddammit … he couldn't imagine her married to Dima, either. The hot anger that spilled down his spine at the very idea was enough to make him sick. He wanted to keep that motherfucker *far* away from her.

But how?

The thought was still lingering in the back of his mind when he turned the corner at the end of the hall of his loft that led to the stairwell. Roman was still trying to come up with a plan when he felt a crack land on the back of his skull.

^{\text{THE}}AGREEMENT

He didn't even see the bat coming. Everything went black when his body hit the ground with a thud.

• • •

It was the blinding ache in his ribs that finally brought Roman around to consciousness. The painful throbbing at the back of his head was a close second, though. Both were intense enough to push him to the edge of unconsciousness again, if only because the second he felt the pain, he wanted it to go away.

Roman crawled off that edge, forcing himself to open his eyes wide, and still wasn't able to see anything at all. Dingy darkness surrounded him, a mustiness crawling into his lungs with every breath and making him want to puke from the smell alone. He couldn't tell if it was just his swimming vision giving up on him or the actual lack of lighting in the space.

"Rise and shine, sweetheart," came a dark voice, and a low chuckle from within the shadows.

Too close to him, really.

Roman blinked into the darkness, attempting to move if only to settle the swelling nausea. He quickly discovered that his wrists were tied together—stretched high over his head, the rope connected to a chain wrapped around a wooden beam.

His toes grazed the ground.

Barely.

Like an animal ready to be skinned, he hung there, *helpless.* Roman tried not to panic—he did. It didn't work.

Fuck.

This was the end.

This was how he would die. After every stunt he pulled over the years—all the outrageous shit he managed to do, and the trouble he found time and time again ... Roman was going to die like this.

Jesus Christ.

Sorry, Papa.

His ma, too.

They didn't deserve this.

"Down here," came the murmur.

Roman tilted his head down, finding Maxim's face staring back from down below. His brain was beginning to connect the dots—painfully so.

Maxim sat on his haunches, right in front of Roman's feet. A smoky cigar rested between his fingers in one hand, and a baseball bat waited in the other.

For some fucked up reason that Roman couldn't decipher, the man was shirtless. All his tattoos were on full display, the story of a high ranking bratva vor inked across a canvas of sweat-dotted skin.

Maxim had clearly taken liberties with the baseball bat before Roman even regained his consciousness. Why else were his ribs on fire?

"The fuck is this shit?" he managed to groan. "What did I—"

His words cut off from the dryness in his throat and mouth that had his muscles closing around the sound trying to escape. He wouldn't ask for water when, given his current state, it would be a sign of defeat to a man like Maxim.

"You know exactly why you're here," Maxim said as he eyed the cloud of exhaled cigar smoke. It filled the darkened space with the sharp, bitter stench of tobacco fog and only made Roman's ribs throb more when he had to breathe deeper through the smoke. "You should have kept your hands to yourself."

Of course.

Why wouldn't it be about Karine?

"How long?" Roman managed to ask.

How long did he know?

Maxim smirked, but it only felt cold when he replied, "Does it matter—you're lucky I left you alive for this long, no?"

No, but it gave him an answer all at the same time. Maxim allowed him to fall into a false sense of security, leading him to believe he suspected nothing for days about his daughter's involvement with Roman. That whole time—he was planning.

ᴛʜᴇAGREEMENT

This, apparently.

Strung up to a beam, held accountable by a baseball bat, in what appeared to be a basement of some kind.

Roman almost respected Maxim for that. Except he knew enough now about the man's life and business to confidently say he didn't deserve any of his respect. Not when he treated his daughter as nothing but currency.

Flowers shouldn't be hidden from the sun.

They wilted.

"Didn't your father teach you loyalty?" Maxim asked, the cigar resting at the corner of his mouth while he drummed his fingers to a bent knee. "Loyalty to the *boss*? The respect of it all—any of it?"

As far as Roman could tell, no one else waited in the shadows. It seemed like it was just him, and the boss. Maxim stood, then, slowly stretching to his full height. He took a moment to pace back and forth in front of his captive's stretched form.

"I'd at least like an answer," the man said.

Fine.

"You are not *my* boss," Roman replied, knowing what it would likely earn him. Still, he wanted it clear—*all* of this. "And you're not my father."

As he expected, that wasn't the answer Maxim wanted. He lunged for Roman, lifting the bat to crash it down on Roman's head, but he stopped at the last second.

Stepping back to look at him one more time, Maxim shook his head, the disgust thick in his tone. "Good thing—had you been my son, I would have castrated you for doing that to another boss's daughter. A lesson you wouldn't soon forget. I might still."

Well, then ...

Maxim continued on, seemingly unaware of the way Roman had flinched at the threat. "You would have gone far, Roman. You already were—you left me no choice here. All you had to do was do your job, stay loyal to my bratva, and keep your fucking nose out of my business."

Roman let out a laugh that melted into a cough from the pain. "So, it's not just about Karine."

233

That earned him an arched brow, and a wicked sneer, saying only, "How long did you think your little friend could snoop around—asking questions he had no business asking—before word got back to me?"

Fucking Marky.

To be fair, it wasn't his friend's fault. Marky only did what Roman demanded—he'd known the risks when it came to digging for information surrounding the Yazov family. Back home, no one would have said a thing when Roman showed up asking for details.

Surprise.

He still wasn't in New York.

Apparently, Roman forgot to act like it, too.

"How did you find out about us, then?" Roman asked, each breath and word measured to ease the pain.

It was the only thing left now. Everything else Maxim said was true—no point in denying it. He did fuck his daughter, and snooped around the bratva's business. Roman played where he had no business being. He wasn't loyal to them beyond paying his dues.

Maxim wiped his forehead with the back of his hand, the bat swinging with it as he swiped away sweat. Roman got a whiff of that sour stench from where he was hanging, and it made him wonder how long the man had been swinging before he woke up.

The double vision, aching ribs, and constant throbbing said more than Roman cared to know.

"It doesn't fucking matter how I found out," Maxim said flippantly, waving that sweaty hand and bat high. "Nothing you say will change my mind about tonight."

"*This* is the punishment for sleeping with your daughter?"

"You think a few cracks from a baseball bat is what you get for fucking her? You're going to *die* tonight, Roman Avdonin. I hope it was worth it."

"My father—"

"Won't forgive me," Maxim interjected with a nod, "but he will understand. An unfortunate byproduct of your choices—I'll lose my only friend."

He actually sounded sad about that, *pained.*

ᴛʜᴇAGREEMENT

Roman still wouldn't apologize.

What difference would it make?

With only a push of the bat's tip against his chest, Roman's ribs sent agony ripping through his body and straight up his spine. The groans that left him were inhuman—the sound a wounded animal might make as it lay dying. The action sent him swinging from the pole, back and forth, softly. The pain was still *unreal*, and only got worse with every slow second.

Maxim wasn't oblivious to Roman's plight, and in fact, smiled at the sight in front of him. Proud of his work, clearly.

"There has to be something else," Roman added, teeth clenched.

He needed to work through the pain to get to the truth. That was the thing he hadn't missed in all this—what he bet Maxim didn't want him to point out.

Maxim said nothing in reply, but his gaze hardened.

"It has to be more than Karine, right?" he asked the man, his breaths coming in short, hard bursts. "More than me asking questions. It has to be."

"No, actually."

Bullshit.

"You wouldn't kill the me over that. You wouldn't risk what my father will do to you for *that*. At least have the balls to tell me—"

"You don't get to demand anything from *me*."

"Not really great at doing what I'm told, or haven't you figured that out yet?"

Yeah.

His arrogant nature just had to go and show itself at the worst possible time. This time when Maxim took a step toward him with the bat raised, Roman had no doubt there would be nothing to stop the swing from landing against its intended target.

His fucking skull.

The first one wouldn't kill Roman, they both knew that. However, a few more blows from that bat certainly might. Or … did the man intend to leave him alive for a while? What was Maxim going to do, then?

That was the worst part—not knowing how this would end. There was still nothing Roman could do about it.

His hands were literally tied.

And then he remembered …

The plan.

The fucking plan.

How could he forget the plan?

TWENTY-ONE

"They're going to kill you on the day of the wedding."

The words left Roman's mouth in the same breath that Maxim started to swing. He knew the man had heard him—the shift in the air was instant. That, and the bat didn't land on top of his fucking head.

Maxim flinched, still holding the weapon high. "What the fuck did you just say?"

Quiet, but it still felt like a roar.

Roman shifted in his constraints, trying to ignore the way the rope bit into his wrists the longer he was forced to hang. His limbs ached the longer they stretched unnaturally, his muscles feeling like they were tearing under his skin.

"I said they're going to kill you the night of the wed—"

The bat fell from Maxim's hand, stopping him from saying anything more as he lunged forward, bringing his face right up close to Roman's. Cold, hard eyes locked onto his. Seconds ticked by.

One.

Then, two.

Maxim only asked, "*Who* is going to kill me?"

Roman had to make a conscious effort to keep his eyes open, the pain and hard breathing threatening to take him under. Sweat dripped down his forehead, the beads down to the point of his trembling chin.

He was quite a sight.

No doubt.

Still, Roman hadn't begged.

That counted for something.

"*Who*," Maxim snarled.

The loud yell making Roman jerk against the rope. Even the chains rattled from his sudden movement. His captor waited, but the bat was still close enough for him to reach, though.

That couldn't be forgotten.

Figuring the only thing that was keeping him alive was the fact he had something to say, Roman started to tell the man, "I overheard a conversation, Leonid and—"

Maxim spun away from him, scoffing hard. "Fuck them. Fuck the both of them. Leonid and Dima want to take a shot at me?" He turned back with a wild smile—maniacal almost—before he thumped his fist against his bare chest. The news didn't seem to be, well ... *news*. "I'll be right here waiting for them."

Roman's brows knitted together. No, it wasn't Dima. He opted to keep that information silent, even if only for a moment longer, as he watched Maxim lose his calm. It was the first time he started thinking about who Leonid's partner actually *was*. He heard him say the name Katina—hadn't forgot it since. A name he didn't know, and one no one in the Yazov Bratva used for any woman who was around enough to be talked about.

So, who was she?

And why didn't the boss know about her?

"I did every fucking thing I needed to—made sure those two shits didn't bite the hand that fed them," Maxim said, facing Roman fully again. "*My hand.* Do they really think I agreed to this match because I *want* Dima as my son-in-law?"

^{THE}AGREEMENT

Who cared?

All that mattered to Roman was that the baseball bat had been forgotten for now. That gave him a few more seconds to figure out how to keep Maxim distracted long enough to keep him talking—or for the man to allow Roman to talk.

Either way ...

"You arranged the marriage to appease them—*why?*" Roman asked.

Maxim's gaze met his for only a moment before darting away.

At the chance to ask another question, Roman did. "Because you were expecting them to plot against you? Did you think you could get ahead of it that way?"

"I would have been surprised if they didn't. I thought the marriage agreement would solve the problem before it began. Tie them to me in a way, yes? A win-win, if you will. Leonid would get what he wanted—his son married to a pakhan's daughter."

"Clearly, you were wrong. What he wants is to be the boss."

Roman simply connected the dots, he hadn't actually heard those words from Leonid—but it was the only thing that made logical sense. Maxim wasn't denying it, either.

In fact, the man just stared at an empty spot on the wall behind Roman. He had another thought, then. A *win-win*, he'd called it. Like Leonid got what he wanted, and so would everyone else.

What did they get?

"And what about Dima?" Roman dared to ask.

Maxim startled at that, like he'd been shoved hard, as his gaze slammed back into a sore, tired Roman. "What about him?"

"What does he get from the marriage?"

"Karine. That's what he wants. What he's always wanted."

But that meant having her, too. She would be his—under his control, Dima's to possess in any way he wanted. *Forever.*

"And you're willing to just ... what, hand your daughter over to a man like that?" Roman hissed through another wave of pain, but his anger was still clear in every single word that ripped out of his mouth. "Fuck you."

Maxim turned his back to him at that statement, making Roman unable to see his face or expressions. Was he pissed off at the disrespect, or actually considering what was said between them?

Would it matter?

Roman still thought there was one person left in Maxim's *win-win* equation that he hadn't pointed out. The boss himself. Protection from a possible plot on his life certainly didn't seem like enough when he could just cut out the middleman and kill the assholes if he couldn't truly trust them.

What else was there?

"And what do *you* gain from this?" Roman asked.

Maxim looked over his shoulder at him, a gleam of wonderment coloring his expression as he stared at the beaten and bruised man hanging in front of him. The man who may have just saved his life. Did he realize that?

"Let me guess," Roman choked out through another agonizing cough, "I bet you gain everything—you'll finally be rid of her. Karine."

There was a part of him that ached for her, too, but in a different way than the pain currently flexing through his body with the smallest movement. Sweet and naive Karine. She had clearly agreed to the marriage to please her father, on top of her other issues that had become abundantly clear to him, and she had no idea he was just using her as a pawn. She was nothing more than a small piece in a big game.

One she couldn't play.

"She doesn't belong to me. She doesn't belong *here*."

Maxim's voice coated with hatred. The man's disdain for his child stunned Roman for a moment. He couldn't relate to that. At all. No matter what shit he'd done to his parents—to his father, specifically, a far better man than him—they still loved him. Not once had he heard them speak about or to him the way Maxim just did about his own daughter.

"She needs someone who wants her," Maxim added quieter.

^{THE}AGREEMENT

And that was *Dima?*

"She needs help," Roman snapped back.

That wasn't the response Maxim wanted if the way his burning gaze and red face turned on Roman was any indication. "And suddenly, you're an expert? The fuck do I need your advice for—a privileged *boy* without an ounce of respect or loyalty?"

Even hanging like he was, battered and exhausted, Roman still bristled at the insult. He refused to rise to the bait, knowing good and damn well it wouldn't do anything for him to do so.

Instead, hoping the man would hear him this time, he said, "I can see enough to know she needs *real* help—probably a professional diagnosis of her condition, and the right kind of treatment. None of the medication you keep feeding her like candy is going to help. Not unless she gets seen by someone who knows how to handle her situation." Roman briefly considered asking Maxim if he knew about Katee—that he suspected Karine and Katee were the same person. Even if one was seemingly a child, and the other, a grown woman. That Katee was an alter—an identity that fractured from somewhere in her mind, maybe to keep her safe or to deal with her situation. Whatever it was.

He decided to keep that piece of information to himself, just in case he wasn't able to get out of there alive. If that happened, he wouldn't be able to help Karine. And if her alter, Katee, was one of the ways she survived, then who was he to stop her from protecting herself?

Maxim scoffed, muttering, "I'm not taking her to a shrink. I don't need some balding fuck with a degree on his wall to tell me what I already know about her. She is *crazy*. Has been for years. And yes, if someone wants her, and it works to my favor like this has, then I don't see the problem."

How?

God, how could he think like that?

Roman flinched, then, and not just because of the way his ribs burnt with pain. He couldn't stand the sound of Maxim's voice. Karine's name on his lips. She was who she was—whether she was perfect or not shouldn't matter to the fact she still deserved to be loved and cared for like every other human with a beating heart and a soul.

She certainly had those.

Or … he thought so.

"So, you're just going to hand her over to him. Like a *weak* man would—a scared man who doesn't understand, can't comprehend, what they're looking at when they see her. That's what it is, right? You're scared of her."

It wasn't even a question.

Roman didn't need to ask what he now knew. Everything he had been missing was suddenly right in front of his face. He hated what he was looking at. The irony wasn't lost on him, though. She terrified her father because she wasn't *okay* by his standards, but clearly Maxim didn't see it the same way. He didn't see she was like a small kitten trying desperately to hide away from a big, mean world all at the same time. Did Karine even know the power she really had?

He didn't think so.

"What makes you think you know *anything* about me, you sorry sack of shit."

Just like that, Maxim's rage returned. A wave that crashed against him, unable to keep himself from drowning in it again. He stormed at Roman with his bloodshot eyes narrowed, his chest and shoulders heaving.

"I know too much, that's the fucking problem," Roman growled, using the last seconds he had to toss out the final card trick in his pocket. The one thing that *might* save him, if it mattered. "And you're wrong—it wasn't *Dima*. I don't know what Dima knows, but Leonid plotted against you with someone named Katina."

Once again, the name unsettled him. Something felt wrong, even as he said it. And he could tell that he was right to feel that way based on the way Maxim came to a full stop just inches away from him, his shoulders lifting higher as his chin tipped up.

Staring Roman down, Maxim's words came out slow, and *hard*. "What are you talking about?"

"I didn't stutter."

Not without effort, though.

ᵗʰᵉAGREEMENT

"*Katina*—not Dima, Maxim," Roman said, his voice hoarse now.

Maxim didn't move an inch. "Katina is dead."

"He was on the phone with her. I heard what he said—do you have proof of her death?"

Maxim's breaths suddenly exploded from him in fast bursting pants that sounded like a dog huffing at the end of its chain. His fists tangled into his hair as he snarled under his breath, turning away from Roman at the same time.

The man was just seconds away from losing his shit, and Roman was prepared. What else was he supposed to do now? The only thing he could do with his hands tied—*talk*. It was the only thing, next to stealing cars, that he was actually good at.

"Do you have proof?" he asked again. "Who is she?"

"*Shut up!*" Maxim roared at him. As fast as the man exploded, the unsettling calm returned when he added, "Yes, I have fucking proof. She was my oldest daughter. I *buried* her."

The two men glared, silence stretching on in the dank, musty basement.

It just didn't make any sense to Roman. How and *why* was Leonid speaking to Katina—if she was dead? And if so, then who was she?

Someone with a personal vendetta against Maxim, apparently. Enough to want to see him dead.

Roman didn't have the chance to think about it for long. That pain he'd been fighting finally took him under, dragging his consciousness with it.

Great.

• • •

Roman came back to when violent shakes rocked him awake. The pain was the first thing he remembered—*felt*—but the gravity of his situation came back just as fast. More surprising was the reason why he was shaking so hard the chains above him rattled.

243

Maxim had fished a knife out from somewhere, and was cutting the ropes where they'd been tied to the chain over Roman's head.

Before he could even ask why, he fell to the floor. Feet first, too, but the impact sent shock waves all through his body, and the weakness in his muscles and bones was too much to keep him standing for long before he crumbled to the floor.

Clenching his teeth to stop from groaning, Roman struggled against the dirty floor to stand as quickly as he could. Even if it was on shaky legs and bent knees.

The feel of the solid floor underneath his feet reassured him. Maybe there was still a chance he'd be able to make it out alive tonight.

By the time he was up and able to breathe—albeit, with pain that he tried to soothe by wrapping an arm around his tender chest—Maxim had retreated to the far corner of the room where he'd deposited his shirt. With his back turned to Roman, he started putting it on.

Roman rubbed his wrists where the ropes were still wrapped, before pulling the ruined constraints off while he did. Raw and red—probably swollen, too, but he couldn't tell in the low light—his wrists and fingers felt like needles pricking into his skin everywhere as blood rushed through the appendages. The tips of his fingers and fingernails had turned purple, but he figured that would get better now that the blood was circulating again. The pain in his hands was nothing compared to his ribs and the rest of his muscles.

Fuck.

Considering Maxim still had him under his control, why he cut him down was a goddamn mystery, but one he was happy with. Roman's mind didn't linger on the questions for long because he was more concerned with the man now pacing in the corner of the basement.

Under his breath, Maxim muttered to himself, face drawn into a scowl. "Katina ... Jesus Christ, I should have *seen it.*"

Roman stilled, listening closer only to hear Maxim ask, "But *when? Fuck.*"

ᴛʜᴇAGREEMENT

All at once, the thing he'd thought was off became blindingly clear to Roman.

If Katee was one of the alters invented by Karine, was Katina—

"I'll let you live," Maxim said suddenly, staying in his corner though he'd turned back on Roman in his distraction. "I'll forgive you your transgressions—I won't even make you fucking beg for your life. Though I damn well *should*."

Roman stood firm, staring the man down because he wasn't about to start showing weakness or fear now. "For what?"

Because there had to be a trade. He expected nothing different, but he didn't believe for a second it was going to be something entirely in his favor. Strangely, he thought *but I can deal with that, if it means she*—and just like that, he stopped his thoughts from running further.

Not that it mattered, he *knew*.

Roman just wanted to make sure Karine came out safe from this. Safe from Dima. Wasn't it the least he could do? Wasn't she *owed* that, considering everything?

He had no doubt—there wasn't a soul in the city of Chicago that gave a shit about her beyond what they could use her for. Even her own father basically said it—his actions *proved* it.

Who did she have?

No one.

So, he would. He'd give a fuck. At this point, it was the only thing he cared about.

He wondered if saying that out loud might help his case, but Maxim interrupted him before he could make the mistake. "You're to leave. *Now.* Go back to New York—go wherever the fuck you want to disappear to. If I ever hear you mention anything about the Yazovs to anyone, *anywhere*, I will find your balls and feed them to you. Before I mail your severed cock to your mother, of course."

Roman swallowed hard, but stayed quiet.

Maxim arched a thick, dark brow. "Do you understand what I am saying to you? No one can know. Not a soul."

Even just a few days ago—Roman would have laughed at a proposition like that. Nobody told him what to do. Not even his own father. Not his *grandfather*. Maxim meant fuck all to him. Even if the man had a sliver of Roman's respect, he didn't anymore.

But Karine…

She meant more.

More than his stupid pride.

So, he listened to Maxim's offer. And considered it.

"You're just going to let me walk away?" Roman asked. "Why do I find that hard to believe?"

"Not alone. You take her with you."

Roman's pulse picked up speed, but he kept that calm exterior.

There was no way …

What was happening?

"I don't want to hear about her ever again," Maxim continued, "and especially *not* about Katina."

Roman's brows crossed—something still wasn't right. "You need to tell me everything you know about your daughter and her condition."

A bitter smirk formed on Maxim's face. In a blink, he seemed a whole lot older. Maybe it was the way he pressed the tips of his fingers into his forehead as he shook his head.

"I don't have to tell you anything," Maxim replied in a sigh, long and tired. "I'm giving you a gift by sparing your life. You fucked her—you can have her. She's yours. Just get her away from me. And when—if—you think you've figured it all out, know that it's already too late. The agreement is final. There's no going back. Not fucking ever. If you want to leave alive, then you take her with you, and stay gone."

Just like that.

Karine was his.

This was what he wanted, right?

Had he really asked for this?

The weight of the choice came to rest so heavy on Roman's shoulders that his feet felt cemented to the ground from the pressure. And yet, it didn't really matter about the questions people would have, or the work it would take to keep her safe. She was his responsibility now.

Roman's choice was made.

His life to save hers.

The two men stood staring at each other in silence for a minute longer. It was all they could afford. Roman didn't care to know what raced through Maxim's mind. All he really wanted to do was get out of that basement, find Karine, and get her as far away from the city as he could before dawn broke.

Her father didn't love her, never cared for her, couldn't wait to be rid of her. So, *fine*. She meant something to Roman—she wasn't worthless to him.

He'd make sure she knew it, too.

TWENTY-TWO

Tonight, there would be no dreams. It was so close, though—the day that would change *everything*. Katina knew the others wouldn't be able to handle it, so she shuttered them away.

Karine wanted to sleep.

Katee had to play.

Katina was the only one between the three who wouldn't disintegrate into a puddle of useless tears knowing they were going to be forced to marry Dima in two days. But not before Maxim paid for it—*answered* for all of it.

Wide awake and stretched out almost naked under the sheets of her bed, Katina enjoyed the moonlight pouring in on her. A cool stream of light against the backdrop of black shadows. She felt like that, too.

Cold.

Dark.

She didn't know where Karine was. As the day of the wedding drew near, Karine grew more and more out of it.

THE AGREEMENT

Lately, she rarely knew what was going on around her. The medications she had tried to stop taking had returned full-force back into her life. She begged and threatened Masha for them—manipulated to get them, even. That wasn't Karine at all. She needed them again, just to make it through the day.

Katina stepped in to help more than she usually would, or the girl was going to kill herself.

As she stared at the silvery light that filtered through the room from the veranda's doors, she could almost see him standing there. *Roman. Her* memory of him was fragmented—pulled from what she knew, not what she'd done. It was Karine who wanted him.

Obsessed over him.

Seduced him.

Katina was just there in the background, not living it, not really remembering it, either. Except, she couldn't seem to shake off how he made Karine feel. A peculiar feeling. Like she didn't need to run. Hide. Fight. *Survive.*

She could just be.

Karine liked the idea of just *being.*

Katina, not so much.

A knock on the bedroom door didn't even earn her interest, as she assumed it was Masha. Katina blinked hard, trying to bring back Karine's voice. Usually, she spoke like her, and responded to Karine's name, too. That made it less confusing for the others around her. And oftentimes, she had ulterior motives for wanting people to believe she was someone else.

Except Leonid.

That was a different business. They both wanted the same thing, and in two more days—they would have it. The prick could fuck off to do whatever he wanted, then. As long as she got what was due, too.

A proper give and take.

However, instead of Masha, someone else opened and stood at the door. The looming shadow of his tall, broad-shouldered frame filled the doorway, and she knew who it was immediately.

Even though *they* hadn't met before.

Technically.

"Karine?" Roman asked, stepping further into the room when she pushed up to her elbows. His voice came off deep, velvety smooth, and masculine, too. The concern still rang through.

Maybe she could understand why Karine liked to fantasize about the man. He *was* something to look at. She sat up, and stared at him blankly. *Waiting*, really, for him to figure out what she thought—after Karine's last meltdown with him—should be obvious by now.

Karine was a lot of things.

People, sometimes.

Katee, yes.

Katina more often.

Herself with him.

Roman searched her eyes as Katina tilted her head to the side, and a smile curved the corner of her mouth. Realization settled over his face slow. She enjoyed watching it, honestly. He recognized her, or rather, he recognized who she *wasn't*.

"Katina."

The breath she let out was relief. There was something to be said about not having to pretend—it certainly made her goals easier to reach.

"*And?*" she asked back. Just as fast, Katina demanded, "Why are you here—where is Masha?"

Roman raked a hand through the short-trimmed, thick dark hair on his head. A tug started somewhere in the pit of her stomach when she considered what it would feel like to have his beard scratch the sensitive skin on the insides of her thighs while she rode his face.

She could see it now. His appeal. Why Karine was so possessed by him. Why Katee, even though she was just a girl, was so drawn to him, too. Pretty people attracted pretty people.

"Well?" she asked sharply when he said nothing.

Roman let out a hard breath followed by a clipped laugh. It sounded like *disbelief*. Just as fast, he shook it off to say, "We have to go. You're coming with me—you're not staying here."

Katina almost laughed aloud at that. Who did he think he was—what did this man think he was doing, or *going* to do, save them? At the same time, she couldn't help but be bemused at how careful he was not to show that her very obvious, *new* alter had took him off guard. That was hard to do.

She arched a brow. "Why should I go anywhere with you?"

"Because right now, Katina," he said, crossing the space until he stood next to her side of the bed. "I am the only person in the world you can trust."

He leaned over the side of the bed, bringing his face close enough, so she could breathe in his scent. She didn't think he did it for that purpose, but didn't miss the opportunity all the same, because he simply seemed to stare into her eyes. Like he wanted her to look back and see the truth.

Despite herself, she wanted to believe him.

Still, she asked, "Tell me why I should."

"Maxim knows—your shit with Leonid, *you*."

Katina stiffened, tipping her chin up to look down at him.

He continued, not letting her have time to respond before he said, "This is what Maxim wants, too. He isn't going to come after us if we leave now—we know nothing, say nothing, but he wants *you* gone."

At that statement, her nostrils flared. The only true show of her anger, but she couldn't say this man knew *her* tells.

This wasn't how it was supposed to go. She was so close to getting what she wanted—for Maxim to get what he deserved, and she *needed* to be here to watch it happen.

Roman slowly straightened up again. "Would he kill you if you stayed? Do you know the answer to that?"

Katina chewed on her inner cheek to keep from screaming her frustration. *No.* This was not how it was supposed to go. She didn't need rescuing—she needed revenge.

Seemingly unwilling to wait for her answer, Roman walked back to the bedroom door, stopping at the threshold to look at her again. He wasn't about to give her a second chance. "Well, you coming?"

Yes, she was.

She had to.

• • •

Katina knew Masha would have to come with them. She liked her well enough, although Karine was way too attached to the woman, as far as she was concerned. Katee called her Maria—an English equivalent to her Russian-given name—and was similarly reliant on her. Katina couldn't quite say the same, but as she hadn't been with Masha for nearly as long as them, she wasn't sure they would have made it alive without her.

Besides, if they left Masha behind, she didn't know what Maxim might do to her.

Roman didn't dispute her on it when she suggested Masha accompanying them. In fact, he'd been quick to agree the woman might be a help to them all. And he said it just like that, too.

Through the reflection in the rearview mirror, she watched Masha sleep in the backseat, her head leaning against the window. Oblivious to the miles of freeway passing them by, and warm under a jacket Roman had offered for her to use as a blanket. Only one thing made her pause about Masha.

Katina didn't know what Masha did or where she slept when she wasn't with her. It was obvious the woman didn't get much rest. She was Maxim's slave. Yazov property. She never gave her a reason to think she would hurt or act against them, but where did her loyalties lie?

Maxim probably wouldn't miss Masha's presence if he was now aware of the plot underfoot in his organization—he'd be even less concerned when he realized how deep the betrayal truly ran, too.

The sun peeked through the sky in the horizon, sending vivid streaks of orange and purple across the backdrop of thin, sparse white clouds. As far ahead as she could see, asphalt sprawled before her. Fields and grazing cattle surrounded both sides of the vehicle. She had never seen such a landscape before, but it was beautiful.

_{THE}AGREEMENT

Natural.

Wild.

Free.

The only thing that had ever scared her was how badly she wanted exactly that—*to be free.*

She didn't know their destination, where Roman was driving them to, but she couldn't bring herself to ask, either. She just wanted to keep staring out of the window—like that, sitting there, empty of thought and devoid of feelings. For once, not needing to be *on*. Sitting beside him returned those feelings she remembered Karine having and obsessing over constantly.

Safe, warm, hopeful.

And then there was him.

Handsome, curious, *sinful.*

Glancing at him, just for a split-second, she didn't want him to think she was staring at him. She didn't want him to mistake her for Karine. They were not the same people. They knew and saw different things that made them who they were. She wondered if he would understand that—if he truly understood them.

Roman was in profile, his knuckles whitened as he clutched the steering wheel hard. He focused on the road ahead of them, but also kept glancing in the rearview mirror. Never forgetting to check that they weren't being followed.

"Aren't you going to ask me where we're going?" he finally asked, breaking the silence that had existed between them for what felt like hours. It couldn't have been longer than one, maybe two. She didn't mind that time stretched on.

Katina looked in the rearview mirror, too, making sure Masha was still asleep. Not that it mattered if the woman overheard *her* talking—out of all of them, she was the one the nanny often feared.

For good reason.

"No, I trust you," she replied.

She didn't look at Roman again even though she wanted to—if only to enjoy the view.

Katina couldn't remember Karine ever being attracted to a man before. She didn't trust men. Neither did Katina, to be fair—she hadn't even trusted Leonid to get the job done, but she was at a point where he was her last option.

So, why Roman?

Why had she picked him?

Well, she hadn't.

Karine did.

Katee, too.

They trusted him, but they weren't here. She was—and so far, she didn't have a reason to *dis*trust Roman.

"Well, I'm glad you trust me, but I have some questions for you," Roman murmured, watching her from the corner of his eye. "Don't feel like you have to answer, but—"

"What?" She clasped her fists tightly, feeling the pinch of her fingernails digging into the palms of her hands, not sure she wanted to hear his question but still saying, "Just ask."

Roman tightened his grip on the steering wheel more. He checked the mirrors again as the question slipped from his mouth. "Why did you plot to kill your father?"

Katina's gaze narrowed.

Anything but this.

She turned away to observe the trees that passed them by in a blur of green as they left the miles of fields behind. Her eyes were unable to focus on just one. She wished he hadn't asked her that question.

Specifically, *that* way.

A few more moments of silence passed, and she felt the brush of Roman's hand on her knee. Her instinct usually dictated her to jerk away, to react violently to a man's touch—but she didn't. This time.

She met his gaze, then, and he took his eyes off the road to look at her, too.

"You don't have to answer that," he said.

"He's not *my* father."

"Karine's, then, but you—you have the sister's name, right?"

"She's dead."

Roman didn't even blink. "And you're definitely not."

"*Definitely* not. He's not my father."

Beside her, he nodded. "And the rest?"

THE AGREEMENT

Right.

The why.

Why did she do it—*try* to do it.

Katina was unsettled at the quiver in her voice when she whispered, "Maybe someday, I'll tell you."

If he noticed, he didn't say. Roman nodded, and that was that. Perhaps she expected him to fight her for an answer—to threaten and lay down ultimatums like most men did when they didn't immediately get their way. As it turned out, he wasn't like any man she had ever met before.

He wasn't going to force anything.

"Aren't you curious about Karine? Isn't she the one you want?" Katina asked.

She found herself as curious as she was afraid of his answer. And she wasn't quite sure why.

Roman shrugged, replying, "I'm sure wherever she is, she's safe. Because of you—I suspect. And Katee."

"Maybe. Katee only wants to play. Me—I had no other choice. No one else was going to step in and do something, so I did. If she didn't kill herself, someone else probably would."

If he was shocked at her frankness, he didn't show it. Roman's eyes did narrow a bit as he stared straight ahead at the road. She couldn't help but wonder what was running through his mind, and no matter what he said, Katina knew she was right.

He *did* want Karine.

"You know, I've read a few romances—watched some movies—and in all of them, the hero saves the woman he loves. But the only love Karine knows is painful. Left her feeling ashamed and degraded. A love that was unworthy, that she used against those around her in order to survive."

She wasn't the *chatty* type, but the words kept spilling.

"I don't believe in happily ever afters," Katina added, lifting one shoulder in a shrug when he glanced over at her. "And this isn't a romance, is it? You're not a hero. You don't love me. You don't even love Karine."

She didn't want him to answer. It would hurt her if he agreed with her, which she knew he would, but she hated liars even more. He didn't seem like the type to lie.

Instead, he said, "There is a lot we don't know about each other, Katina."

Blood rushed to her cheeks.

What did that mean?

Better yet, what did she want to hear?

"Is this how you love?" she asked, honestly curious. The risks and decisions he'd made surrounding Karine certainly didn't feel ... *safe*. Even if they were good. "Uncontrolled and uncontained? Erratic and unexpected? Risking it all? Crazy love doesn't scare you?"

He barely even thought about it, the words coming out easily. "That's the only way to love—if you're gonna. What good is giving someone the world if you haven't ruined it first to get to them?"

The next breath stuttered in her lungs.

No.

This wasn't some fairy tale romance—and he certainly wasn't a hero. That didn't mean the man couldn't sound like one, and that only interested Katina more. Because then she found herself thinking ... *do bad men make good heroes?*

Could they?

If they even existed.

"What happens now?" she asked lowly, turning back to the window and the racing scenery.

"I don't know," Roman replied, "and I especially don't know what happened to Karine and Katee back in that house, but they're not going back there. *Ever.*"

Katina swallowed around the large lump that had formed in her throat, knowing she *shouldn't*, and still telling him anyway, "The worst things happened to them there."

• • •

Want more of Roman and Karine's story—check for book 2, THE PROMISE at www.bethanykris.com/thepromise, to continue the trilogy or ...

^{THE}AGREEMENT

Here's a sneak peek:

Chapter 1

The mind was a messy thing.

A fickle thing.

Karine's was even worse. Her hair blew in the breeze coming through the rolled-down window, while she kept her face turned away from Roman because she didn't want to meet his eyes. The intensity she always found staring back from the striking blue gaze distracted her in ways she couldn't explain, and the last thing she needed was to drown in them.

Hell.

She was already drowning in herself, after all—in her mind, the hellscape was a dying carcass circled by the vultures that were her thoughts. Things she didn't want to see, others that she's worked so hard not to know … she couldn't possibly deal with an overwhelming man, and the violent currents inside her mind at the same time.

Karine also didn't know what to say to Roman without it sounding like an attack. Instead, she remained silent, her stare locked beyond the window at the passing scenery whether she was actually seeing it, or not.

So did Roman.

The only sound came from Masha's soft, rhythmic inhales and exhales from the backseat. She seemed content to sleep, probably the longest stretch of rest she had for the first time in decades. It was also entirely possible that she had helped herself to the pills she used to ply Karine with—they did say what was good for the goose was good for the gander.

Every time Karine glanced in Roman's direction, she found him glaring at the black patch of road stretching on ahead of them. A hardness had set into his handsome features that made her pause with each glance she stole his way. He gripped the steering wheel tight until his knuckles turned white, and his mouth shut. The entire drive had been that—it felt like.

Unbearable silence.

Unexplained anger.

She didn't know how much further they had to go—never mind where he planned for them to end up. He rolled into her life at the worst possible time, seemingly unaware but too curious and interesting for his own good, and she barely knew him at all.

Except she wanted to.

A dangerous thing for someone like her.

Karine almost had to wonder what was broken inside Roman Avdonin that made him do the things he'd done. What he still was doing, even. It would have made sense—maybe—if the other woman who hid within herself was one who had lusted after and seduced him, and then spent the night with him.

Karine would be lying if she said a part of her didn't blame him. That didn't change how she felt sitting beside him, not knowing where they would go—safe. She had no choice but to trust him now.

What else could she do?

"Are you scared?" Karine suddenly asked, breaking the silence that had become something else that was just too much for her to handle. Yet, it was also something she could control.

And maybe if he talked, then that loudness in her head might quiet. If only for a moment … God, she'd take a single second.

Roman didn't have a particular reaction to that question—almost like he had been expecting it. "Scared of what?"

The way he almost growled the words had her blinking back in response. His rumbling annoyance didn't seem to be directed at her asking, but she still shrunk subtly back like it might be. Roman chanced a quick look her way, his shoulders gently rising at the tilt of her frown, before he continued to concentrate on the road ahead.

"Sorry—I'm just tired," he said.

Karine let out the breath she'd been holding and nodded.

^{THE}AGREEMENT

From the corner of her eye, while she stared at his chiseled profile, she noticed the New York State sign zoom past.

"I meant them—back in Chicago," Karine replied, softly. "Are you scared of them?"

That was all she needed to say for him to know exactly who she was talking about. She didn't really think he needed a clearer picture.

"I didn't realize I had any reason to be afraid of them," Roman murmured.

Karine swallowed the lump that formed in her throat, promising to keep her fears locked tight in her chest, thumping there with every beat of her heart. He didn't know what he was talking about—he still said it with enough confidence to convince someone else he might.

But not her.

Even if she wished he could.

Maybe he genuinely didn't know how things operated in Chicago, but Karine's entire life had been an unfortunate lesson in the topic. Her father might be distracted with the plot to assassinate him, but it was only momentarily. She was supposed to marry Dima in two days—agreements like those weren't broken without someone answering for it, too.

Last night, the risk had seemed worth the choice, but as the sky cleared with the light of the morning breaking through the dark clouds, she sat in the passenger seat unsure of herself.

Of her decisions.

Of his.

She had grown up around those men—she doubted the ones he came from were the same. Even though there were times of her life that she couldn't remember, she didn't wonder at all about this. Those men weren't going to let her simply escape into the sunset. A deal had been made, and there were men who would make sure she kept her end of the bargain, one way or another.

Karine hadn't gotten away with anything in her life—she certainly didn't think the universe was going to start now.

Despite a sheltered life, she had in fact lived long enough to see a woman face the consequences of not seeing an arrangement through. Her wedding to Dima might not happen when it had been originally planned, but that didn't mean it was anywhere near void.

Roman hadn't even mentioned the wedding.

How could she trust this man?

What did he have to gain by saving her—or was it keeping her? Was it possible that he would do all of this just because they slept together once?

Same body, different girl, came a cackling glee from somewhere in the recesses of Karine's mind. She blinked away the taunt, but it lingered all the same.

She forced herself to talk so that voice wouldn't. "I'm supposed to get married tomorrow. Do you realize that?"

Roman said nothing, but his narrowing eyes while he continued to stare straight ahead said he was listening. That didn't mean he liked what he heard.

"I don't think you truly understand what that means. They're going to come looking for me," Karine said, the steady stream of her thoughts tumbling out in fast sentences she couldn't control. "It's not like they'll sit back and file a missing persons report with the cops or something."

A dark cast washed over Roman's face while he acted as though the feverishness of her rambling wasn't concerning. He was so good at doing that, she'd noticed.

Already.

It only urged her to continue.

"Dima expects his bride to show up, to get what he wants, and if he doesn't—"

"The wedding isn't going to happen," Roman interjected, the calm in his tone belying the coldness that settled in his gaze. "Not too many people know about it, anyway. I don't think most of the Yazov bratva even knows, only those involved directly within the city limits. They had only just started delivering the invitations. By hand, mind you. There's time for them to make a decision that doesn't include returning you."

But not likely.

Karine wasn't dumb.

A mess, yes.

THE AGREEMENT

Dazed, at times.

Not stupid, though.

"Everything was set up," she whispered, picking at her fingernails to soften the sound of her own voice saying things she hated. "We were going to exchange vows in the rose garden. The wedding dress was picked out for me, I didn't even have to think about it. Masha was going to do my makeup."

Karine spoke mechanically, aware of how she sounded but unable to stop repeating everything that she had been told by others. Her father. Dima. Even by Masha. Over and over again.

She had spent a lot of time preparing herself for her marriage to Dima. There was no real choice presented to her, she couldn't stop the wedding—it was out of her hands.

Karine had already been sworn to Dima, and there was no escape from that. No matter how far she ran.

"I'm going to say it again," Roman said, turning to meet her gaze with a clenched jaw and expressionless. "Know it will be the last time I say it, Karine. There will be no wedding tomorrow. You're not marrying that motherfucker. Not ever."

She swore every muscle in his body tightened and coiled in the seat next to hers—like a snake ready to spring. If the conviction he spoke with couldn't convince her, his anger that flared at the suggestion certainly might.

Karine sucked in a sharp breath, shaking her head as she told him, "I don't know what you're doing, I don't understand it at all."

Roman didn't even blink when he replied, "Neither do I."

*

"Why did you do this?" Karine asked, well-aware that some time had passed since she last said a word. Within the city limits, everything was new to her. Each building, every block … she tried to take it all in, and Roman said nothing while she did so. She'd never been anywhere but Chicago. Yet, even there, she hadn't done much exploring of her own city. At Roman's questioning glance, she added with a shrug, "Take me, I mean?"

It was a question that wouldn't leave her alone—the problem was that she could come up with a million answers of her own, and none of them were good. He didn't answer straightaway, but he didn't seem like he was trying to come up with something just to say it, either.

Was he ignoring her—changing his mind about bringing her with him, maybe?

She couldn't decipher this man. His mind was a place she couldn't reach, but she suspected it was nothing like her own. Her belief that he wouldn't hurt her, not for as long as he assumed responsibility for her, did nothing to assuage the other questions she had.

Like what if he woke up tomorrow morning, and decided he didn't want to deal with her anymore?

It was then, as she tried to avoid his gaze that kept slipping her way, that she noticed the bruising on his wrists. The blackened-blue marks were too fresh. She'd been thinking he kept holding tight to the wheel because he was angry—those grimaces and hard stare was further proof— but suddenly, she didn't think that was the case at all.

Karine couldn't help but ponder if those bruises were in anyway connected to what caused him to walk into her bedroom in the middle of the night, and take them away. She had a feeling he wouldn't tell her even if she asked him.

"I don't remember any protests when I suggested this plan last night," Roman replied, arching a brow her way as he rolled onto a bridge behind a line of taxi cabs.

She didn't miss it.

How careful he was—how he posed each word as to not suggest something that might set Karine off. He clearly hadn't forgotten that breakdown in her bedroom the night they spent together.

Karine chest tightened all the same—she didn't have the words, or maybe the vocabulary, to explain to him how overwhelmed she was. At everything, constantly. He didn't make it better, even if he might sometimes make it easier. He had offered an opportunity that couldn't be refused, but now she wanted to know the truth.

What did it actually mean?

Before she could ask; Roman continued speaking. "You could ask me about your father, about—what he's done or is going to do. You could ask anything, Karine, but what you do is question my intentions. What makes you think I had a choice in any of this—that even this car that isn't mine is somehow part of my plan?"

He didn't look at her while he spoke that time, but she was suddenly grateful for that. Not even the obsessive, undeniable attraction she felt for the man was enough to soothe the way his words stung her skin.

She had asked.

At least he was honest.

Karine tried to find an appropriate response, but the words were lost to her murky mind as Roman pulled the vehicle off the road, and into the underground parking lot of a tall apartment building with windows that looked like panes of chrome, and high, black brick walls. A thrill ran down her spine at the sight.

She didn't know much about New York, but at the very least—well, the movies had been right.

It was glamorous.

*

The lobby of the building had clearly been designed with the outside in mind. Chrome accents twinkled in the tile under their feet while black brick made up the walls, and even the face of the reception desk that they passed in a hurry. Roman walked like he was, anyway. It took two of Karine's steps to keep up with his one.

Masha trailed far behind them, still as quiet as ever. All the years that she'd served the Yazov household taught her how to make herself invisible, and blend into the background when not required.

Karine stared up in awe of the rows of hanging chandeliers made from twisted chrome along the high ceilings of the lobby. She barely even cared that their bright lights made it hard to see what was ahead of her when she looked away.

Roman definitely had good taste.

And money.

The man and woman at the reception desk greeted them with smiles as they passed—Roman didn't offer a reply as he headed straight for the elevator. Karine, at least, returned their smiles with her own, but couldn't say it felt very true.

He carried one bag in his loose grip—hers. It was the only one he'd been able to pack in a hurry. Only what you'll need for a couple days, I can replace everything else, he had told her earlier as they drove into the state. She'd already noticed how he had no bags of his own. Did he really have no belongings in Chicago—nothing that he held dear enough to bring back with him?

They stood at the elevator doors until they spread apart with a loud ding. It was clear by the size and available space that it wasn't made for more than a couple people at a time.

"Which floor, Mr. Avdonin? I'll take the next one," Masha said, making her voice heard before they entered.

"Fiftieth," Roman replied without a glance over his shoulder. "It'll open right to it."

Just as fast, he placed a hand to Karine's lower back and urged her inside with the pressure of his palm. The doors slid shut behind them, and she caught sight of a quiet Masha before they closed. Alone with him in the confines of the elevator, she clutched her stomach, the wave of claustrophobia starting the second the floor seemed to jump under her feet.

Maybe then would have been a good time to point out to him how she didn't enjoy closed spaces. Her anxiety went through the roof, forcing her to ramble or babble nonsense for nothing more than the distraction it provided.

She said the first thing to come to her mind, but she wouldn't pretend like the thoughts hadn't been bothering her for a while. "You said you had no choice—so you didn't want to take me with you? Is that what you meant?"

The elevator lifted faster than she expected it to. She was able to watch the numbers change on the digital screen over the doors rapidly while the pressure and speed vibrated underneath her feet.

Roman didn't look at her, not even once, keeping his hand firmly stuffed in the pocket of his pants while his other held tight to her bag. Instead of answering her question, he simply asked, "You talk a lot when you're nervous or scared, huh?"

Karine chewed on the inside of her lower lip, muttering only, "Sorry—I can't stop it."

"That's okay. Didn't say it was a bad thing, did I?"

Wasn't it?

Before she could mull the question—or his words—over, the doors slid open again and welcomed them into what appeared to be another lobby. Only much smaller, with one entire side of the space being dedicated for floor-to-ceiling windows that overlooked the buildings across the block, and the street below. They passed leather bucket chairs placed on either side of a electric fireplace on the way to the door at the other end of the small corridor.

"The whole floor on this side of the building is the apartment," he said, making Karine realize he was paying more attention to her than she thought.

How much did a place like this cost?

"It seems—"

"Modern," he filled in when her words stopped forming altogether. "And the deed to this side of the floor was a gift to me from a family friend involved in the development when I ..." For a moment, his gaze slid to her as he seemed to consider the words he wanted to say. Then all at once, he just decided to apparently say them when he shrugged and said, "They gave it to me as a gift when I joined the family business. Some people tried to make a game out of it—who could get the best gift. Got three cars out of that, too, so hey. Not too bad."

Karine blinked, unsure of how to respond. Roman seemed to enjoy her stunned silence, the grin stretching across his lips making her heart race a little faster. It screamed wicked—all sorts of fun. It didn't seem like the time, but he could probably make her willing without even trying. And she liked it.

Roman pulled a keycard from his wallet, and slid it through the electronic lock at the end of the small entry. The door unlocked and opened on its own as he nodded a head toward the dimly lit space that greeted them. His voice was kinder than she expected when he said, "You should have a look around, make yourself at home. Might be here for a while, right?"

She stared at him, considering that—would it be such a bad thing?

Instead of waiting for her mind to come up with its own answer, Karine pushed open the door and stepped inside the apartment. Roman made his way in behind her, reaching beyond her shoulders to flick on a row of switches that lit up the open-concept floor of space to her view. Black marble pressed into the soles of her shoes while high, vaulted white ceilings waited overhead. She could see through the main floor of the space to where a long, glass dining table welcomed guests into a kitchen full of stainless steel, white marble countertops, and more black brick.

Roman remained at the door while she took slow steps further beyond black marble pillars to see the living space and entertainment section overlooking more floor-to-ceiling windows, but these were different than the ones in the entry. Curved outward in a domed shape. The life and buzz of an unknown—but strangely beautiful—city stretched out in front of her.

This high, it was like she was floating in the air above it.

"You still didn't answer my question, Roman," she said, enjoying the view but knowing he'd left something unsaid. Karine didn't like that. Turning away from the windows, and forcing her stare up from the shiny black marble under her feet to meet his gaze, she couldn't allow herself to get carried away. Not in anything. Not even in him until she had an answer. "You didn't want to take me with you, did you? You were forced to."

If he was shocked at what she asked, Roman didn't show it. Lucky for him that he didn't have to answer her question, either, because the approaching footsteps from the entry they had just come from had Roman turning away.

Masha didn't seem at all aware that she had interrupted them. Karine hated to admit that she was relieved at the sight of her—she wasn't sure if she wanted to hear what Roman's response would be.

She had a habit of doing that. Asking, but not wanting to know.

Karine was fine to let Roman busy himself with showing Masha where things were and disappearing with her down a back hallway where he said one of three bedrooms and the main bathroom could be found.

She remained standing where she was—quiet by the glass wall where she could see the hustle of a city. Where she really didn't have to think.

Of course, she still did.

Overthinking.

Entirely numb.

Who was Roman?

Who was he really?

Despite being told to explore, she didn't do much as Roman and Masha's voice carried out from the back hall. She did marvel a bit at the touchscreen panel on a pane of the glass that controlled everything from the automatic blinds covering the glass dome-shaped walls to the massive, curved flatscreen television next to the oversized, squared leather sectional. There was even a full-fledged bar at the corner of the living space, melding between there and the dining space.

The apartment seemed fit for a man who had priorities for a good time, and few responsibilities. A bachelor's life. There she was, ready to disrupt it all.

She still couldn't come up with a single good reason why he would have willingly done this—taken her.

"Hey."

Roman's firm, but not unkind tone, had Karine jumping in her skin. She hadn't heard him come back into the room. Spinning around, she found him standing at the entry of the hall, his shoulder pressed into another one of those black marble pillars as he looked her over.

Masha was nowhere in sight, clearly having chosen to stay out of focus. Maybe wisely.

Karine licked nervously at her bottom lip, determined not to blurt her thoughts, and making a conscious effort to keep the words inside the longer he stared and said nothing.

"What?" she eventually asked.

A little too sharply.

Roman still gave her a crooked smile—it was just as tempting as everything else. Then, he told her, "Just because I was forced in to taking you doesn't mean that I didn't want to."

She hadn't expected that.

"Why?" she asked.

Seconds ticked on as he took in a deep breath, and his shoulders rose and fell from the effort. His reply wasn't what she was looking for, "I don't really have an answer for that, Karine."

"That's a lie."

If he could say he wanted something, then he should be able to say why. Besides, everything else about her life was a lie. It wouldn't even hurt her feelings if he lied about this, too.

"The real question is whether you want to know the truth," Roman returned just as fast, never once breaking her stare. "Because that requires accepting certain things, you know? I think we've both established you have—just a bit— of a problem doing that in different aspects. Think about it."

That truth was cold.

He also wasn't wrong.

Karine chose not to reply, and that time, it wasn't hard to keep the prattle of words induced by her anxiety and fears inside. Maybe he knew her better than she was willing to admit.

She still thought he shouldn't.

XO,
BK

ABOUT THE AUTHOR

The author of too many novels to count, Bethany-Kris is a Canadian, lover of much, and mother to four sons, a glaring of cats, and a pack of dogs. A small town in Eastern Canada where she was born and raised is where she has always called home. With her boys under her feet, a snuggling cat, barking dogs, and a spouse calling over his shoulder, she is nearly always writing something ... when she can find the time.

Find where to follow BK and stay up to date with all her books news at www.bethanykris.com.

www.ingramcontent.com/pod-product-compliance
Lightning Source LLC
Chambersburg PA
CBHW072348020726
47506CB00004B/1048